Praise for *Jesse's Girl*

"A fun, sexy, suck-me-in read."

—Katie McGarry, author of *Nowhere But Here*

"Kenneally branches out with this book while keeping all the elements readers have come to love about her books: friendship, family life, romance, strong female characters, and a glimpse at past characters… *Jesse's Girl* is the perfect summer novel hitting all the right notes."

—*VOYA*

"Highly enjoyable."

—*Kirkus Reviews*

Praise for *Breathe, Annie, Breathe*

★ "In this expertly paced and realistic romance, Kenneally gives Annie's sorrow a palpable weight, but she writes with such ease that Annie and her goals become exceedingly likable and familiar and never overwrought."

—*Booklist*, Starred Review

"*Breathe, Annie, Breathe* is an emotional, heartfelt, and beautiful story about finding yourself after loss and learning to love. Her best book yet."

—Jennifer L. Armentrout, *New York Times* bestselling author of *Wait for You*

Praise for *Things I Can't Forget*

"Kenneally's books have quickly become must-reads."

—*VOYA*

"Entertaining and poignant."

—*School Library Journal*

"[A] compassionate and nuanced exploration of friendship, love, and maturing religious understanding."

—*Publishers Weekly*

Praise for *Stealing Parker*

"Another engrossing romance from Miranda Kenneally with a hero who will melt your heart."

　　—Jennifer Echols, author of *Endless Summer* and *Playing Dirty*

Praise for *Catching Jordan*

"A must-read! Whoever said football and girls don't mix hasn't read *Catching Jordan*. I couldn't put it down!"

—Simone Elkeles, *New York Times* bestselling author of the Perfect Chemistry series

"*Catching Jordan* has it all: heart, humor, and a serious set of balls. Kenneally proves once and for all that when it comes to making life's toughest calls—on and off the field—girls rule!"

　　—Sarah Ockler, bestselling author of *Twenty Boy Summer* and *#scandal*

"Sweetly satisfying."

—VOYA

Defending Taylor

Also by Miranda Kenneally

Catching Jordan

Stealing Parker

Things I Can't Forget

Racing Savannah

Breathe, Annie, Breathe

Jesse's Girl

Defending
Taylor

MIRANDA KENNEALLY

sourcebooks
fire

Published by Sourcebooks Fire, an imprint of Sourcebooks, Inc.

P.O. Box 4410, Naperville, Illinois 60567-4410

(630) 961-3900

Fax: (630) 961-2168

www.sourcebooks.com

Library of Congress Cataloging-in-Publication data is on file with the publisher.

Printed and bound in the United States of America.

VP 10 9 8 7 6 5 4 3 2

For my sister, Holly, who followed her dreams of working in theater.

Before

When I was a little girl, Dad installed a gumball machine in our house. But instead of just giving me the candy, I had to pay for it by doing chores.

Now I'm seventeen, and Dad hasn't changed one bit. If I want a new purse, I start saving my allowance. My father made his own way in life and expects the same of me. He loves drilling mantras into my head: I will work hard at everything I do. I will model integrity and compassion. I will lead by example.

I will fully support his Senate reelection campaign.

To be honest, I don't see him much. Only on parents' weekend and holidays. His secretary schedules his rare visits to St. Andrew's, my boarding school, so I know when my parents will be rolling onto campus. I know in advance to yank my plaid uniform skirt down a few inches and pull my sock up over my bluebird ankle tattoo.

I tell Ben not to hang around.

He is here on scholarship, and my mother never hesitates to

let me know I can do better. *Taylor, why don't you spend time with Charles Harrington? The governor speaks highly of his nephew.*

Mom wants me to date somebody with "proper breeding," as if I'm a horse or we live in Regency England.

But it doesn't matter what she thinks. I adore the boy who came over to congratulate me after I scored the winning goal against Winchester and then asked me to homecoming.

I love my school in the mountains surrounded by thick green trees and blue skies. I love Card House—the dorm I share with the fourteen other girls on my soccer team—where every night, I sit down to lasagna or beef stew with a black lab named Oscar curled up at my feet.

I won't lie—this school is tough. It kicks everybody's ass. I study and study and study. I probably spend more time on homework than sleeping.

But who cares? St. Andrew's is my favorite place in the world.

After I Fall

Mom hates coffee.

She won't keep the stuff in the house. She claims it will make my skin sallow and my bones brittle, but I can't function without a cup every morning. So I stop for a fix on the way to my new school. The windows are rolled down, the cool wind is tangling my hair, and I pretend I'm driving to the beach for a vacation.

I smile at the dream, but my body knows the truth. My fingers are clenched around the steering wheel.

Last week, I was worrying about normal stuff: homework, a soccer game against Hamilton County, college applications, a tough math test. The list went on and on and on.

This week? Everything's changed.

I park my Buick in the lot of Donut Palace. After everything that's happened, I'm surprised my parents let me keep the car. Dad wanted to take it away, but Mom defended me, saying, "Edward, she's a senior! It would embarrass me if Taylor had to walk to school or take the bus." Mom shuddered at the idea of public transportation, while Dad rolled his eyes.

At least my car probably won't stick out at my new school. Although other kids at St. Andrew's drove Porsches and Bimmers, Dad bought me a used car that was older than the dinosaurs. With its dark-green paint, it even looked like one. Everyone teased me, calling it the Beastly Buick or the Beast for short. I laughed and shrugged it off because *that's my dad*.

Yeah, he's the senior senator from Tennessee, but he's all about being true to his roots.

He expected that of me too, and I let him down.

I climb out of the car and open the door to the little café. Intoxicating scents of coffee and cinnamon lace the air. I examine the menu. Dark roast or hazelnut? I normally drink lattes, but it's going to be a long day, and I need as much help (caffeine) as I can get. I decide on dark roast.

The barista takes my order and fills a paper cup with steaming coffee, then hands it to me. I walk to the sugar station, and as I'm slapping a Splenda packet against my hand, a Hispanic guy wearing a *Santiago's Landscaping* T-shirt walks up and begins pouring skim milk into his cup. I watch him out of the corner of my eye, admiring his buzzed dark hair, easy smile, and lean, muscular body that must spend a lot of time hauling big bags of mulch. He catches me checking him out.

"Hi," he says.

"Hi." I don't meet his eyes because I don't want to give him the impression I'm interested. I reach for the half-and-half and start pouring it into my cup, accidentally knocking my plastic lid on the floor.

"Want me to get you a new lid?" the guy asks.

I bend down to pick it up, then wipe it on my jeans. I shake my head. "No need. Five-second rule."

That makes him smile. "I haven't seen you in here before."

"I never come in here." *Because I haven't lived in Franklin in years.*

"What's your name?"

He leans toward me, and I inhale sharply, ignoring his question. I can't lie to myself. Landscaper Guy is completely my type—well, he would've been my type when I was dating. After Ben, I am not anxious to get involved with a guy again.

Love is just not worth the pain.

"I've got a little time," he starts. "Do you want to sit—"

"Gotta go." I rush out the door, careful not to spill my hot coffee. Tomorrow, I'll have to pick a different café so I don't risk running into the cute landscaper.

Maybe I need a mantra. No. More. Boys.

I now understand *culture shock*: it's me experiencing Hundred Oaks High for the first time.

A lot of kids go here. Five hundred? A thousand? There are so many I can't tell. At St. Andrew's, there were only forty kids in my entire class. We lived on a calm, sprawling, green campus. Walking down the halls of Hundred Oaks feels like last-minute Christmas shopping at a crowded mall.

Two guys wearing football jerseys are throwing a ball back and forth. It whizzes by my ear. A suspender-clad male teacher is hanging a poster for the science fair, while a couple is making out against the wall next to the fire alarm. If they move another inch, they'll set off the sprinklers. At St. Andrew's, kissing in the hall was an über no-no. We snuck under the staircase or went out into the woods. Ben and I did that all the time.

Thinking of him makes me stop moving. I shut my eyes. Dating Ben was stupid. Going into the woods with him was stupid. Thinking about what happened makes me so mad, I want to rip that newly hung science fair poster off the wall and tear it apart.

A boy shoves past me, slamming my arm with his backpack. That's what I get for loitering in the middle of the hallway with my eyes closed. He looks me up and down. "You coming to Rutledge Falls this afternoon?"

"What?"

"Paul Simmons challenged Nolan Chase to a fight. Rutledge Falls. Three o'clock. Don't tell the cops."

A fight? Where the hell am I? Westeros?

A girl bumps into my side. "Watch it!" Flashing me a dirty look, she disappears into a classroom with a group of friends, chattering away.

Seeing those girls together reminds me of my best friends, Steph and Madison. Right now, they're probably gossiping before trig starts. I miss Steph's cool British accent and Madison's cheerful laugh.

I take a deep, rattled breath. And then another. I feel trapped, like the time I got locked in my grandpa's garage and no one found me for an hour and I banged on the windows until my fists turned purple from bruises.

I can't believe I had to leave my school. My home.

All because I made one stupid decision.

I check my schedule. My first class is calculus 1, the most advanced math course Hundred Oaks offers. Just a week ago, I was taking an advanced calculus quiz at the University of the South. St. Andrew's is one of the best prep schools in the country, and they offer seniors the opportunity to take courses at the university, which is up the road. Even though I was still in high school, the professors treated me just like a college kid. I was only in the course for two weeks, but still. It was insanely difficult. The truth is, unlike everybody else in my family, I hate math. I have to work at it harder than anything else in my life.

But if I didn't take college calc, there's a good chance I wouldn't get into an Ivy League school. I need to go to a top-tier school because that's what people in my family do. My father attended Yale, and my sister Jenna is there now. According to Dad, my brother Oliver—Jenna's twin—is a traitor for going to Princeton, but I think Dad respects him for having the balls to make his own decision.

Me?

When Dad called me into his home office last night, he barely looked at me as he pored over my new schedule. The silence was killing me.

"I don't know how Yale will still consider me if I'm not taking all AP courses," I said. "Hundred Oaks only offers AP chemistry."

Dad sighed, took off his glasses, and set down my schedule. "I'm incredibly disappointed in you, Taylor."

I looked him straight in the eyes. His quiet restraint worried me. I'd never seen him so upset.

But I was upset too. He rarely had time to call me when I was away at school, but he could spare a few minutes to comment on my one screwup? After how hard I've always worked?

Over the years, I've done hours of homework every night. I had a 4.2 GPA at St. Andrew's. A 1520 SAT score. I was on track to be valedictorian. I was captain of the soccer team and on the debate team. I did everything I could to show Yale that I worked hard. That I am a unique individual. Because that's what Yale wants.

But my one misstep has muddied my glowing record.

Dad ended our conversation with a death knell.

"Tee, I gave you all the tools you needed to succeed," he said. "I've paid for your private school education since first grade, and you squandered it by getting kicked out."

"I'm sorry," I said, my face burning. "I'm going to keep working hard at Hundred Oaks though."

"You're damn right you will."

My father had me so flustered, I wasn't thinking straight when I said, "Maybe Yale will still take me because of who I am."

"You mean because of who *I* am." Dad rubbed his eyes. "I've always taught you kids the importance of integrity, and the minute you got into trouble, instead of owning it, you called me to bail you out. And now you're doing it again. Using my name to try to get ahead."

I hung my head. "I'm sorry, Dad."

"I love you more than anything, but you have to take responsibility for what you did. You'll have to figure college out on your own."

"What does that mean?" I asked slowly.

"It means I'm not lifting a finger. I won't be calling the alumni association or the school president to put in a good word for you."

"But didn't you do that for Jenna and Oliver?" I blurted.

He put his glasses back on. "You need to own up, Tee."

So here I am, glancing around the unfamiliar halls of Hundred Oaks. The school is neat and orderly, but it doesn't look completely clean, like no matter how hard you scrub, it still looks old. *At least it's not juvie.*

I step into my math class, which is already filled with kids. I choose an empty seat at a wobbly wooden desk and stare out the window at the sunny, seventy-degree September day. I bet at St. Andrew's, my world politics teacher is telling my friends, "Gather your books. It's a beautiful day out. Let's have class in one of the gardens."

I check out the problem set on the whiteboard. I could do this level of math years ago...

My former guidance counselor told me that colleges look for trends in our GPA and activities over four years of high school. So that means when colleges see my application, they will see:

1. I'm taking easier classes;
2. I'm no longer doing debate;
3. I've lost my soccer captainship this year; and
4. I was expelled.

I have never simply given up when calculus got a lot tougher or an opponent ran faster than me on the soccer field. So I refuse to believe my entire future is over because of one mistake.

I just need to figure out how to move forward.

Tease

I miss everything about St. Andrew's but especially Card House.

It was filled with leafy green plants and overflowing bookcases. Oscar the dog followed me everywhere. At night, I sat down for dinner with my friends, and we talked about guys and homework and soccer over spaghetti. Afterward, we'd all pile onto couches to watch TV and gossip more about boys.

Today, I go home to a mansion that could pass for a museum. Not a cool museum, like the Field Museum in Chicago, which has a T. rex skeleton named Sue on display. My house is more like a giant white art gallery with only a couple of landscapes. It's so fancy, a ticket booth, hired guards, and a gift shop would fit right in.

Dad works really hard to give our family a comfortable lifestyle, but that doesn't mean he'll let us coast. He always says, "I'll provide enough for you to get started in life—but not enough for you to do nothing."

Our housekeeper, Marina, greets me with a snack of peanut butter and crackers and hands me my mail—a pile of college catalogs.

"Thanks, Marina."

"Anytime, baby."

"Have you heard from Jeff lately?" That's her son who's an Air Force captain serving in Afghanistan. She's so proud of him.

"I just talked to him this morning. He's not sleeping too well. I'm worried about him."

"Next time you talk to him, please tell him I said hi."

"He'll be so happy," she says genuinely.

When I climb the stairs, Mom doesn't come out of her room to greet me. Dad had to go to Washington, DC, for a couple days. Mom loves the life of a senator's wife, attending campaign events, throwing parties, and doing charity work for Vanderbilt Hospital. She was Miss Tennessee back in the day and went to the Miss USA competition in Atlantic City. Normally she'd go with Dad to DC, but she had to stay here to make sure I don't get into more trouble. Mom cares a lot about appearances—for good reason, since that's what politics are all about—so she's been very pissed at me the past few days. What happened didn't just get me kicked out of school and embarrass me; it embarrassed the entire family.

I inhale deeply, steeling myself, hoping she's not *as* angry, and poke my head into her room. The shades are drawn, and she's burrowed under the covers.

Without Dad here and if she doesn't have any charity events, Mom has a hard time filling her days. And if she doesn't fill her time, she starts thinking about her sister and gets depressed. Up until a couple years ago, Mom spent a lot of time with her twin sister (twins run in our family), but unfortunately, my aunt Virginia passed away after a long fight with lymphoma. Mom was devastated and didn't come out of her room for weeks. Knowing Mom's tendency to be dramatic, the press wasn't kind to her.

"Those assholes," I had said, poring over the *Tennessee Star*. The paper had reported the rumor that Mom didn't attend the Tennessee anniversary celebration because she was having a nervous breakdown. "Why are they saying these things?"

"They think rich people don't have problems," Jenna had replied, "And because we're rich, we shouldn't be allowed to complain. Money changes a lot of stuff, yeah, but not everything. We're allowed to feel shitty."

I can always trust my sister to tell it exactly like it is. For instance, just this past summer, Jenna mentioned she's worried my parents are arguing about money more. I'd noticed the same thing. I didn't voice it aloud though.

Ever since Aunt Virginia died, Mom and Dad have had philosophical differences about wealth. Mom thinks that life is short, and since we have the money, we should be living it up, staying in fancier hotels on trips. Hell, she thinks we should be going on more trips in general. To experience the world.

And Dad is still Dad.

I shut Mom's bedroom door with a click, letting out a sigh of relief. For a second, I was worried I'd have to talk to her. She's been snapping at me, which is uncharacteristic for her. Normally, she floats around graciously like Duchess Kate.

I continue up the stairs. My parents' room is on the second floor, and Oliver, Jenna, and I are on the third. When we're all home for holidays and school breaks, it's always rowdy and loud up there. Oliver loves blasting rap music—for some reason, the boy lives for clubbing—and Jenna is always screaming at him to turn the music down so she can read "a hot sex scene." Jenna loves historical romance novels.

Today, it's quiet and lonely.

Chewing on a cracker, I change into athletic shorts, a sports bra, and a T-shirt. Then I take a long run up and down the rolling roads of Franklin. With each step, I feel the tension bleeding out of my muscles, but the moment I get home, I'm alone with my thoughts again, and my shoulders clench back up.

Dinner? I sit at the long empty table with only a buzzing phone to keep me company. Texts from my friends, telling me everything I'm missing, wanting to know if I'm okay. St. Andrew's is about two hours from Franklin, up on Monteagle Mountain, but students can't leave without advance permission from their parents and the school, so I probably won't be seeing my friends anytime soon. Sure, kids sneak off campus sometimes, but it has to be worth risking a week of detention.

Mom joins me for dinner way after I've finished my

salmon and salad. I'd been staring out the window, pissed off at Ben—and glad he's not around—yet missing him all the same. It's complicated.

"Taylor, I'd appreciate it if you'd dress for dinner. Your outfit"—she pauses, scrunching her nose at my running gear— "is inappropriate for the dining room."

"I'll try to dress more like Jenna in the future," I say dryly, but Mom's too busy scrolling on her iPad and forking lettuce into her mouth like a robot to notice my attitude. When Dad's away, she might as well be married to that iPad.

The loneliness gives me an idea. "Mom? Can I get a dog?"

She looks up from her screen. "Why?"

"For company. I miss Oscar—"

"Who is Oscar?"

"The dog at Card House. Can I please get one?"

"It would mess up the carpets."

Spoken like a person who has never had a dog and doesn't understand the happiness they bring to your life.

Mom adds, "Besides, you should be thinking about what you did wrong."

How could I forget?

My phone buzzes, and I sigh when I see his name flash across the screen. Right before I left campus for the last time, I broke up with him by text, but he won't stop calling.

"Who's that?" Mom asks, staring at my phone.

"Ben," I mumble.

"That boy is not good enough for you," she says.

It's true. He's not good enough for me, but not for the reasons my parents think. Mom never approved of Ben because he's a scholarship kid. Dad didn't mind that my ex-boyfriend isn't well off, but ever since Ben asked about internship opportunities in my father's Chattanooga office, he hasn't been a fan. Dad thought Ben was using me to get ahead.

I don't approve because I tried to help him—and he abandoned me when shit hit the fan.

Mom goes back to scrolling on her iPad. My phone buzzes again. I turn it to silent so I don't have to listen to more texts coming in. Madison complaining that soccer practice sucked this afternoon without me on offense. Steph telling me how Madison has changed her clothes four times since classes ended today, trying to figure out what to wear when she hangs out tonight with Chris, this guy she likes. Every other text is about how angry they are St. Andrew's kicked me out. I miss my friends…

Ben's texts are always the same: Tee, please call me back. Please.

I told him it was over, and now he wants to explain. To work things out.

Well, fuck that.

I text him back: We were over the minute you didn't help me like I helped you!!

He does not respond. Which is heartbreaking, but not surprising. If he admits the truth, he'll get kicked out of school and he'd lose his scholarship and probably his future along with it. Getting admitted to St. Andrew's was his big break in life. His chance to rise above his poor upbringing.

But what about me? I could turn him in, but I don't betray the people I love. Loved? Love. Ugh. Like I said, it's complicated.

I pick up my dinner plate to take it to the sink to rinse. At Card House, we all took turns doing the dishes. I've always enjoyed it, to tell you the truth. *Swipe left, swipe right, round and round and round.* The repetitive motion, like running, helps me let go of my worries and relax.

After I'm finished, I'm not sure how to spend the rest of my night. Write an essay for Yale about why they should be thrilled to admit a liar to walk their hallowed halls?

With a sigh, I go to my room and lie down on my bed. It's cold and empty without Oscar's warm body curled up against my side. The dog must be wondering where I went. Will he eventually forget I was ever there?

I gaze around the room at the stylish yellow and gray walls with pink accents. I haven't unpacked my boxes from St. Andrew's yet. I have no pictures of friends. I haven't yet displayed the artwork and knickknacks I picked up at museums all over the world. Other than some dirty clothes scattered on the floor, it's like I'm in a guest room at a B&B.

It's like I'm a guest in somebody else's life.

Before day two at my new school, my phone lights up as I'm sitting at my vanity, drying my long, amber-colored hair.

I set down my hair dryer and answer it. "What's up?"

"Thought I'd check in before I head to class in a few," Oliver replies.

"You actually go to class?" I tease. My brother would never skip. He's dedicated to his schoolwork, just like me.

"How'd school go yesterday?" he asks.

"Honestly? I can't even remember it. I went to class, but I don't know what I heard."

I fill my brother in on my talk with Dad and how he won't give me a reference for Yale. This doesn't surprise Oliver. He doesn't bother trying to make me feel better, saying "Dad'll come around," because he won't. Once Dad makes a decision, there's no changing it.

"I need to beef up my résumé," I say. My freshman through junior years are covered, but I need activities for my senior year—and fast. I have an interview with the Yale admissions office scheduled for early October. Without a reference, all I have to stand on is my résumé. Jenna told me that a world-famous youth cellist attends Yale. Another guy who was nominated for a best supporting Oscar at age twelve for his role in an artsy film about apartheid in South Africa is in Jenna's philosophy class. I don't feel special at all.

"What's happening with soccer?" Oliver asks. "Any chance you can get on the Hundred Oaks team?"

"I'm gonna talk to the coach today. See if there's room for me."

"Of course there's room for you," my brother says with a laugh. "Doesn't Hundred Oaks suck?"

"Yeah," I say quietly. St. Andrew's has played Hundred Oaks in the past, and we slaughtered them every time. Last year, I scored four goals against them in one game. And now I have to go see the coach and grovel to play for them.

"Did you meet anybody nice yesterday?" Oliver asks.

I slump in my vanity chair. "I didn't talk to anyone."

"Why not? That's not like you."

"I wasn't ready. I still can't believe this is happening."

"I guess you haven't seen Ben, huh? You miss him?"

I pull the phone away from my ear, squeezing my eyes shut. "No. I broke up with him."

"What?" Oliver blurts. "How come?"

If I admit the truth about what happened, Oliver will tell Mom and Dad, and then Ben will get kicked out of St. Andrew's. If that happens, my sacrifice will be for nothing. Even though I'm pissed at Ben for hanging me out to dry, I won't snitch.

"It won't work out with him at school and me here," I lie.

"Yeah," Oliver replies. "Remember when Jenna screwed

things up with Jack Goodwin because she couldn't handle the long distance?"

"I remember."

Mom loves that Jenna always acts like a perfect lady. She wears snowy-white pearls without complaint, and you'd never see her out of makeup. She goes to Bible study, for crying out loud. That's not all there is to her. Imagine the smartest, most beautiful girl in the room who is kind of like a bad-girl version of Hermione Granger. When Mom and Dad aren't around, she's more crass than a sailor, which I've always found highly entertaining. But Jenna has always been sort of…horny.

Mom doesn't know Jenna cheated on her ex-boyfriend Jack— son of one of the richest men in Tennessee and one of Dad's biggest campaign supporters—by sleeping with an exchange student from France. If Mom knew that, she'd have a heart attack. I don't condone Jenna cheating on Jack, but I don't care that she likes fooling around with guys. Girls are in charge of their own bodies, desires, and feelings.

"But I thought you liked Ben," Oliver says, bringing me back to our conversation.

I didn't just like him. I loved him. We lost our virginity to each other. Now I don't think I knew what love is. Obviously Ben couldn't love me, because when it came time to stand up and tell the truth, he didn't. I took all the blame so he wouldn't get kicked out of school. I assumed because of who my dad is, the administration would give me community service or make me clean the bathrooms or do dishes for a month. I never imagined that they would expel me.

When I called Dad to beg for his help, he said, "You got yourself into this. You'll have to work through the consequences."

I thought I could handle the sacrifice I made to save Ben's scholarship, but I can't. Deep down, I was hoping he'd defend me and come clean, telling everybody what happened was his fault. He's the reason I don't plan on dating again. Because you gamble when you give a guy your heart.

I bet wrong.

Before my second day of school, I stop at Foothills for coffee. This diner is from the Stone Age.

I step inside, expecting to find woolly mammoths and cave drawings, but instead, a bunch of old men sitting in vinyl booths look up from their newspapers. They're all, like, eighty years old. Perfect. Well, perfect in the sense that none of these men are going to tempt me like that hot guy at Donut Palace yesterday.

It's not so perfect because, well, I get nervous around the elderly.

It goes back to eighth grade when my school choir visited a Chattanooga nursing home. We were singing Christmas carols to a large group of residents when this old man stood up from the audience and made a beeline for me. He grabbed my elbow, then demanded we play gin rummy.

Since then, I steer clear of old men, which is difficult when your father wants to keep his senate seat. He's always making me attend events, like the local bingo night. I wouldn't mind if I actually got to play for real. But a senator's daughter should be seen, not heard, and that's impossible when yelling "Bingo!" I've won a lot of games without anyone knowing.

I pass a booth of old guys who are complaining about the Titans offensive line, walk up to the to-go counter, ring the bell, and that's when it happens.

"Tease."

I'd recognize that slow, deep voice anywhere. Over the years, he stopped calling me Tee like everyone else and had nicknamed me *Tease*. Why on earth is he here? Isn't he in college at Cornell? Is it his fall break? Oh God, talk about the last person I want to see!

"Tee?"

I slowly turn toward him.

Ezra Carmichael.

The guy who filled my thoughts for years and years.

The first time I met him, I was ten. For elementary school, I went to a private girls' school, so I hadn't met many of my brother's friends. It was Oliver's twelfth birthday party, and he had invited a ton of boys over to the house for video games, swimming, and a game of football. Mom said they had to play two-hand touch, but as soon as she went to the back patio to drink mint juleps with the other moms, Ezra announced to the boys that they were playing tackle.

"No wimps!" he said, and of course, none of the boys tried to bow out. You had to play tackle or you'd be considered a pansy forever.

With hands on my hips, I stood on the porch in my little red dress and announced, "I want to play!"

"No way!" Oliver said.

"Let me on your team or I'm telling Mom you're playing tackle and you'll be in trouble!"

Ezra scowled. "Just let her play, Oll. She can be on my team."

The other team kicked off. I sprinted forward and somehow managed to catch the ball. "I caught it!" I yelled, and Ezra waved his arms, screaming, "Run!"

I took off for the end zone, my red skirt flapping in the wind. I was nearly there—and then this whale of a kid tackled me into the ground. A rock gashed my forehead.

I felt blood trickling down my face as Ezra slid to a stop in front of me. He pulled off his sweaty T-shirt and held it to my forehead, stopping the flow of blood. It hurt like the devil, but I couldn't cry in front of these boys, especially Ezra, who had stood up for me and argued to let me play. So I bit down on my lip.

He crouched over me that day. "Tee? You okay?"

"Did I score?"

Ezra burst out laughing, and that's when I knew I wanted to marry him.

When we were in high school together, I spent a lot of time secretly doodling *Ezra + Tee* and *Tee + Ezra* in the margins of my notebook, then scribbling over it so no one would see. I thought our names sounded perfect together, looked perfect together, and thus we would be perfect together. But he didn't think so. Or at least I don't think he did. I base this assumption on the fact that even though he flirted with me, he never made a move, and I chickened out the few times I might have had a chance to.

After what happened on my sixteenth birthday, we stopped hanging out. So of course, he'd show up again when my entire life is falling apart because *karma*.

His deep voice calls out again. "Tee."

I open my eyes and face Ezra Carmichael.

Modeling Integrity

Ezra is at the sugar station, pouring half-and-half into a steaming cup of coffee. The sight of him turns my knees to JELL-O. Dark, cropped hair. Serious green eyes that glance away from mine to make sure his coffee isn't overflowing. The way he licks his lower lip when he's concentrating. I've rarely seen Ezra out of a white button-down Oxford shirt, khakis, and blue plaid tie, which is the dress code for guys at St. Andrew's. Now he's wearing holey jeans spotted with paint and a bright-white T-shirt that is magnified by his warm tan. He's carrying a construction helmet under his muscled arm.

"What are you wearing?" I blurt.

His cheeks flush at my outburst. "What are *you* wearing? Where's your uniform?"

I look down at my jeans and cardigan. It's been weird trying to figure out what to wear—I've never had to pick out school clothes before. I own one pair of jeans, because when I'm not at school or soccer practice, I wear dresses and skirts to parties and political events.

"I don't need the uniform anymore," I finally reply.

"But you're a senior."

"I am, but I'm going to Hundred Oaks now…"

His eyes go wide. "Why?"

"You don't know?"

"Should I?"

"I figured everybody knew. I bet the guys on the International Space Station even know." Ezra's face is blank. "It was all over Facebook," I tell him.

"I didn't see anything, I guess," he says quietly. This is not a surprise to me. He doesn't have a Tumblr or Twitter account. He never posts anything on Facebook. At least not in the past several months. *Not that I noticed or anything.* I'm no stalker. Well, not *all* the time.

It's weird that he's never online. My brother's phone is practically fused to his fingers.

"Are you home for fall break already?" I ask.

He rubs the back of his neck, meeting my eyes for a long moment, and just as I'm asking why he's holding a construction hat—"Isn't it a little early for Halloween?"—an older man dressed in a T-shirt and dirty jeans comes into the diner and waves at him.

"Ezra, man, let's go!"

"Take care, Tease," he says, then hurries out the door and jumps into a truck with a construction logo on the side. As they drive away, he stares at me through the window.

Okay. So that was weird.

I definitely went through my first day of school in a haze.

I don't remember seeing any of these people yesterday. Which is odd because my calc teacher has the most Biblical beard I've ever seen. Seriously, this guy could've given Moses a run for his money. How did I miss *that*?

After first period, I go to the school office to find out who the soccer coach is, and the receptionist directs me to the athletics hallway where I find the office that says "Coach Walker—Soccer."

I knock on the door.

A man opens it, and I sigh, relieved that he doesn't have a Biblical beard. He's a normal guy, probably in his early thirties. He is chewing gum and wearing the typical coach's uniform: khakis, a ball cap, an unflattering polo shirt the color of corn.

"Yeah?" he asks.

"Hi, I'm Taylor. I was hoping to talk to you about the soccer team."

He smacks his chewing gum. "For the school newspaper or yearbook or something?"

"No, I play. I know tryouts probably already took pla—"

"We'll take you."

"What?" I scrunch my eyebrows together. "Don't you need to know if I'm any good?"

He shrugs. "We've only got twelve girls this year. We could use the help."

There were only about a hundred girls total at my old school, but we still held tryouts every year. We couldn't risk having a bad player, or we'd lose. They only have one sub? St. Andrew's always had at least three.

"So you play?" he asks.

My voice cracks when I admit, "I used to play for St. Andrew's."

His eyes perk up. "Oh, so you're the new transfer student the principal mentioned? The one who was kicked out—"

"I don't want to talk about it."

"Sheesh. Fine. Our first game is Saturday. We practice every day after school from three to four o'clock, except for on game days and Fridays. Can you make it today?"

I nod, hardly believing that practice is only an hour long. That's not enough time to run a few miles, do drills, *and* scrimmage.

"I'll be there. I can't wait."

"Good," the coach says with a smile.

I find myself smiling back.

Technically, with the amount of drugs St. Andrew's found in my possession, I could've been required to finish high school in juvie.

Last Monday, my parents took me to juvenile court to face the music. While my offense was not severe enough for cops to arrest me and send me to detention, I was still required to appear in the judge's private office to face charges.

"Taylor Lukens, come forward," the judge in dark robes said. It was like approaching Professor Dumbledore for breaking school rules at Hogwarts. Honestly, that would have seemed more normal than going before a judge for possession of drugs.

Mom and Dad stood to my right, while Dad's lawyer stood to our left. I felt so flushed with shame, I could barely lift my head to face the judge. Mom gently held my elbow.

"Want to tell me what happened?" the judge asked.

Dad's lawyer gave me a pointed stare. He said if I told the truth, the judge would be more lenient. But I couldn't tell the *truth* truth, or Ben's future would be over along with mine. On top of that, Dad would be even more pissed that I attempted to use his position to bail out a friend.

I could imagine his reaction: *"You lied for your boyfriend and expected me to clean it up? And when the going got rough, you snitched on him to save yourself? That is the opposite of modeling integrity."*

So I told the same "truth" I had told Mom, Dad, and their lawyer:

"The pills were mine, Your Honor."

"Why did you have so many? Were you selling them?"

"No, Your Honor. I had them to help me study."

They believed my lie. Before I went to court, I had to take a drug test. Sure enough, they found Adderall in my system, and it had never been prescribed to me. On occasion, I took it to stay awake to study. So did my friends. Ben knew someone on campus who sold Adderall and would buy pills for me when I asked. There were about thirty pills and a tiny bit of weed in the backpack, but our lawyer argued I had no intention of selling.

I had no priors and had never been in trouble before, so the judge said I could attend public school, but I have to meet with the school counselor on a daily basis, which I start today.

During my free period, I head to the counseling office. I plan to use the time to my advantage. I'm hopeful the counselor can help me figure out the right approach for my college essay.

"I'm Taylor Lukens," I tell the receptionist, and she quickly ushers me into Miss Brady's office. The counselor is an attractive woman in her twenties, wearing a pearl necklace and earrings, and she seems to have an affinity for cat artwork and inspirational posters. I take a seat in a lime-green armchair that must be from the seventies and stare at a poster of a snowcapped mountain that says *Inspire*.

"So, tell me about yourself."

I wipe my sweaty palms on my jeans. I should go buy another pair after soccer practice this afternoon. That would give me something to do so I don't have to go home and be lonely. I love the idea of having plans—even if they are with myself.

"Taylor?"

"Yeah?"

"I asked you to tell me about yourself."

"Oh. Sorry. I'm a senior. I have a 4.2 GPA. I'm sure you already have my transcript and test scores."

She glances down at the opened folder in front of her. "That's wonderful. But what about you? What do you like?"

I squeeze my knees. "I like soccer…and dogs."

She smiles, even though I'm cringing at how immature I sound.

"Do you have a dog?" she asks.

"I want one, but my mom said no. The house dog at my old school, Oscar, spent more time with me than anybody else."

"You must miss him."

I clear my throat and stare at my lap. Then I nod.

Then silence.

"I hate to put you on the spot, Taylor, but in order for you to avoid court-mandated rehab and for us to continue our sessions, I have to ask if you've been using Adderall or any other substance."

I stare straight at her and speak with a strong, steady voice. "No, I have not."

"Do you have any Adderall in your possession?"

"I do not." I never had more than three or four pills at a time. I still don't know why Ben had *thirty* pills. Part of me doesn't want to know why…

The counselor clicks her pen. "Why were you taking it?"

I decide to be upfront. There's no need to lie more than I already am. "To stay awake and study."

"You must feel a lot of pressure."

With a father who grew up middle class and went on to become a United States senator, doing great things is expected in my family.

My sister was president of the Tennessee chapter of the National Honor Society. His freshman year of college, Oliver wrote an opinion column for the university paper, the *Daily Princetonian*. Because success comes so naturally to them, sometimes I think I put more pressure on myself than anybody else does.

"I want to go to a good college like my brother and sister," I finally reply.

She clicks her pen on. "Where are you planning to apply?"

"I had been planning on applying early decision to Yale in November…" My cheeks flush with embarrassment. "Everything we talk about is confidential, right?"

The counselor twirls her pen between her fingers. "I have to report to the judge who handled your case, but otherwise, this is just between us. I won't share anything you say with other students or teachers."

"Okay…" I take a deep breath. "I've been working toward Yale for years… After what happened, will they still take me? I'm scared."

She jots down a note on the pad in front of her. "There are always options. We can work together to find the one that's best for you."

Is she trying to manage my expectations? Does she think Yale is off the table? The judge assured me my record would be sealed.

"I'm not giving up," I tell her.

She nods, continuing to write. "Do you know what you want to study?"

"I hope to major in business with a minor in politics."

She raises an eyebrow. "Like your father?"

It's not a surprise she's bringing him up. He's been a senator for eighteen years. That's longer than I've been alive. But I'm not some clone of his like Miss Brady probably thinks. I have my own thoughts and ideas. A more liberal point of view.

For a time, I considered majoring in art history because I love going to museums and learning about the past. But Dad always says that in this economy, I need a solid major, something that could lead to many different successful careers. This was coming from the man who some have touted as a future Secretary of the United States Treasury or even the next governor.

I get what he's saying. As much as I love museums, a business major would have many practical applications. Such as working at Lukens, Powell, and Associates, my family's firm. My grandfather built the firm from nothing, and Dad turned it from a solid business into a multimillion-dollar operation. Grandpa and Nana are in their seventies and have retired to Naples, Florida, but Grandpa keeps a close watch on the business.

Dad has always said Oliver, Jenna, and I can apply for jobs there after college, to keep the firm in the family, which sounds very *Godfather*-esque.

Wait—after what happened, would Dad and Grandpa still want me to work there? I inhale sharply and end up gasping.

"Taylor? Did you hear me? Are you okay?"

"Hmm?"

She looks concerned. "I was wondering how you deal with stress and pressure. What do you like to do in your free time?"

"I study. Work on college essays. At my school, I ate dinner and hung out with my friends, played with Oscar. I spent time with my boyfriend…" I let my voice trail off. Will the sting of betrayal ever stop?

Miss Brady's eyes don't leave mine. "Have you made any friends here at Hundred Oaks yet?"

"No."

"Are you going to try?"

"I'm sure I'll meet the girls on the soccer team." Making friends is not really my priority right now. I need to get my future back on track first. If I can't get into college, I don't know what I'll do.

And now for the mother of all questions. She stares me down and asks, "How do you feel?"

Not so good. I would feel guilty saying that though, because my life is not bad whatsoever. Not when you compare it to people living in poverty or being persecuted for their religion.

"I'm fine," I lie.

Again.

At lunch, I sit down beside a window in the cafeteria and unpack the boring lunch Marina packed for me. Mom obviously chose it—a plain chicken breast, quinoa, and a kale salad. I dig into my homework as I eat. *If I want to spend time with my friends tonight, I need to get my homework done during school hours.* Then I remember where I am. My friends aren't here; I have no plans for tonight.

I set down my pen and fork and stare out the window. I don't want to keep wallowing in my own misery—that's not who I am.

I decide to group-text Steph and Madison: Saw Ezra today!!!

Mads: The Asshole!

Steph: Lick him!

Ugh. Steph always thought I should've pushed harder to find out why Ezra skipped my sixteenth birthday party after he told me to save my first dance for him, but I was too embarrassed and fed up. Previously, two other guys had asked me out, but I had said no, just in case Ezra decided to stop flirting and make an actual move. After he missed my party, I wasn't going to waste another second on him. Madison agreed with me and started calling him The Asshole. Steph, however, said she *knew* Ezra was in love with me, but he wasn't pursuing me because of his friendship with my brother.

Mads: Tee, I don't care how tasty he looks, u aren't licking him. BTW, Ben won't stop asking about u.

Me: What does he want?

Mads: YOU, obvs. He misses u. What happened with y'all? Can't believe you dumped him! It's all anyone's talking about here!

Me: I told you. I don't want to do long distance. I'll never see him. What if either of us ended up cheating, like my sister did with Jack?

Lies. All lies.

Mads: But Ben loves u!

Steph: Tell us about Ezra! How'd he look? Is he still lick-able?

Mads: Of course he is. A boy like that doesn't just suddenly become un-lick-able, even if he is The Asshole.

I change the subject because they are no help.

Me: Mads, what's up w/ Chris?

Mads: He's totally lick-able!

Me: Eeeeeep!! <3

Steph: Gotta go. Trig time. Chat later.

Next, I text my brother about Ezra.

Saw Ezra today at Foothills dressed up like a construction worker! Why is he here?

My phone dings ten seconds later. No clue. We haven't talked in a couple weeks.

He's ur best friend.

I know.

Then why haven't you talked to him?

He hates texting & he's never online. We've been trading phone calls. Keep missing each other.

I thought he goes to Cornell?

He does. Gotta get to lab. TTYL.

The plot thickens.

No Matter What...

The school office gave me permission to go home during last period study hall to change into shorts and a tank top for soccer practice. I decide to wear my lucky smiley face socks over my shin guards and braid my hair into a long plait. I speed my car back to school with only a couple minutes to spare. Dad always says five minutes early is on time.

Feeling like myself for the first time in a week, I am grinning as I park next to the lush green soccer field. I hop out of the car and rush past an outdoor basketball court, where a bunch of guys are playing shirts versus skins. Because they are high school boys and are evolutionarily wired to do so, they whistle and catcall at me as I jog over to the benches where Coach Walker is standing next to two orange coolers.

"You made it," he says, smiling as he reads from a paper on his clipboard.

I bounce on my toes, raring to go. "Yup. Where's the team? Isn't it three o'clock?"

He pulls his phone out and checks the screen. "It is."

Instead of explaining where the other girls are, he starts tapping buttons on his phone and seemingly loses all interest in me. I edge to his side and peek at his screen. He's checking Facebook.

I decide to use the time to stretch. I bend over and touch my toes. Next, I cross one leg over the other, then lean toward the ground again. Someone whistles loudly. I glance up from touching my toes to find the guys have stopped passing the basketball and are staring at me.

The tallest one sticks his thumb and forefinger in his mouth and whistles again.

I ignore the silly boys and go back to stretching. I work on my arms, hamstrings, and calves, and still no team. Coach Walker is still typing on his phone. He and Mom should hang out together with their electronic devices.

A minute later, a skinny guy steps onto the field carrying a stats book, a set of orange cones, and a mesh bag full of soccer balls. He's probably a freshman or sophomore, and with his floppy brown hair and freckles, he's sweet looking. But I don't know *what* to say about his T-shirt that says in huge bold letters *Not Even Flexing*.

When he sees me, his eyes grow wide behind his glasses. "Hey. I'm Danny, the team manager."

"I'm Taylor. So you're into soccer?"

"Not really. I'm here to meet girls."

I raise my eyebrows. I'm the only girl here so far. He better not get his hopes up about me, but I can tell what he's thinking thanks to his big smile.

"Danny, where are the other players?"

"Still in the locker room, but I'm not sure what they're doing because I'm not allowed inside."

Good to know.

Danny pulls out an air pump and begins making sure the balls are fully inflated. I take a deep breath and wonder what I've gotten myself into. It's at least 3:10 p.m., and I'm still the only player here. If the team's first game is on Saturday, we're losing valuable practice time. Especially if we're supposed to be done by four o'clock.

What if I'm the only one who shows up to practice? I imagine standing in front of a goal, defending against a team of eleven other girls all by myself. Sounds like a bad sitcom.

The basketball boys start whistling again. Girls are trickling out of the gym door. Not only are they late, some of them aren't even wearing shin guards. Coach Clark never would've stood for that. She benched anyone who didn't show up prepared. One time, I accidentally forgot mine and didn't get to play the entire game, even though Madison had an extra pair I could've borrowed.

My new teammates walk toward the field, gossiping and laughing. I feel a pang in my heart when I remember how I used to walk to practice with Steph and Madison. They're probably doing that right now. Are they thinking of me?

When my new teammates see me, the chatter stops. The smiles disappear.

I recognize a few from my new classes. The tallest girl, the only one I remember from last year, steps forward. I don't know her name, but she has big, expressive hazel eyes and long black hair that's pulled back in a ponytail. She's also one hell of a player. She places a hand on her hip as her eyes roam over me.

"What is *she* doing here, Coach?"

"Taylor's new to Hundred Oaks, and she's joining the team. Now we have enough players to have two subs! Isn't that great news?"

"Yeah, great news," the girl says, staring at me like I have the plague.

I step forward and hold out my hand. "Taylor Lukens."

"I know who you are," she says, ignoring my handshake. "You're the snobby rich girl who laughed in our faces last year after your team beat us."

"I was happy we won the game. I wasn't laughing *at* you."

"You may as well have been. The other girls on your team did."

Uneasiness settles over me when I remember how some of my teammates had laughed at Hundred Oaks after we pummeled them 6–0. But I wasn't one of them. I was in line to be this year's captain, so I had to be a role model. I can't say I wasn't laughing internally though, and thinking about that makes me feel like a terrible person.

"Are we good enough for you *now*?" she adds. "Did all your

40

expensive soccer camps not pay off? Someone better take your position on the St. Andrew's squad? Daddy couldn't convince them to keep you?"

"Nicole, c'mon. Just drop it," Coach Walker says, and I'm grateful. It was becoming difficult to hold my tongue. Coach adds, "Let's get stretched out, okay?"

My new teammates sit down on the grass and begin to stretch whatever way they want. One girl fiddles with a complicated-looking metal knee brace. I feel bad for her—she must have torn her ACL or something. Not only is that painful, you always have to wear a brace while playing after that kind of injury. Another girl does splits, like a gymnast, showing off more than actually stretching. At St. Andrew's, for the two weeks I was captain, I had my team stand in a big circle and do the same stretches together. It builds cohesiveness and camaraderie. Since I've already stretched and each girl is doing her own thing, I decide to use the time to juggle a ball with my feet. It's a good way to practice control and improve balance.

I begin kicking the ball up over and over again to myself, sometimes using my head and chest to control the ball. I bounce the ball back and forth off my thighs.

"Show-off," a girl says. It's not even a mutter; she wanted me to hear it.

I'm tempted to call her a slacker for being late to practice, but I hold my tongue. I'm trying to be the bigger person in this situation.

"All right, let's scrimmage!" Coach calls, handing out neon-green mesh pinnies to half of us, splitting us into two groups. Nicole ends up on the green team with me. I'm actually kind of excited to see how we play together, given how good she was last year.

"What about drills?" I ask the coach. "Are we doing them after we scrimmage?"

"Nah, we have a game Saturday. We'll use the time to simulate real game conditions."

"Drills are important though. Good mechanics will help us in the game."

"Taylor," Nicole says. "Listen to Coach. Get your butt on the field. You're on D."

"I play forward."

"I said, *you're on D*."

Okaayyy. I jog out onto the grass and take left back, loving how my cleats sink into the dirt. It's only been a week since I've played, but it feels like a hundred years.

I notice our net is empty. I look to the younger girl playing center defense, who must be a freshman or sophomore. She's wearing one pink sock and one yellow. Her legs are super skinny; I bet she's quick on her feet.

"Hey!" I call to her. "Where's our goalie?"

"We only have one. She's playing for the other side."

Great. Our team doesn't have a backup goalie? What happens if she gets hurt? Given that we only have thirteen girls, we'll be in a rough spot if *anyone* is injured.

"What's your name?" I call out to the girl with the colorful socks.

"Sydney."

"I'm Taylor."

"I know." She gives me a nervous smile.

Coach blows the whistle. The other team kicks off, and I streak forward to engage them. Nicole steals the ball and dribbles straight toward the goal. Their defense chases after her. She darts left, then right, and shoots. The goalie doesn't stand a chance. The ball sails into the upper right corner of the net.

"Woo!" Nicole yells, then accepts high fives from the other players on our team. I look at the goalie. She slaps the goalpost, looking humiliated. *I'll talk to her after practice*, I think, to tell her Nicole is a formidable opponent and any goalie would have an issue defending against her.

After we get back into position, the other team kicks off. Nicole immediately steals the ball and scores again. Okay, I can handle her doing that twice, but after she does it a third time, I totally snap.

"C'mon, Nicole!" I shout. "Pass the ball. The rest of us need to practice too."

Everyone stops.

Nicole storms my way and hovers over me. "What did you say?"

"I said pass the ball."

Out of the corner of my eye, I see the shocked expression on the girls' faces. A few are laughing, but most just glare at me.

43

I don't regret yelling at Nicole, but it's not the best start with the team.

"Get back on defense," Nicole barks, then jogs to her position.

I glance over at Coach Walker. He's shaking his head, looking distressed. When he offered me a spot on the team, I bet he didn't think I'd be this vocal. But I have a lot riding on this team.

My future…my spirit.

I run on my own after practice.

Doesn't Coach Walker understand that if we don't run at least three to four miles a day, our team won't have the endurance to last an entire game, much less win one? Today's practice consisted of a half-hour scrimmage during which Nicole showed off and everyone else chased the ball around like kindergartners. Whenever I rushed for the ball, Nicole went out of her way to boot it out of bounds. Some team player.

After practice, I tried to share a few words with the goalie, Alyson, to encourage her, but she told me to mind my own business.

Hopefully, our game on Saturday will go better.

I run up Spring Hill, down Spring Hill, past the crumbling flour mill that closed ten years ago, around the sheriff's station, avoid looking at the cemetery because it scares me, and go back out into the country.

Running reminds me of how Ben and I used to jog before

dinner sometimes, him training for basketball and me for soccer. We enjoyed being alone together—away from our classmates, who unfairly judged him.

He had a hard time at St. Andrew's. Beastly Buick aside, my classmates knew my father is wealthy, so they treated me like one of their own. But nearly every day, some asshole would make a crack like, "You're really into dating down, huh, Lukens? You must like 'em on their knees."

I speed up. Run faster. Harder. Run, run, run. Forget, forget, forget.

When I reach my driveway, I sprint the quarter mile to my house. I dart up the back porch stairs, then lean over onto my knees, panting hard. Air is all I need, all I want. I feel good, and I grin.

Once I've caught my breath, I open the back door, and I'm heading for the stairs to my room when I hear voices in the formal living room. *His voice.* All the air *whooshes* back out of my body.

I enter the living room to find Mom talking to Ezra.

He stands when he sees me, ever the gentleman. After a long moment of us staring at each other, Mom breaks the silence. "Taylor, isn't it nice that Ezra stopped by?"

I swallow hard as I look into his green eyes. He's changed clothes since I saw him earlier. Instead of jeans and a T-shirt, he's wearing a crisp white button-down with the sleeves rolled up his forearms, navy pants, a silver watch, and chestnut-brown leather shoes. Definitely Ralph Lauren and Prada, but I doubt he knows that. His mother always picks out his clothes. Just like my mother does with Oliver.

He checks me out too. I took off my shin guards and cleats earlier, but I'm still wearing the same tank top and short shorts I wore to practice.

"I remember those socks," he says, nodding at my smiley faces. "Those are your lucky ones, right?"

"What are you doing here?" I ask.

"He dropped by to see how we're doing!" Mom says. Seeing Ezra is a treat for her. "I'll go pour us some iced tea while you two get caught up."

"Thank you, ma'am," Ezra says.

He watches her leave the living room, then turns back to me with a slow smile. A smile that gets my lady parts all revved up. Stupid lady parts.

I glance down at my white tank top as I take a seat on the couch. Yup, I'm covered in embarrassing sweat stains.

Only once I'm seated does Ezra sit back down. I had forgotten how much I love the dark freckles on his tan nose and cheeks.

He speaks first. "I've missed you."

I lift an eyebrow. "I'm surprised you're in Franklin."

"I was surprised to see you too… I talked with Oliver," he says softly with a knowing look in his eyes.

"Great, so you heard everything."

"I'm so sorry, Tee."

I bite a hangnail dangling from my thumb. The pain distracts me from my thumping heart. Ezra has gotten cuter and cuter over the years. Now, I'd call him handsome. And buff. His tan forearms are corded with muscles. He's a man.

"How do you like Hundred Oaks?" he asks.

"The soccer team isn't that good," I say, knowing he'll understand, since he was the St. Andrew's goalie for four years.

"Are you okay?" he asks with genuine concern.

I give him a curt nod.

"Do you want to talk?"

No thanks, I don't care to gut myself. It took forever to get over Ezra. Only when I met Ben did I think there might be more than one guy for me, and look how that turned out.

I internally repeat my mantra. No. More. Boys.

I decide to go on the offensive. "I texted Oliver this morning. He didn't know you're here."

"He knows now."

"Why *are* you here?"

He turns to stare out the window into our garden. The sun is beginning to set. "Would you want to go out tomorrow night?"

He's asking me to do something on a *Friday night*? Everybody knows that's date night. *Is he asking me on a date?* "To do what?"

"To talk. Maybe over dinner?"

I don't even bother asking if he means as friends or more. It doesn't matter. I will not put myself in a situation where a guy could hurt me again.

I stand up from the couch. "I'm sorry, Ez. I can't."

He hops to his feet in gentleman mode. "No dinner. Got it." He lifts an eyebrow. "Maybe I could get us into the Cumberland Science Museum after closing? We'd have the whole place to ourselves."

My eyes go wide. Of course he'd have a connection. I bet his family knows the curator or something.

He's good. Real good. He knows exactly how to entice me. Museums. Set me loose in one, and I could stay for weeks, reading all the little placards describing each exhibit. When Mom finally convinced Dad to visit Europe, I went to the National Gallery in Vienna. I couldn't stop staring at the Venus of Willendorf, a tiny statue of a voluptuous woman carved twenty-five thousand years ago, in a time when no one was voluptuous, when humans were cold and hungry. I wanted to know more about who carved that woman. I loved thinking about how much the world had changed since then. My parents finally had to drag me away before we missed our train to Prague. Museums are my Kryptonite.

Still, I say "no thanks" to Ezra's invite.

"If you're grounded, I could talk to your mom—"

"No, now's just not a good time. I need to take a shower, so I'll see you around, okay?"

The confusion in his eyes is strong and clear. I'm hurting him. But I'm saving myself.

It was two years ago. I was stepping into chemistry class when he took my hand.

"Tease," he said in a playful voice. "Your parents sent me an invitation to your cotillion."

"Yeah?" I said softly. I knew my parents would invite him to my sixteenth birthday party because he's my brother's best friend. On top of that, the Carmichaels have more money than God and have always supported Dad's politics.

Ezra tugged on a strand of my hair. "You'll save your first dance for me, right?"

I swallowed hard. The weekend before, Ezra and I had been watching a movie with my brother and his girlfriend in the common room of Harvey House, his dorm. I'd been lounging on the floor in front of the couch where Ezra was sitting. He kept tapping my shoulder, and when I'd turn around to see what he wanted, he pretended he hadn't touched me.

When my brother left to go make out with his girlfriend, Ezra patted the couch next to him and smiled. With a deep breath, I crawled up to sit beside him, close enough that our thighs touched. At seventeen, Ezra was two years older than me, and he played goalie for the soccer team. He'd had a slew of girlfriends, all of whom were sweet to me, but I had to hate them on principle because I was in love with him. His experience with girls intimidated me. My sister told me he'd lost it when he was fifteen, with a girl on a mission trip to Panama. I prayed it wasn't true, even though it likely was.

It was a nice surprise to hang out that night. According to Oliver, Ezra generally spent Saturdays running poker games in Harvey House, gambling with other boys for real money. Instead, he was sitting on the couch with me. I shivered with excitement. He'd finally stopped looking at me as his best friend's annoying little sister. I knew this because when I wore my first real string bikini that past summer, he checked out my boobs.

During the movie, he threw his arm across the back of the couch, behind my shoulders. I caught him looking at me out of the corner of his eye, and for a few minutes, he gently played with my hair.

Nothing else happened that night—well, except for people getting eaten by dinosaurs during *Jurassic Park*—but I could feel the crackle of anticipation between us. I'd saved everything for him. My first kiss, my first hookup, my virginity. I wanted him to have them all.

But on the night of my cotillion, after I'd spent an entire day at the spa prepping for what was going to be the best night of my life, I waited.

I waited and waited for Ezra.

His parents, who had also been invited, came over to wish me a happy birthday. "We sent a car to the school to collect Ezra for the party," his father grumbled, "but our driver said he wasn't at the dorm."

Mrs. Carmichael clutched her husband's elbow and spoke in a rushed, worried voice. "And he's not answering his cell."

"Typical Ezra," his father said with a grimace, squeezing his champagne glass so hard, I expected it to shatter.

Oliver, who'd come home with me on Friday to help get ready for the party, had no idea where Ezra was either. "I hope nothing's wrong," my brother said. He and Ezra were completely loyal to each other, and Oliver couldn't believe Ezra would purposely miss my birthday.

Guests came to the tent in our backyard, drank champagne, danced under twinkling bright lights, and left.

And he never showed.

Jenna gave me hugs and passed me tissues as I cried.

The next day, I heard from Madison that he had snuck off campus, driven down to Chattanooga with Mindy Roberts, and hooked up with her.

He missed my sixteenth birthday party to fool around with another girl.

Monday in the hall at school, I confronted him. "I got my hopes up…and then you didn't show. Waiting for you sucked."

With a red face and watery eyes that wouldn't meet mine, he said, "I'm so sorry I missed your party, Tee. Seriously."

But he gave no excuse.

That wasn't good enough. I'd been waiting for him, for our moment together, for years. Well, no more. I would like other guys. Better guys. Guys who wanted to kiss me. Guys who didn't leave me hanging. Guys who didn't flirt without ever making a move…

I decided to stop crushing on him, but no one else made me shiver with the slightest touch. Made my heart beat frantically just by appearing before me.

Then I met Ben, and I forgot all about how Ezra had let me down. Of course, Ben turned out to be a mistake too. Boys just aren't worth the letdown.

Here in the present, I tell Ezra that I need to do my homework.

He holds my gaze for a few moments, then pulls his car keys from his pocket. "You have my number if you want to talk."

He starts toward the foyer right as Mom is returning to the living room with a tray of iced tea. He kisses Mom's cheek, and before he leaves, he turns to look at me again.

"Who cares if the soccer team sucks? If you want to play, play."

Then he's gone.

I can't stop thinking of Ben.

After Ezra left, I holed up in my room. The shock I felt earlier this week is slowly starting to wear off, and my emotions are bleeding through. I'm trying not to cry, but it's hard. How could Ben love me and still do what he did?

He loved me. I felt it every time he squeezed my hand. His hugs were the best, and he lived for kissing me.

"I love your lips," he'd say when we'd sneak under the staircase for a quick make out session between classes. Sometimes, his hands would inch under my plaid skirt and cup my bottom through my underwear.

Just thinking about it turns me on. Well, *that* would be a way to pass the time. I hop up to lock my door, lie back down on my bed, and close my eyes. I don't need guys. *I can take care of my needs myself.*

But when I slip my hand down into my underwear, I discover that's not exactly true. What's the fun in making myself feel good if I don't have a guy to fantasize about…touching me, smiling at me, groaning at my touch?

The first time Ben and I went to third base, I got scared. I'd never touched a guy *there* before, and when I saw him naked, I was afraid that when we did have sex, it would hurt. I knew he was a virgin too. What if we did it all wrong and it sucked? From the look on my face, Ben could tell something was up.

"What's wrong?"

I looked down at his body. It was bigger than I expected. "I don't see how it will ever work. You know, if we—"

He gently touched my cheek, urging my face to meet his. "Don't worry, Tee. If and when you're ready, we'll figure it out together. I love you no matter what."

My phone buzzes, jolting me from the memory. Ben's picture flashes on the screen. I don't pick up. Hot tears burn my eyes.

The last time he and I were together was last Friday night. The night I took the fall for him.

That Thursday, St. Andrew's had a game against Grundy County. When I scored the second goal, my team circled me with hugs, jumping up and down, and the thrill carried me until the end of the game. I was pumped about our win, but I had to scramble for a quick dinner before studying for my first college test.

I had signed up for advanced calculus and economics at the University of the South. Along with those two college classes, I was taking four high school classes, including AP trigonometry and AP chemistry. I'd wanted to take an art course about color theory but couldn't fit it in the same schedule Oliver and Jenna had taken their senior year.

To stay awake to study for my calc quiz, I took two Adderall pills Ben had gotten for me. He knew who to get them from. I didn't take pills regularly or anything, and I had no stash, but it wasn't the first time I'd used them. If I was going to be the best student, then I needed to be alert when it mattered most. After I made it through the test—I think I did okay, though I wonder if I'll ever find out—I was practically shaking from the stress. My right eyelid was twitching, and all I wanted to do was sleep, but I was too on edge.

Ben called after I frantically texted him about my freakish eye twitch. "Babe, you need to relax."

"What if I failed the quiz? You know how much I hate calc."

"Tee, you knew the material backward and forward. I know you did great. It's Friday night. Come outside with me."

I met him on the Card House porch, where he kissed me long and slow, then twined his hand with mine. I handed him my sweater to put in his backpack, in case it got chilly later. Then he led me toward the woods beyond the soccer field.

"What are we doing?" I asked.

"Relaxing," he said with a big goofy grin. He patted his backpack, the black one I had bought him for his seventeenth birthday over the summer.

In the woods, Ben found a small clearing. He collected sticks and built us a cozy campfire, like we had done on a few other occasions. From his backpack, he nonchalantly pulled a two-liter of Coke and a bottle of Jack Daniel's.

"Where'd you get that?" I exclaimed.

"Brought it from home. My brother got it for me." Ben mixed us each a cocktail, and we leaned against a fallen log, staring up at the stars above the lush trees. With each sip of Jack, I relaxed into the romantic atmosphere. My eye stopped twitching. I took my ponytail out of its tight knot, letting my hair tumble down my back. I felt like I'd lost ten pounds.

My boyfriend unbuttoned my shirt and slipped a hand inside

as I loosened his blue tie and unzipped his khakis. He pushed up my plaid skirt, pulled down my panties, rolled on a condom, then crawled on top of me. We had been sleeping together for a few months. At first, it made us both nervous, but I was totally in love, and sex was becoming more comfortable. This was one of the times it felt really, really good for me. When we were finished, I adjusted my skirt back into place, let out a contented sigh, and curled up in his arms. But I wanted to cry—I had to get up in six hours to drive to Nashville for a debate tournament.

"All I want to do is sleep in," I murmured to Ben. "Maybe I'll skip. I'm exhausted."

He stroked my hair and back. "Shh," he said, and I snuggled closer. We both knew I couldn't skip. The college acceptance committees wouldn't care that I was tired. All that mattered is that I had perfect grades and was perfect at all my activities. Colleges want awesome students, not failures. I could not be a failure.

Right as I started to nod off, Ben whispered, "I need to use the bathroom," and left me curled up in front of our campfire. My eyelids felt heavy. I couldn't keep them open.

That's the last thing I remember.

I woke up with a pounding headache to a flashlight shining in my eyes. What time was it? Had I missed curfew? Where was Ben? He couldn't be far. I spotted his backpack. The fire was still crackling. It must have been only a few minutes since Ben had left for the bathroom.

Two dorm mothers stood before me. They'd found the bottle of Jack, and when they searched the backpack to see if I had more liquor, they found a little weed and silver packets with rows of little white pills. Ben was nowhere to be seen.

I was groggy and didn't have time to think, to weigh the consequences. I didn't even have time to wonder why Ben had all those pills. I just knew that the teachers thought the backpack was mine because my sweater was in it and I was the only one there.

Dad's *modeling integrity* motto flew out the window when Ben appeared in the clearing with a panicked look on his face. I gave him a subtle shake of my head, silently willing him to keep quiet. My mind raced. *Ben's on scholarship. He'll get kicked out. My dad's a senator. A school trustee. They'll give me detention. Or community service.*

The dorm mothers already thought the pills were mine.

I didn't correct them.

What Won't Dad Do for a Vote?

Where in the hell should I get coffee?

If I go to Donut Palace for a proper latte, I might run into that landscaper again.

But if I go to Foothills, which does not have proper lattes, there's the very real possibility Ezra will be there…and the slight possibility that one of the old dudes might want to play gin rummy like that man at the nursing home.

Starbucks by the interstate it is.

By the time I drive out there, the parking lot is packed. Who knew the interstate Starbucks was so hot right now? I find a spot on the side lot and am walking up to the entrance when I do a double take. *Wait. Is that Mom's Lexus?* Oh my God. If she's been hiding a secret coffee fetish, I am going to kill her. And then force her to buy us a Keurig.

I slide inside to find Mom schmoozing with Tennessee citizens. It's a meet and greet. Mom and Dad often ask me to go to these events whenever I'm home. It's weird she didn't invite me to stop by before school.

I wave at Mom. She sets down her white paper cup and rushes over to me. "Taylor, what are you doing here?"

"Getting my coffee fix."

She purses her lips. "You know it's not good for your skin."

"But it's great for my soul," I say, feigning seriousness. "What are you drinking anyway? Black coffee with a shot of espresso, I hope."

"It's green tea."

I make a face. "Green tea tastes like grass."

"Taylor," Mom whisper-yells. "Stop that. The camera crews will be here any minute."

That's when I spot Dad.

He's staring me down from behind the counter, where he's wearing a green apron and holding a white cup and Sharpie. Dear Lord, what *won't* Dad do for a vote? If he had to, I bet he'd shovel elephant poop at the Nashville Zoo.

Dad has a tough race coming up in November and is doing everything he can to rock the vote. Hence the Starbucks excursion. Tennessee has always been super conservative, so his real competition is usually during the Republican primary in August, which he won by a landslide. But this time, the Democratic opponent—Harrison Wallace—is getting a lot of voter support. He's young, cool, and seems very real in his TV commercials, which play over and over and over. Especially the one where he's unloading groceries from the car like he's a regular guy, even though he's been a congressman for six years. He wants to move from the House to the Senate.

Dad stops playing barista and comes over to me. "What are you doing here?"

I nod at the marker and cup in his hand. "I'll have a grande skim latte, please."

Despite his obvious discomfort at seeing me, he actually laughs at my joke, but Mom scowls. When an elderly woman pushes her walker by us, Mom's frown turns into a smile, and they exchange pleasantries. It takes the lady a good twenty seconds to move out of earshot. Then Mom turns to me again.

"Shouldn't you be at school?"

"I need my caffeine first. Dad, do you need to know how to spell my name for the cup? It's T-A-Y—"

"I've had enough of your sass," Mom says, glancing around Starbucks. "We'll talk about this later. You need to get to school before the cameras get here."

"Are you embarrassed by me?"

They hesitate for a moment before saying, "Of course not!"

But they are. And I'm not sure whether to feel hurt or ashamed or angry. Hurt because they're my parents, and even if they've always been a bit overbearing and expected a lot, up until today, they had always been proud of me and wanted me by their sides.

Ashamed because I fucked up big-time, and I can't blame them for being embarrassed by me. I'm embarrassed by me.

But I'm also angry because I've always done exactly what my parents asked of me. Sure, I bent the rules here and there, like when I used my sister's driver's license to get my ankle tattoo, but overall, I've been a very good daughter. Have they forgotten the *real Tee* all because I made one mistake?

"I'll see you later," I mutter and turn to leave. My parents don't try to stop me. I climb into the Beast and drive toward school.

"God, they suck!" I yell to my empty car.

At a traffic light, I lean my head against the steering wheel. Coffee. I still need coffee. I will not survive without it. I quickly flip a U-turn and speed down the four-lane.

Five minutes later, I swing open the door to Donut Palace and beeline to the counter. "Grande skim latte, please," I tell the barista.

"It's on me."

I groan under my breath. The sexy landscaper is back. I mentally repeat my *No more boys* mantra, give him a curt smile, and say, "No, thank you."

"C'mon, you know you want me to buy you coffee. A coffee that's hot and dark, just like me."

I snort and burst out laughing. "You did not just say that."

"How about it?" He winks at me.

"No, thank you." I turn back to pay the cashier.

"C'mon, bab—"

"She said no."

I whip around to find Ezra. Landscaper Guy eyes Ezra, who's wearing a *Hall's Construction* T-shirt.

"Dude, why would she want a construction rat when she could have a *landscaping lion*?"

I crack up again.

His pickup line was so ridiculous, I expect Landscaper Guy to send a horny pelvic thrust in my direction, but he vamooses when Ezra gives him the glare to end all glares.

I can't say I'm not glad the landscaping lion ran off to rejoin the pride, but I'm not thrilled to see Ezra again either. My heart skips at the sight of his green eyes.

No. More. Boys.

When I give my debit card to the cashier, Ezra hands the woman a twenty-dollar bill. "I'll get yours."

"You don't have to do that," I say.

"Would you rather the *landscaping lion* buy it for you?" he says with a laugh.

"I can pay for it myself."

Hearing the hard edge of my voice, Ezra lets me buy my own latte.

Ezra places an order for a coffee and six cinnamon doughnut holes, then turns to me.

"I figured you might come here," he says.

"How'd you know?"

"You love lattes, and this place has the best ones in town. You always ordered them at the Friendly Bean at St. Andrew's."

I smile a little. He noticed that when we were in school together? "Donut Palace is so much better than the Friendly Bean," I say.

"Yeah, I'd forgotten how much I love the doughnut holes here."

The barista calls my name and holds out my drink to me. I take it and nod at Ezra's tee. "What's the shirt for?"

"I'm working for a construction firm."

"Why?"

He looks into my eyes for a long moment, then shrugs. "I just like it."

As a kid, Ezra loved taking things apart and putting them back together. Computers, car engines, microwave ovens. It drove everybody batty. One time, Ezra convinced my brother to disassemble Dad's riding lawnmower. My father grounded Oliver for a week for not being assertive enough to stand up to Ezra. Another time, Ezra got detention at school for taking apart a teacher's SMART Board.

So it's not totally surprising he likes construction. But why is he doing it during the school year?

"What about college?" I ask. "Aren't you going to get in trouble for missing classes?"

Ezra's coffee is ready. He picks it up at the counter along with a white paper bag of doughnut holes. "I'm not going back this semester."

I touch his forearm. "Is everything okay?"

"I'm fine." He stares down at my hand on his skin. He clears his throat, then gruffly says, "Look, I need to get going."

I take a long sip of coffee and watch him stalk out into the parking lot. What's up with him?

Then I remember he's not my problem, and I don't want him to be.

I made it to the weekend!

I celebrate by going shopping at the Gap for new jeans, followed by a long run. After showering and dressing to earn Mom's approval, I head down to the kitchen to see what's happening for dinner.

There, I find Mom and Marina working on hors d'oeuvres. Two platters filled with lean meats, cheeses, olives, and a loaf of bread sit on the granite countertop. Mom is circling a separate veggie platter like a vulture.

I slide onto a stool at the island. "What's going on?"

"Peter and Maura Phillips are coming over to discuss your father's campaign," Mom replies, popping a baby carrot in her mouth. She passes me a cocktail plate and gestures for me to grab anything I want. I choose a few olives and a slice of salami.

"What'd you do this afternoon?" Mom asks.

"I drove over to the Galleria and got some jeans."

"Did you get any other clothes?" she asks eagerly. Mom loves shopping.

"Nah. I didn't want to use any more of my allowance."

She furrows her eyebrows. Then a sly look crosses her face,

and she smiles conspiratorially. "Do you need anything else besides jeans?"

Every year, Dad gives us kids a clothes budget, but Mom has always felt it wasn't enough—certainly not enough money to buy clothes *befitting a senator's kid*, so she's been known to slip us some cash here and there if we need something in particular, like when I needed a new outfit for the governor's Independence Day Ball this past July. According to Mom, nothing in my closet "would do," so she swore me to secrecy and swept me off to Nordstrom for a new cocktail dress.

"I could use leggings and a few more shirts for school," I whisper in case Dad is lurking about.

"We'll get you some," Mom says with a smile. "You know, you could probably afford more clothes if you'd kick that coffee habit."

"Get us a Keurig and I'll stop blowing money on lattes."

"Amen," Marina says, while Mom rolls her eyes.

I pop an olive in my mouth, then open the folder Miss Brady gave me during counseling today. It's a list of all Hundred Oaks' clubs and activities.

"What's that?" Mom asks.

I scan down the page. "I need to choose another extracurricular besides soccer."

"Why? Don't you feel like you have enough on your plate?"

I shrug. "Not as much as at St. Andrew's. I need to add to my résumé, or Yale will wonder why I started slacking during my senior year."

"But Taylor," Mom says quietly, not meeting my eyes. "Don't you think you should relax a little? I don't want you turning back to Adderall."

"But my early decision app for Yale is due November first! I can't stop working now, Mom." My voice is full of desperation. "Not after all these years."

"I know you work hard, Tee," Mom says, squeezing my hand. "But we can't risk another incident like this."

Another incident?

"You need to concentrate on taking care of yourself right now," she adds. "I'm sure Yale will accept you. You're a Lukens, for God's sake."

Clearly, she is not in the know. "Dad said he won't give the alumni association a heads-up that I'm applying."

Mom practically chokes on an olive.

"My application is no different from anyone else's," I add. I have killer grades, and I do amazing work. I shouldn't need a *name* to get ahead. I can do this on my own. And I'm going to do everything in my power to get in.

Dad strolls into the kitchen, looking tired, probably because he flew back from DC this afternoon, but he perks up when he spots the food. He loads a cocktail plate to the brim with cheese and ham, which earns him a slap on the wrist from Mom.

I continue to pore over the list of clubs and activities. Maybe I could do Quiz Bowl. I mean, who doesn't like shouting answers at the TV when *Jeopardy!* is on?

The Dinner Club sounds fun too, but it turns out to be cooking. I'd join if it were only about eating. Then there's the Polar Bear Club. They jump into freezing cold bodies of water. Ooh, skeet shooting!

Not much on this list appeals to me. I sigh.

"What are you up to, Tee?" Dad asks as he uncorks a bottle of red wine.

"Trying to pick another club to join."

Mom glares at Dad. "Edward, I really don't want Taylor overextending herself. I'm worried. She should be focusing on her studies and soccer, not joining random clubs so Yale won't think she's a slacker."

Dad pours a dollop of wine, sniffs it, and taste-tests it. "Taylor and I had a talk. She knows it's up to her to get into college. But I never said she has to join clubs."

"You're missing the point, Edward." With a heavy sigh, Mom pours herself a large glass of wine. "Don't you think you take your values too far? We're not all perfect." Mom disappears to the living room to wait for her guests and chug her wine. I don't blame her.

The kitchen is silent as Dad stares after her and tops off his wineglass. He rubs his eyes, then pulls up a briefing on his iPad. Part of being a senator is reading briefing papers all the time.

I click on a pen and begin crossing out clubs that there's no way I'll join.

~~Outdoor Grilling Society~~
~~Gospel Choir~~
~~Knitting Klub~~
~~Robotics Club~~
~~Polar Bear Club~~ *oh hell no!!!*

Out of the corner of my eye, I catch Dad looking on as I work, smiling.

After how much I've screwed up in the past two weeks, I never thought he'd smile at me again. Which is a relief. But I'm still kind of angry because Mom's right. We're not all perfect. Earlier this week, I felt like Dad had given up on me. And now he's happy that I'm looking at a stupid list of clubs? Why do I have to work so hard to make him proud?

Can't he love me for me?

A New Team

I wake up early to have a good breakfast before my first Hundred Oaks soccer game. Marina makes me a fiesta omelet with peppers, onion, avocado, Monterey Jack cheese, and a salsa dipping sauce.

"Thanks," I tell her. "This is my favorite."

She beams, wiping her hands on her apron. "It's your mother's too, but she takes hers without the cheese."

"Sacrilege."

"I completely agree, baby."

While I eat, I jot down ideas for my common app essays. There are two prompts to choose from. *Describe a significant event or risk you have taken and its impact upon you,* or *reflect on a time when you challenged a belief or idea. What prompted you to act? Would you make the same decision again?*

Neither question appeals to me. Up until a week ago, I'd always played by the rules. Sure, I drink alcohol when I have the opportunity. I drop the F-bomb pretty fucking frequently. I binge-watch *Game of Thrones* when I should be sleeping. But when it comes to school, I've always done my homework. I've never challenged a teacher. I haven't really taken any risks.

A few years ago, when Oliver, Jenna, and Ezra went on a mission trip to build houses in Mexico, they snuck out to nightclubs after the chaperones went to bed. I'm a loser by comparison. During the two months I spent working in Haiti, I read the Harry Potter series for a second time and never once stepped foot on a dance floor.

I set down my pen. I have no idea what to write for this essay.

I stuff one last bite of omelet in my mouth, kiss Marina's cheek, and head to my car.

Today's a special day for soccer, in that teams from our region will all come together at a sports complex in Murfreesboro, where there are seven soccer fields. It will be a chance for us to watch other teams and learn what to expect from them the rest of the season.

St. Andrew's is one of only two private schools in Middle Tennessee, so we always play against public schools. I know all about the teams in our district. We're playing Lynchburg today. Last year, they were tough, and unless a bunch of their best players graduated, Hundred Oaks will bite the big one today.

On the way to school, I drop by Donut Palace for my latte. At 7:00 a.m. on a Saturday, the coffee shop is deserted. I feel a pang of *something* when Ezra doesn't appear out of nowhere to bother me.

Of course, I am the first person to arrive at Hundred Oaks. I get there even before the coach. Hell, I'm here before the damn bus driver! If someone was late at St. Andrew's, Coach Clark made the team run extra laps while the late person watched from the sidelines. That's cruel and unusual punishment: you feel guilty, *and* your entire team is pissed at you.

While waiting for the Hundred Oaks squad, I lean against my car and sip my latte, trying to take my mind off how I have nothing to write about for my college essay. Does that mean I'm a loser? Does that mean I haven't *lived*? The only real risk I've taken is covering for Ben, and it turned out badly. Besides, I can't write about that on my application. People would find out the truth, and I'd get in more trouble for lying, and he'd get kicked out of school. Which he deserves.

But then I think about his home life. Ben grew up on the outskirts of Birmingham. His mom works at the Piggly Wiggly, a small grocery store. His father is a coal miner. Ben has an older brother and three little sisters, and his parents can barely afford to support them. Ben hasn't been to the doctor or dentist in years because it's just not an option for him. I've always admired that he applied for a St. Andrew's scholarship. It will take him far. I can't be the person responsible for taking that away from him, even if he was the one in the wrong.

I'll never forget the time his family drove up from Alabama to watch him play basketball. His mother was so proud, she cried, and his father clapped the entire game.

My parents never had time to come to my games at St. Andrew's…

I shake the sad thoughts from my head.

Dad always says that if I can't figure out a problem, I should think about something else entirely. Just get my mind off it. So I push essays to the side and concentrate on enjoying the warm sun on my face. It's mid-September. Fall starts next week. It won't be warm much longer.

About a minute before the team is supposed to leave—where is everybody?!—a dusty truck creaks into the parking lot, shaking and shuddering to a stop. An old man hobbles out and makes his way to the school bus, unlocking it.

Oh no. I'm alone with an elderly bus driver.

I reach behind me and open the driver's side door. I'm trying to sneak back into my car when he speaks.

"Hi there."

"Hi."

"Ready for the game? Lynchburg's pretty good, right?"

I pause, surprised that somebody actually brought this up. At practice the other day, Coach Walker devoted absolutely *no time* to discussing strategy or the other team's strengths.

"Yeah, they're tough."

The bus driver unlocks the door and opens it, then begins to hobble up the stairs. "Well, c'mon then."

I shut my Buick's door and follow him, choosing a seat in the middle of the bus. I slide onto the ripped, green vinyl and pull out my phone.

Jenna sent me a text: Kick some motherfucking ass today!

Well. That was blunt. But my sister makes me smile.

I also find a short email from my father:

> I hope your game goes well.
> —Dad

At least that hasn't changed. Between his work and travel schedule, he never shows up to games, but he's always wished me luck. It makes me smile.

I feel the bus shake and glance up to find other players getting aboard. *Finally.* I smile at them. Nobody smiles back except for Sydney, the freshman with colorful socks who was nice to me at practice the other day.

Nicole appears in front of me, filling my vision. "Get your ass to the front. We sit based on seniority."

We did that at my school too. As captain, I would've sat at the very back of the bus this year. Whatever. It's just a bus seat. I pull my bag onto my shoulder and edge up the aisle to the front until I'm sitting behind the coach and across the aisle from Danny, Soccer Manager Pervert Extraordinaire.

Did he just lick his lips at me?

Ugh.

I slip in my earbuds so I can listen to music to get pumped for the game. Then, while all the other girls are braiding each other's hair and gossiping, I dig into my chemistry homework, which is due Monday.

By the time we reach Murfreesboro about half an hour later, I'm itching to play. The fields are filled with players passing balls back and forth. The smell of coffee and fried egg sandwiches wafts from the concession stand. I can't wait to start running.

We don't play until 10:00 a.m., so the team spends time getting camped out in a field where other teams have set up tents to shield players from the blazing sun. Fall may only be a few days away, but it's still freaking hot outside.

I sit down cross-legged and pull my Adidas cleats from my bag. Two girls sit down across from me. I think their names are Brittany and Chloe. Chloe's the one who hurt her knee and has to wear the robotic-looking brace. I like her super short blond hair; it's trendy and mature. I'm opening my mouth to ask about her knee when they start chatting with each other.

"How'd it go with Jamie last night?" Chloe asks, adjusting the strap on her brace. "Did you hook up?"

The other girl—Brittany—squeals in response. I guess that's a yes.

"Was it good?"

"No, it was great." She grins. "His parents were out at a movie, so we had time to go up to his room."

"Did you do it?"

Brittany shakes her head and giggles. "Not yet, but he was plenty satisfied, Chlo."

"I'm surprised y'all aren't already going at it like rabbits. You've wanted him long enough."

"I'm thinking about it," Brittany says, blushing. "Maybe next time."

I smile to myself, remembering a very similar conversation I had with Steph when I was trying to decide whether to sleep with Ben.

That's when Brittany notices I'm listening. "Mind your own damned business, traitor."

Traitor?

Chloe shrugs at me, but it means nothing, because she doesn't say a thing. I change my mind about wanting to join their conversation. I look around at the other girls. All of them are talking and playing on their phones. It's like I'm not even here. I hug my legs to my chest, not meeting anyone's eyes until it's time to warm up.

Coach calls out, "Pair up for passing drills."

Everyone quickly finds a partner except for me. I'm unlucky player number thirteen. It reminds me of recess in elementary school, when inevitably one kid is always picked last.

"Can I get with you and Chloe?" I ask Nicole, still anxious to see how we might play together.

"Didn't you hear Coach Walker?" Nicole snaps. "He said pairs. Not threesomes. Is that the kind of shit you're into? Two guys at once?"

I put a hand on my hip. "Sounds great to me. Who wouldn't want two hot guys?"

Chloe and a few other girls snicker, and Nicole sneers when she sees the team's giving me attention.

Sydney edges closer to me and whispers, "You shouldn't antagonize her. It's just making it worse."

I shrug. Nicole doesn't scare me.

Since I don't have anyone to pass with, and I'm not going to start a *threesome*, I juggle the ball like I did at practice the other day.

After drills, Coach Walker and Nicole lead the team to field four, where we will play Lynchburg. We sit down on the sidelines and stretch as Coach goes through the lineup. "We've got Nicole at center forward. Alyson in goal. Chloe on right forward. Brittany—halfback. Taylor—center back."

"You're *starting* her?" Nicole blurts. "Are you sure about that, Coach? She just joined the team."

"Taylor's good, Nicole. She'll help us win."

I can't help but grin, even though I hate playing defense. It's not that I'm bad at it. I just like leading the charge.

The ref blows her whistle, letting us know it's time to take the field.

"Let's bring it in," Nicole says, putting her hand out. Everyone piles their hands on top. "One, two, three, Raiders!" everybody yells, and I jog out onto the grass and take my position.

The whistle blows a second time, and Nicole kicks off.

Lynchburg immediately steals the ball back, because they are really good, and start making their way down the field, effortlessly passing the ball back and forth between their players. They call each other's names and cooperate. They remind me of my former team.

As center back, I'm the last line of defense before our goalie. I quickly glance over my shoulder at her. She's crouched, hands outstretched, ready to take on the world. I dart forward to engage with the Lynchburg striker. She fakes left, but my reflexes are good. I thrust my right foot out and dislodge the ball from between her feet. Rearing back, I boot the ball up the right side of the field to Chloe, who dribbles a few feet before the ball is stolen away again.

Lynchburg is better than most teams in our district. That's just the way it is. But I'm not going to give up. Over the next twenty minutes, Alyson stops two shots on goal, and I manage to boot the ball away about ten times, but Lynchburg is wearing us out. Sydney is not bad on D. She's helping out a lot back here.

Then it happens. Thirty minutes into the game, a Lynchburg forward launches a shot into the upper left corner of the goal.

"Dammit!" Alyson yells, covering her face with her goalie gloves.

"It's cool," I say, clapping my hands. "You're doing great. We got this."

Sydney smiles gratefully over at me, but Alyson drops her hands to give me an ugly look that would make even Hope Solo cringe. "You never should've let her get that shot off, Taylor!"

With a sigh, I turn to face the field as the ref toots the whistle. Time for round two.

Chloe kicks off to Nicole, who dribbles up the center of the field but loses the ball when a defenseman boots it away. One of our midfielders—I think her name is Beth—takes control of the ball and hustles past Lynchburg's right defender. Holy shit! She might actually get into scoring position.

Then she trips and falls. The ref blows his whistle. I take off running toward her. *Is she okay? God, I hope she is.* I reach Beth and squat beside her.

"What's wrong?" I ask.

"My ankle." She clutches her cleat.

I look around to find Coach. He's taking his sweet time making his way across the field. None of our other players come over. What gives? The St. Andrew's girls would all be sprinting her way.

This team is just getting ridiculous.

When Coach Walker reaches us, he helps Beth get to her feet. "What did you hurt this time?"

"My ankle."

I help Coach lead her off the field. As soon as we're at the benches, she reaches into her tote and pulls out an ice pack, prewrap, gauze, and tape. I peek inside her bag, and it's packed to the brim with first aid supplies. It's like a mobile hospital.

"I hope you feel better," I tell her, and she looks up at me with quivering lips and shiny eyes.

"Thanks," she gasps.

I jog back onto the field, passing Chloe. She grabs my elbow. "Beth does this every game."

"Does what?"

"Fakes an injury."

"You can't be serious."

"She gets off on the attention. It seriously pisses me off." Chloe glances down at the brace on her knee. Even from this distance, I can see the pinkish-white surgical scar. I shudder, thinking of the pain she must've gone through. She hasn't been particularly nice to me, but I feel for her. You don't fake using a brace like that one.

"Don't give Beth any more attention, got it?" Chloe says before jogging off.

Shaking my head, I get back into position. The ref blows his whistle, indicating a Lynchburg player should throw the ball back in from the sidelines.

We're down one-nothing, and Nicole continues to be a ball hog: she seems to have a complete inability to pass the ball. A few times, both Chloe and Brittany are completely open, but Nicole attempts fancy footwork, trying to outmaneuver Lynchburg. But they are so aggressive and so in step with one another that any play Nicole tries fails.

"Pass the ball to Chloe!" I scream at her, but she ignores me.

My yelling seems to inspire both Sydney and Coach Walker. "Pass the ball!" they holler.

Chloe gives me a shrug at one point, obviously grateful for my efforts, but why won't she yell back? Why is this team made up of wimps when it comes to Nicole? I will admit that great players can be intimidating. The better a person is at a sport, the less likely other players are to want to cross them. It must go back to the *survival of the fittest* or something. I mean, would anyone question LeBron to his face?

While I'm thinking about this, Lynchburg makes another play for our goal. Two players barrel toward me, passing the ball, talking to each other, completely in sync.

I charge at one, but she passes at the last second, and the other girl slams the ball into our goal.

2–0.

Hell.

"C'mon, Alyson! You still got this," I say, giving her a pep talk. "They've taken, like, a hundred shots, and you've stopped most of them."

Instead of yelling at me, this time she nods and jumps up to slap the crossbar above her head. Then she claps to get back into the zone.

Chloe kicks off, barely tapping the ball to Nicole. Nicole immediately makes a break for it, dribbling up the middle of the field. A Lynchburg defenseman boots the ball back to our side. I'm closest, so I run to meet it. I prepare to pass it to Brittany, but then I think, *why?* She'll just pass the ball to Nicole, because she's a lemming.

I hate lemmings.

I take off with the ball.

"What are you doing, Lukens?" Nicole yells.

I ignore her and dribble past our forwards, totally leaving my position, heading for the goal. I lean back, plant my foot to aim, and boot the ball toward the upper left corner of the net. It sails in, and I jump up and down.

"Score!"

I turn around, expecting my teammates to surround me with celebratory hugs, but I get nothing. A few look relieved, but most are staring at Nicole, who looks insanely pissed off. Ugh.

"Get back on D, Taylor!" she shouts.

I run past her on the way to my position and say low enough so only she can hear, "Fine by me if you want to lose."

Okay, that was pretty bitchy of me, I'll admit it. But I want to win. I want to have something positive to write on my college applications. But even more than that, I want to be part of a team. A team that shares secrets and confides in each other, trusts each other, laughs together. Hundred Oaks is not a team. *Team members pass the damn ball.*

At that moment, I hear a familiar British accent. I look off the field to my right to see my old teammates passing by with cleats hanging around their shoulders. Arm in arm, Steph is laughing with Madison. They don't even notice me...

The ref blows his whistle, and Lynchburg kicks off.

I tell myself to start running.

Our First Dance

I didn't get to talk to Madison and Steph after the game.

By the time ours was over, their game had started, and our bus was getting ready to leave. I couldn't believe Coach didn't want to stick around to check out the competition we'll face this season. He probably has plans to spend the rest of his day checking Facebook.

The only good thing that happened is Alyson, the goalie, sat with me on the bus for a few minutes to say thanks for the good defense today. Even though she'd been kind of bitchy earlier, she seemed grateful for my efforts against Lynchburg. I told her she played awesome, saving twice as many goals as St. Andrew's did against that team last year. When she moved to sit with the rest of the seniors in the back, I filled the silence by listening to music.

Later that afternoon, I find Dad sitting at his desk, typing on his computer. Both of his cell phones are beeping, and the TV is blaring Fox News. A squawking voice spills out of the speakerphone on his desk.

"Is that a parrot on the line?" I joke. "Hey, can we get a pa—"

"We're not getting a parrot," Dad replies. My parents know me and my animal obsession too well.

"Senator, we need to get out in front of this," a voice on the phone says. "You have to make a statement about what happened. Remind people of your strong antidrug stance. Wallace's people are just waiting for your poll numbers to go up again. Then they'll leak something to the press about her drug use—"

"Perhaps she should go to rehab," another voice fires back. "That'll show how seriously you take this."

"She doesn't need rehab," the other man retorts. "The tests found only nominal amounts of Adderall in her system and nothing else. We just need to make a statement!"

Dad looks horrified that I overheard all that and starts jabbing a button on the phone, turning the volume down. I can still hear them. Dad sighs and gives up trying to get the phone to cooperate. "Randy, Kevin, let me call you back," my father says before hanging up.

Randy is Dad's campaign manager, and Kevin is his chief of staff. It's late on a Saturday afternoon, and all these people do is work. It sucks, but I get it. You either work hard, or you don't succeed. Losing the election would not only leave Dad without a position, but all of the people in his DC, Nashville, and Chattanooga offices would lose their jobs too.

It makes me feel guilty that Dad and his guys have to give up their day off to talk about me. I'm the reason they're doing damage control in the first place. At the same time, I hate that I'm a pawn in their political game. It's humiliating.

I sit down in the armchair across from Dad. He looks at me with a tired expression. Campaign season always runs him down, making his hair turn grayer and the wrinkles around his eyes more pronounced. Campaigning is worth it to him though. Hardly anyone knows the president asked him to be Secretary of the Treasury, but Dad turned him down. He prefers being a senator so he can set his own agenda and focus on what he thinks is best for Tennessee, like the farm bill and tax policy. He loves his job.

"How was the soccer game?" he asks.

"We lost. It's every girl for herself out there. Nobody passes the ball."

His mouth fades into a frown. "Maybe you can figure out a way to lead the team."

"But I'm not the captain."

"It's just a title…you don't need that in order to lead," Dad says. "I'm sorry I couldn't make it today."

"Me too," I mutter. "It would've been a perfect campaigning opportunity. But you probably don't want to remind voters we're related."

"Taylor!" Dad pauses to rub his eyes. "This situation is already hard enough without your attitude. What did you need? I have to call the guys back."

"Can I apply to Webb?" I ask.

Webb is a boarding school about an hour from here. I don't know anyone there, but I feel like I might fit in better than at Hundred Oaks.

Dad scrunches his forehead. "Why?"

"They have a better soccer team."

He turns his attention back to his computer. "I'm not paying tuition for another boarding school."

"I checked their website. They offer scholarships to students with outstanding grades and test scores. I figure it's worth a shot to see if they'd be interested in having me."

The determination in my voice gets his attention. He swivels in his chair to face me. He doesn't speak for a long moment. "I'm sorry, but no. You're staying right here where your mother and I can keep an eye on you. If I'd known the sorts of…activities you were involved in, I never would've let you stay at St. Andrew's."

"Webb has more AP courses and a debate team," I say, my voice taking on a desperate tone. "I think if I go there, I'll have a better chance of getting into Yale."

"You should've thought of that before becoming involved with drugs." Dad rubs his eyes again. "I still don't understand. You've never shown any interest in…in that lifestyle."

"I needed to stay awake and study," I say quietly.

"All the more reason for you to stay here and go to Hundred Oaks. It should be more manageable for you."

I shut my eyes. All my hard work. Years and years of pushing myself. All down the drain, because people never notice good news. They flock to the bad.

"You've been seeing the school counselor, right?" Dad asks quietly, his gaze meeting mine.

I'm insulted he has to ask. I look him straight in the eyes when I respond, "Yes."

"Good."

I stand up. "What time are we leaving for the Goodwins' party?" Mr. Goodwin, a millionaire horse-farm owner, is hosting his annual Tennessee Harvest party and most definitely invited lots of people Dad will need to schmooze with in advance of the November election. It's only a little more than a month away. "I saw the invite on the kitchen counter."

Dad clicks his pen on and off. "Why don't you sit this one out." It's not a question.

"But I love going to the Goodwins'. I haven't seen Jack in forever."

"Randy and Kevin are worried people will learn you got kicked out of school."

"People already know. It was on Facebook."

"We don't want the news to spread any further. You need to keep a low profile, or this could turn into a scandal, which would damage my campaign."

"Me getting kicked out of school a scandal? C'mon. That's nothing compared to what the governor's son did. I mean, Simon got drunk and streaked through downtown Nashville."

"And then he went to Europe for six months until everyone forgot about it. It's only been a week since you were caught with pills. Speaking of which, I'm glad to hear Marina hasn't found any more drugs when she's gone through your room."

I gasp. They're going through my stuff? Frantically, I try to think if I have anything embarrassing in my drawers. Did Marina find my condoms? Would she tell Mom and Dad about them?

"Still," Dad goes on, "your mother and I want you to be tested on a regular basis. We'll go next week."

Fuck. They want me to do pee tests?

Taking those pills and taking the blame for Ben didn't just get me kicked out of school. It didn't just mess up my dad's job. It changed people's perception of me. From here on out, I'll be the *druggie girl*.

This is why Dad never wanted us to act entitled, because a last name won't protect you. I never imagined how badly—how quickly—this would screw up my life.

"Did you need anything else?" Dad asks. "I need to get back to it."

My face flushes hot at his dismissal. This situation has morphed from what felt like a simple sacrifice to help my boyfriend to my life spiraling out of control. My anger and embarrassment are starting to outweigh my conflicted feelings toward Ben.

I storm up the stairs and into my bathroom and turn on the

shower, because I don't want my parents or Marina overhearing what I have to say.

I sit down on the toilet, swipe on my phone, and tap Ben's name. He picks up after two rings.

"Tee?"

Hearing him say my name just about undoes me. Tears burn my eyes and throat.

"Hey," I reply, choked up.

"How are you?" he asks. "I've missed you so much."

I love you, I want to say. But he doesn't deserve that.

"Those Adderall pills you gave me."

"Yeah," he says softly.

"Why did you have so many?" There's such a long silence, I check to make sure we didn't get disconnected. "Ben? C'mon. What's the deal?"

He inhales sharply. "I bought them from someone in Birmingham to sell at school…to make some extra cash."

"Oh my God," I whisper. How could I have dated this boy for a year and not have known he was a drug dealer? I mean, they didn't find cocaine or heroin in his bag, but prescription drugs are enough to get you in trouble. I should know. "Why did you do it?"

He clears his throat. "Everything my parents earns goes toward rent and food. I was saving money for college next year. Even if I get a scholarship, I'll need something to live on."

Ben and I aren't that different. We both work hard to prove

ourselves. Both willing to do whatever it takes. I pushed myself to stay up all night to study. He broke the law in order to make money.

In that moment, I realize how crazy it is that we work so hard for our futures. The pressure we're under. Sure, I loved St. Andrew's, but I often stayed up all night studying and did tons of extra activities to show that I deserve to go to an Ivy League school. Just how much do we give up by living this way?

"I'm sorry," he says, and I can hear his remorse. But it's not good enough. I thought I could handle my sacrifice, but I can't.

"Don't sell drugs ever again," I say. "Get a job or something. Listen, I need to go."

"Wait! Tee, I love—"

I hang up and start crying all over again. With shaky hands, I tap out a message: **Please don't contact me again. Good luck.**

And just like that, my first love is over with a text.

Against my dad's wishes, I decide to go to the Goodwins' party for several very important reasons:

1. They own a bunch of horses and dogs;
2. they always have a chocolate fountain at their parties;
3. I want to get out of this mausoleum of a house;
4. I need to get my mind off Ben; and
5. did I mention they have a chocolate fountain?

I wear ankle booties that cover my tattoo and a black sparkly halter dress with a tulle skirt that has a high neckline and a plunging back. I'm showing lots of skin, but I don't care. I love this dress. I like the way I look and feel in it.

At the Goodwins' mansion, I pull into the circular drive and hand my car keys to a cute valet. He gives the Buick a dirty look, then he gives me a look that says *Really? You drive this dinosaur?* I return the dirty look he gave my car. I don't care how cute he is. Nobody sticks his nose up at my Beast.

I give my name to a man resembling an 1800s Regency-era butler so he can check me off the guest list. Then a waiter leads me in the front door, through the foyer, and toward the rear of the house. The party's out back in a clearing between the mansion and the Cedar Hill barns. The stalls Mr. Goodwin rents to horse owners cost more than most families' mortgages per year. The Queen of England stables some of her Thoroughbreds at a farm near here, but Mom heard a rumor that she might move her horses to Mr. Goodwin's farm. Wouldn't it be crazy, the Queen visiting here?

In a way, the Goodwins are Tennessee royalty.

I step out the back door onto a terrace overlooking fields of haystacks and one of their barns. A large tent is set up under the stars. I walk inside it, holding my silver clutch. I smile as I wander across the dance floor beneath sparkling lights and a chandelier. The smell of horse poop wafts inside, but it's part of the charm of being here, and I love it.

I spot Dad and Mom schmoozing on the other side of the party next to the bar. I decide to loiter on the opposite side of the tent, because my parents aren't likely to leave the bar and the food is over here. I start loading a china cocktail plate with shrimp, tenderloin, a brownie, and exactly one carrot, because I don't need anyone judging me on my food choices. Hey, I ran for ninety minutes during soccer today. I earned this pile o' shrimp.

I turn around with my plate and narrowly avoid smashing into Jack Goodwin, my sister's ex.

"Tee, hi!" he says, helping me balance my plate before shrimp go flying.

"Thanks for saving my dinner."

He laughs, and so does the girl he's with. She's petite, with a headful of fire-red hair. This must be the new girlfriend Mom's friends can't help but gossip about. Apparently Jack has been "shacking up with the help," which is "just unheard of" because "Jack comes from well-bred stock."

Jack and his girlfriend go to college together about an hour away in Kentucky, and from what I've heard, she practically lives at his apartment. Regardless of how scandalized my mother is by that, I think Jack's girlfriend is gorgeous and has a friendly smile. I heard she's a jockey here at Cedar Hills Farms, which is so badass.

"Tee, I don't think you've met my girlfriend, Savannah."

Carefully balancing my plate, I shake her hand. "I'm Taylor. Nice to meet you."

"You too. We're sitting over there with friends if you want to join us." She points at a rowdy table of people who are laughing and boozing it up. Their behavior is a little more raucous than I'm used to at these parties.

"Uh, sure," I reply. "Okay." It'll be good to hide from Mom and Dad in plain sight. I follow them over to the table, where Jack makes introductions. I already knew Colton Bradford, the mayor's son, but I haven't met his girlfriend Kelsey before. Nor have I met any of their other friends. All of the girls are beautiful and seem happy. Along with Jack and Colton, there's one other clean-cut boy, Rory, and his girlfriend Vanessa, but the fourth guy—Jeremiah—has his hair pulled back in a half ponytail and his shirtsleeves rolled up to his elbows, showing off three circle tattoos on his forearm. He reminds me of one of my favorite soccer players, Graham Zusi. His arm is lazily draped across the back of his date Annie's chair.

If Mom catches me sitting with Jeremiah, she'll probably insist I get a tetanus shot. Still, I'm jealous of the way he can't take his eyes off Annie. It makes me want a guy I can trust. One who will worship me.

Jack himself has always been Mr. Manners, so it surprises me when he kisses Savannah's neck in front of everybody and sips clear liquor from a cocktail glass. When he was dating my sister, I always found him a little vanilla for my taste, but I quite like this Jack, who's telling raunchy jokes with the other guys, obviously trying to piss off the girls.

"What do you call a bad circumcision?" Jack asks. "A rip-off!"

"Ugh, you are so *cut off*," Savannah says, stealing the cocktail out of his hand. Then she downs it in a single gulp, which makes everybody laugh, including me. I don't know these people, but it is nice to just chill out.

Jack plays with Savannah's red hair as he asks me, "So how's Jenna doing?"

"She's good. She's planning to spend next year abroad at the London School of Economics."

"Wow," Jack says, clearly impressed. "Tell her I said hi." He suddenly turns his attention to something over my shoulder. "Carmichael!"

I twirl around in my chair. Ezra. Of course he'd be here. When I was fifteen and wanted to see him every second of every day, I rarely did, and now he's everywhere. Stupid karma.

But boy, has karma been good to Ezra Carmichael. He's wearing a tailored dark-gray suit with a white dress shirt. The top two buttons are undone, showing off a warm tan patch of skin. Seeing it makes my own skin heat right up.

"Hey, Jack," Ezra says. "Can I borrow Tee from you all?"

"Of course," Jack replies. "But let's talk later. I want to hear about the colt I sold your father."

A dark look crosses Ezra's face, but he quickly recovers. "You bet."

"I want to talk to you later too," I tell Jack, copying Ezra's businesslike voice. "Well, actually I just want to see your dogs."

Jack smiles. "We have a new yellow lab puppy."

I squeal softly, which seems to make Ezra happy. He holds out a hand to me. "Taylor. Want to dance?"

Our first dance should've been at my sixteenth birthday party.

"I can't," I reply. "I'm eating my shrimp right now."

"I like this girl," Jeremiah says with a grin.

Ezra, however, slowly lowers his hand, taken aback by my refusal. "I can wait until you're finished."

"Fine," I say, rolling my eyes, even though my heart is fluttering. Ezra goes back to talking with Jack.

"Is he your boyfriend?" Annie whispers to me.

"No, I have a boyfriend named Ben—" I catch myself, shaking my head. "Why would you think that?"

"The way he was staring at you…it was intense. He's hot, by the way."

"Don't remind me," I groan.

Ezra patiently waits while I eat, like, seven jumbo shrimp. To be honest, I start to feel bloated and gross, but I have to eat them all on principle. When I'm finished eating the entire ocean, he extends his hand again, asking me to dance.

I take a good long look at it and think back to a couple years ago, when we sat on a couch together watching a movie and those fingers played with my hair. If I had gotten some guts and leaned over and kissed him right then, would my life have turned out differently, for better or worse?

He leads me to the dance floor, where he sets one hand on my hip and eases me into a fluid foxtrot. He's very good; Mrs. Carmichael probably made Ezra start taking dance lessons in preschool, like Mom did with Oliver. Dancing to the brass band, I feel like I'm in a glamorous, old-timey movie.

Give me a feather boa already.

We dance in silence for several beats until Ezra speaks. "I'm not supposed to be here."

"Neither am I."

"Then why are you?"

"The food," I say, making him smile. "Why aren't you supposed to be here?"

"My parents are pissed at me. They told me not to come."

I push his chest. "Get out. Dad said the same thing!"

"I bet they're regretting it now," Ezra whispers. "We're the best dancers here."

I've been concentrating on Ezra so intently, I didn't notice the small crowd watching us dance.

The trumpet slides into a high note as his hand moves from my hip to my lower back, his palm big and warm against my bare skin. He's a great dancer. Smooth, but not showy. I'm really enjoying it, and I can tell by his smile that he is too.

No matter what I told myself, I knew my heart wasn't over him, but I'm still disappointed in Ezra. Angry, even. He ditched my party to hook up with *another girl*, as if it was any ole Saturday night, and he never admitted it to my face.

I turn my gaze away from him to find my dad standing with Mr. Carmichael. Both men are glaring at us.

"I'm gonna be in trouble," I say, pulling away from Ezra.

His warm hands keep a tight hold on me. "The song's not over."

"You never told me why you came tonight."

He smirks. "For the shrimp."

I slap his chest. "Don't make fun of me. That shrimp was great. But for real, why did you come?"

He hesitates, looking away from my gaze and out toward the barns in the distance. "I thought coming home was the best thing for me, but all my friends are gone."

I can understand why he's lonely. St. Andrew's is a boarding school, and kids came from all over the country. Steph's family is originally from London and now lives in New York City, while Madison is from San Fran. When Ezra's class graduated, his classmates all went to college or abroad or back home.

"So you wanted to see who'd be at this party?" I ask.

"No, I figured you might be here."

What does that mean? He wants to be friends? He's so desperate for company he sought me out at a party where our parents are hanging out?

He pulls me a little closer. It's intimate, the way his fingers gently caress my lower back. His green eyes meet mine. For so long, this was my dream—that he would hold me. Dance with me. Maybe even love me. But I'm not willing to risk getting hurt again. It took forever to get over Ezra the first time.

I leave his arms. "I need to go."

Without another look at Ezra, I rush off the dance floor, spotting Dad in the middle of a group of men. We make eye contact, and all he does is shake his head.

Part of me regrets defying my father.

But damn, that shrimp was good.

Under Pressure

It's time for my daily counseling session with Miss Brady.

During our meetings, she quizzes me about whether I've had urges to take Adderall or any other drug, and she constantly wants to know how I'm feeling. That part sucks. But some portions of our hour-long meetings are great, like when we discuss the college application process and how to make myself stand out on paper.

"Showing strong leadership skills in your activities is key," Miss Brady says. "What did you think of the list of clubs I gave you?"

"Nothing really appealed to me. Especially not the Polar Bear Club. Pardon my language, but there's no way in hell I'm jumping into Normandy Lake in winter."

Miss Brady laughs. "I don't blame you."

"In terms of leadership, I think soccer is my best bet. But it's not going well."

"How so?"

Leaving out the part where Coach Walker spends most of his

time checking his phone and not coaching us, I tell Miss Brady about the problems I'm facing with the team.

"Nicole doesn't want me there. Which stinks, because I think we could play really well together."

"Have you told her that?"

"I haven't had a chance. She's always too busy insulting me and hogging the ball."

Miss Brady folds her hands on top of the desk. "Why do you feel this is happening?"

"Nicole seems to think I'm a rich, entitled snob, but I'm jealous that the girls on the team listen to her and that she gets to play the position she loves. I was looking forward to being captain of St. Andrew's soccer team this year, you know? I've lost all that."

Miss Brady smiles sadly. "Have you told Nicole this? She might be sympathetic."

"I haven't been able to talk to her one-on-one. She's not very personable."

"It might take time to get to know her, earn her trust."

I've never been in a situation where someone straight-up doesn't like me. It feels awful. "Can we go back to my résumé now?" I ask, sick of talking about Nicole.

Miss Brady sits up straight. "Of course." She asks me to tell her about my other past leadership experiences.

"As I said, I was cocaptain of the St. Andrew's team last year, and I was supposed to be captain this year. I was a Girl Scout counselor at camp last summer, and when I rebuilt houses in Haiti, I was a team lead."

Miss Brady stares at me, wide-eyed. "That's a lot of responsibility." Silence engulfs the room. "Taylor, have you made any friends here yet?"

Ugh, I hate this question. She asks it every time we meet.

I keep thinking about Saturday's soccer tournament, when Steph and Madison walked by laughing together. Sure, they've been texting me, telling me what's going on back in Card House—stuff like Oscar is sad and that they miss me—but they seemed fine the other day without me. It hasn't even been two weeks since I left, and life is back to normal for them. Judging by their Instagram pics, they had a ball eating s'mores at the Monteagle bonfire on Saturday night.

"No, not really," I tell Miss Brady. "I haven't made any friends."

"How's your relationship with your parents?"

I shrug. "They're my parents."

I try thinking about Yale, but end up daydreaming about dancing with Ezra at the party the other night. In my fantasy, he surreptitiously glances around the dance floor, then takes my hand and leads me inside the Goodwins' manor house. He puts a finger up to his mouth and whispers "Shh!" and pulls me into a guest chamber where we rip off each other's clothes and—

"Are you listening, Taylor?"

"What?" I glance up at Miss Brady.

"I was saying that I think your educational goals are commendable, but it seems like you put a lot of pressure on yourself."

"I have to."

"Why?"

"People in my family work hard at everything they do. And I need a business degree so I can work at my family's investment firm one day."

"Oh?"

"Yeah, Grandpa built it from the ground up. He wanted a business where the middle class would feel comfortable investing their money, because it can be intimidating."

Miss Brady rolls her pen back and forth between her fingers without speaking, so I keep on talking. Might as well explain why it's so important that I work hard, so maybe she'll get off my back already.

"My sister's really good with numbers, and Grandpa always asks her opinion on how she thinks a particular stock is going to do. She's going to work for him, and my brother's studying to be a lawyer. Grandpa thinks he'd make a great general counsel. Dad worked at the company for fifteen years before he ran for office, and now he helps out by enacting better tax policies in Congress."

"And what about you?"

"I hate math," I admit. "But my family's worked hard to build what we have. I want to keep that going."

She nods and smiles. Then she changes the subject. "I'm

happy you haven't taken any Adderall since you came to Hundred Oaks, but I worry the underlying reason you took the pills could come back."

"What's that?"

"Your mind can't always be on school and test scores and résumés. You need to relax a little. Spend time with a friend. Watch a good movie."

"I did that sort of thing at St. Andrew's sometimes…"

"But you don't want to here at Hundred Oaks?"

Nicole and the soccer team pop into my head. Then I think of Ben, and I cringe. I usually enjoy making new friends, just not right now…

"Would you like to get out of some of our daily counseling sessions?" Miss Brady asks. "Maybe once a week you could do something else. Supervised carefully by me, of course."

It would be nice to have one day a week that I'm not grilled about potential drug use. "What do I have to do?"

A smile appears on her face. "You need to relax more. Have some fun. Prove to me that you're talking to someone else."

"Do my parents count?"

She lifts an eyebrow. "You *want* to talk to your parents?"

"Fair point." I pause. I can't tell her that I covered for Ben, but she should know I'm not willing to trust someone willy-nilly now. "Look, I can try eating lunch with the soccer team, but I'm not ready to let new people into my life. Can we leave it at that?"

Miss Brady taps a pen on her notepad, thinking. "Is there someone you feel comfortable with?"

"My brother, but he's at Princeton."

"Is there anyone here in town?"

Tuesday morning, I drive to the Donut Palace and get in line for my daily latte. Like clockwork, a couple minutes later, Ezra shows up for his coffee and doughnut holes. There must be something addictive in them, because he is obsessed.

"Hi."

"Hi." He stares at the menu on the wall, careful not to look my way.

"How are you?"

He ignores me, seemingly entranced by the menu, which he's not, because he always gets coffee and cinnamon doughnut holes.

"Is something wrong?" I ask.

He crosses his arms. "You ran off the other night."

"I'm sorry…" I take a deep breath. "Last week, you said you want to talk. Did you still want to?"

His eyebrows pop up. "I've got time." He gestures at a corner booth.

After we both have our coffees, I slide in across from him. He sets his wallet on the table, opens his white paper bag, and pulls out a single doughnut hole, which he places on a napkin and slides in front of me.

I bite off half of it and chew. "What kind of construction are you doing?"

"I'm not really building anything yet. I'm still on demolition crew."

"Yeah? What made you decide to do this?"

He takes a long pull from his coffee cup. "Remember those mission trips we used to go on? I liked building houses."

"Why aren't you doing construction then? Why demolition?"

"I'm lucky I got this position. I need to work my way up in the company. Hopefully, I can start actually building something soon."

"You're a Carmichael. You can do whatever you want, Ez."

He takes a doughnut hole from his bag, dunks it in his hot coffee, and eats the whole thing in one bite. After he finishes chewing, he says in a hard voice, "You mean my father can get me a job. I got this one on my own."

"I still don't get why you didn't go back to Cornell this semester. Did something happen there?" *Please God, don't let there be a girl involved.* "A girl?"

"No, nothing like that." He drinks his coffee and looks out the window. I take the opportunity to grab a sip myself. I've barely had any, since I've been playing detective.

"Why'd you run off the other night?" he asks again. "Something upset you, obviously."

I cradle my cup in my hands. "I ended things with Ben for good that day."

His eyes soften. "You all right?"

I clear my throat. "Yeah."

"I thought you left the party because of me. I thought I'd hurt you somehow," he says quietly.

"To be honest, I just wasn't ready to dance with anybody. Even you."

"I wasn't planning that. I just saw you there, and you looked…" A small smile forms on his lips as his mind seems to wander. I don't think he knows he's grinning.

"Looked what?"

He comes out of his daze. The smile disappears. He glances at his watch. "I better get going."

The barista suddenly appears at our table. "I'm supposed to give you this." She disappears back behind the counter as I rip open the envelope. I hope it's not hate mail or a love letter or something.

"What is it?" Ezra asks as he starts standing up to leave.

The card says:

> Let's have some fun. Here are some
> questions to keep the conversation flowing.
>
> —Miss Brady

When I told her I see Ezra at the Donut Palace sometimes, I

never imagined she'd contact me here. Either she's way into her job or she needs a hobby. I glance at one of the questions.

> *Would you rather eat nothing but Cheerios that had fallen on the floor or sandwich crusts for the rest of your life?*

"My guidance counselor is weird," I say, flipping through the little slips of paper. "Can we meet again tomorrow?"

"Why?" He pockets his wallet. "I got the impression you didn't want anything to do with me."

"My counselor says I'm supposed to talk to someone every day."

"And you want to talk to me?"

"I feel comfortable with you." *More than anybody else around here, anyway.*

He smiles smugly. "Seven o'clock tomorrow then. Bye, Tease."

After he's long gone, I say, "Bye, Ez."

My eyes sweep the noisy cafeteria, looking for the seniors on my soccer team. I told Miss Brady I'd try.

I spot Nicole, Chloe, Alyson, and Brittany at a table next to the Coke machine. It's a place to see and be seen. A tableful of rowdy guys wearing football jerseys and T-shirts sit a few feet away.

With a deep breath, I adjust my tote bag on my shoulder and head toward the girls. I walk up in the middle of a conversation.

"I'm totally going to do it with Jamie tonight," Brittany says.

"You say that every day," Nicole replies.

Chloe gives Nicole a dark look. "Britt, you don't have to defend yourself to us. You can do it whenever you're ready—" She stops talking when they notice I'm hovering beside the table.

"May I sit with you?" I ask, looking straight at Alyson. After I helped defend her goal against the Lynchburg team, maybe we've reached a truce.

It seems I'm right, because Alyson shrugs and gestures at the open seat next to her.

Chloe gives me a short smile, then turns her focus back to her sandwich.

"I didn't say you could sit down," Nicole tells me.

"Nicole, c'mon," Chloe whines. "This isn't middle school. Take a seat, Taylor."

"Thanks," I say. I slide into the empty chair, pulling my lunch out of my bag. Marina packed some veggie chili and baby carrots today.

"Anyway," Brittany lowers her voice, "I think Jamie's getting impatient. He says the guys make fun of him in the locker room because we haven't done it yet."

What the hell? This Jamie guy sounds like a dick. I sink my teeth into a baby carrot so I'm not tempted to voice my concerns aloud. If I knew these girls better, I wouldn't hesitate to speak up, but I don't want to get booted from the table thirty seconds after sitting down.

"Britt," Chloe starts, "it's not cool for Jamie to say things like that. Who cares what those assholes say?"

"Seconded," Alyson says.

"Third-ed," Nicole agrees, and they all giggle.

Brittany looks to me, so I pipe up, "Fourth-ed."

"Sometimes I just feel as if I'm the only virgin left at this school," Brittany says.

"That's not true," Alyson says gently.

It surprises me they are talking about something so personal in front of me, but I guess girl talk is girl talk. Plus, I did play my heart out for them the other day.

I'm starting to relax, but then the conversation changes.

"So, Taylor, why'd you change schools?" Nicole asks, staring at me over the top of her Diet Coke can.

I decide to be honest. "St. Andrew's kicked me out."

Chloe, Alyson, and Brittany gasp, but Nicole just looks at me knowingly. "That's what Coach told my mom. But he didn't say *why* you got kicked out."

I pull a deep breath. Swirl my spoon around in my chili. How could the coach gossip about my private life like that? "I'm not ready to talk about it yet."

Nicole side-eyes me.

"But I'm glad to be on the team," I add. "I love soccer. It makes starting at a new school a little easier…"

Alyson gives me a sympathetic glance.

"You're lucky we needed more players," Nicole remarks.

"Nicole, stop being a bitch," Chloe says, and they give each other dirty looks.

One of the football players swivels around in his chair, leaning toward our table. "Yeah, Nicole. Shut it. Can y'all get back to talking about sex already?"

Alyson throws a grape at the guy, and for the first time since I've set foot in this school, I laugh, and it feels great.

Tuesday afternoon, we have a home game against Coffee County, an excellent team.

Last year, St. Andrew's lost 3–2 against them in the division finals. It totally sucked to lose, but it was a great game. My heart had never pounded so hard as Steph and I worked tirelessly to take shots on goal. We both scored once, but it wasn't enough.

I think some of Coffee County's best players graduated last year. Still, they had some great juniors and sophomores, so today will be no cakewalk.

As usual, I'm the first player warming up on the field. It surprises me when Sydney, the freshman who's pretty good, joins me in front of the goal.

"Hi," I say.

"Hey." Her voice is meek, which makes no sense given how good she is on the field. I was pretty impressed by her on Saturday, and she was playing a position she typically doesn't play. She should have more confidence.

"You played well the other day." I pass her the ball I was playing with.

She stops it with her cleat. She looks toward the locker room, almost as if she's embarrassed to be seen talking to me. Or maybe not embarrassed, per se, but scared.

"Pass it back," I call.

With a deep breath, she plants her left foot and kicks the ball with her right laces.

I run to meet the ball, snapping it back to her. I grin, excited to have someone to play with, but Sydney doesn't look like she's having all that much fun.

"What's wrong?"

"Nicole doesn't want any of us talking to you because you teased our team last year."

"Nicole doesn't even *know* me, Syd. I just want to play soccer, okay?"

"That's all I want too."

"I'm going to talk to her privately," I announce. "I don't care what she says about me, but she has to start passing the ball."

"I don't think you should confront her," Sydney replies, biting her lip. It doesn't surprise me. As a freshman, I never would've had the balls to confront the St. Andrew's captain. On the other hand, I very much respected her. Who knows what I would've done if the captain had been a bully.

"If Nicole's not a team player, she needs to be called out for that," I say. "It's not like she can play a game without the rest of you. She can't be everywhere at once, even if she thinks she can."

Sydney dribbles the ball, does a fake, then passes it back to me. "I made all-district on the middle school team last year."

"That's awesome," I say with a smile. Only ten girls make it each year. I never did.

"I was really excited I made the Hundred Oaks team as a freshman," she says softly. "I usually play forward, but Nicole won't let me anywhere near the front line."

"Because she knows you're good. I bet she doesn't want to share the spotlight."

Sydney nods slowly. "My mom says it's only one year. Nicole will graduate, and then I can go back to my regular position."

"That's bullshit. What does Coach Walker say?"

"He doesn't care. He's the freshman guys' gym teacher. Coaching soccer is just an extra paycheck to him."

I hate the bitterness I hear in her voice.

"I want a scholarship," Sydney goes on. "I don't want scouts seeing me play D. It's not what I love. I don't want to end up playing that position all through high school."

"I totally get what you're saying."

That makes her smile, but it fades when the locker room door opens and the other girls begin to trickle out. When I see how terrified Sydney is of Nicole, an idea comes to mind. Dad always says, *"If you want someone to do something, trick them into thinking it was their own idea."*

I smile mischievously to myself, then kick the soccer ball way out in front of me. I dribble toward Nicole, doing a few fancy tricks along the way to show off. As I get closer to her, I pretend to trip over the ball and let it roll out of bounds.

Nicole enjoys this, of course. I hustle to retrieve the ball. Once I have it, I move close to her again. I point over at Sydney.

"Sydney's really good," I tell Nicole. "Thanks for putting her on defense with me. I couldn't do it without her."

Nicole looks from me to her. "Sydney! You're playing left forward today."

The look of pure excitement on Sydney's face makes me so happy. I'll play D for the rest of my life just to keep her smiling like that.

I fake anger toward Nicole. "No, you can't do this! I need her on D."

With a smirk on her face, Nicole tosses a ball in the air and catches it. "You'll just have to hustle more, I guess."

That was ridiculously easy.

As soon as Nicole is off torturing someone else, I watch

Sydney and the other freshman do their drills, which I've been encouraging players to do before scrimmage starts. Julia isn't bad. She has control of the ball and clearly knows how to move. I gaze around at the other girls. Chloe has excellent footwork. A couple others have great mechanics too. Alyson is awesome in goal. And of course there's Nicole. But about half of the team seems to be here simply to have something to do. They don't appear to be all that interested in playing; instead, they gossip and watch the boys playing pickup basketball.

But having seven girls with skills is good. Really good.

Maybe we could make a real showing this year.

I decide to buy Ezra's coffee today.

After all, he's agreed to talk with me, which should ultimately get me out of meeting with Miss Brady once a week. I like the woman, but spending five hours a week with her is just too much.

When Ezra arrives at Donut Palace, he opens the door, looks around, and spots me sitting in the corner booth away from the noise of the cash register. I wave him over, and as he's making his way to me, I check out his Braves ball cap, long-sleeved black shirt, ripped jeans, and work boots splotched with dirt. His biceps and forearms seem to be getting bigger each day. Demolition is physically demanding work.

"Morning, Tease," he says, stifling a yawn.

I slide him his coffee. He lifts the lid and peeks inside. "How'd you know?"

"You order the same thing every day."

"So do you."

"I know what I like."

His mouth lifts into a mischievous smile. "I know what I like too."

He takes a sip of his coffee and sets the cup down on the table. Together we gaze out the window at the farmland to the east, where the sun rose about half an hour ago. That's one of my favorite things about this café—it's on the outskirts of Franklin, and all the green reminds me of St. Andrew's. And with Ezra sitting across from me, it's almost as if I'm back there.

As much as I didn't want to be around him, because I'm afraid my crush will come back, I feel very relaxed sitting here. I sip my latte and sigh.

Then Ezra's cell phone makes a noise like someone bowling a strike. He digs in his pocket and pulls it out. I've never seen him look at his phone before. It's totally un-Ezra.

He stares at the screen for several seconds and laughs. He types back.

"What's going on?" I ask, a little miffed. I hate it when people look at their phones while they're spending time with me. It makes me feel like I'm not worth their time.

"It's my friend Svetlana."

Svetlana?

"From Cornell," he clarifies.

"Oh," I say in a tiny voice. "Your girlfriend?"

His eyebrows pop up. He takes a little too long before responding, "No, she's not."

His cheeks blush pink, and it's not from the coffee. If she's not his girlfriend, then what is she to him? Has he hooked up with her? What kind of a name is Svetlana anyway? I start imagining a Russian gymnast who contorts herself into fancy sexual positions while spying on the United States.

"Do you talk to friends from Cornell a lot?" I ask.

He lifts a shoulder. "Mostly just Svetlana. And my old roommate, Justin."

"Do you miss college?"

"Yeah, I miss my friends and intramural soccer. And I loved my frat."

"Oh. I guess I figured you didn't like it there. Since you're back, you know?"

"I liked all the social aspects of college, especially the Sloppy Joe bar—"

"Sloppy Joe bar?"

"The dining hall had a Sloppy Joe bar on Tuesdays and Thursdays."

My mouth waters at the idea. Unless there's a Sloppy Kale

Joe thing I don't know about, Sloppy Joes will never be served at my house.

"But there were parts of college you didn't like?" I press.

He rests his chin on his fist. "Yeah, the whole *college* part. The classes."

Huh. Oliver and Jenna settled right in at their schools. "Really?"

"The business courses sucked. College writing sucked. It pretty much all sucked."

"Is that why you left?"

He adjusts his ball cap. "I'm taking some time off. I need to figure out what I want to do."

"So you're going back in the spring? Or next year?"

"That's what my father wants…and expects."

As the largest shareholder in the Tennessee Asset Management Group, Mr. Carmichael is the wealthiest man in the state. He's even richer than the royally connected Goodwins. He has tons of influence. He endorsed my dad's reelection campaign. Lots of people depend on Mr. Carmichael. In turn, Mr. Carmichael expects a lot of Ezra.

"But?" I prompt.

"But the longer I'm away from Cornell, I'm not sure I should go back."

"Why not?"

"I don't want to be a business major. The classes…just aren't for me."

"Maybe change your major?"

"Try telling that to my father."

I totally get what he's saying. I care a lot about my future, and I work very hard. But if my parents—my dad in particular—hadn't always been pushing me to be the best I can be, would I work so hard in school? Would I care? I don't know.

"If you could change your major, what would you pick?" I ask.

He stares at his coffee cup. "I'm not sure. I like working on houses though. I like using my hands."

I glance down at his strong, tanned hands and swallow hard.

I hope he didn't use them on Svetlana.

Today Miss Brady left us a prompt that reads,

What's the best gift you've ever gotten?

"That's easy," I say. "Chickadee!"

Ezra bursts out laughing. "I forgot all about him."

"My mom sure hasn't. I can still hear her hollering about that rooster poop on the back deck."

When I was eleven, Ezra came over to our house bearing a gift for me, *just because*. He opened his hands, and out popped a little yellow chicken. It was so cute. I named him Chickadee.

Mom and Dad hated Chickadee, but I wouldn't part with him. He was a gift from Ezra! Then Chickadee grew from a tiny chick into this giant rooster. He attacked anything and everything with his beak and flapped his wings like Dracula.

"Chickadee loved eating chicken," I say. "It was sort of cannibalistic."

"Remember that time he bit Oll's finger?"

I clap my hands, laughing. "Yeah, and after that, Mom thought Chickadee needed a distraction, so she bought those hens. Bow-chick-a-wow-wow," I sing.

"But he wasn't interested in the hens."

"Yup, because Chickadee was gay."

Ezra snort-laughs, which makes me laugh even harder.

"Only you would manage to give me a gay rooster," I say.

"You loved it."

"Yup. I was so sad when Chickadee died."

"But then I brought you that betta fish."

"Mom was much happier about that. She probably thought you'd bring me a baby goat next. Which I would love, by the way."

Ezra smiles widely before drinking from his cup.

"So what's the best gift you've ever gotten?" I ask.

He takes another long draw of coffee before answering my question. "It's not really a gift. It was more of an experience. Dad took me camping in Arkansas for my eighteenth birthday—it was just me and him and the river. We caught trout and cooked it over the campfire. Then we drank beer and just talked. I liked how he treated me like a man."

I smile. "Sounds nice."

"It was. I think it was the longest he and I have ever been alone together. He doesn't usually have time, you know?"

"I get that. Both our dads are busy."

His face darkens. "I doubt Dad and I will ever do anything like that again."

"Why not?"

"He's pissed that I left Cornell. We haven't been talking much lately. I don't really know what to do about it."

I shouldn't pry, because I understand how it feels having people poke around in your business, but I care about him. I need to know more. "So did you, um, officially drop out of school?"

Ezra gives me a hard look. "I took a leave of absence."

"So you can go back?"

"Can we talk about something else?" He peers at the envelope Miss Brady left us at the counter. "Any other prompts in there?"

"You can talk to me," I say quietly. "You know, if you want to."

He eats the last doughnut hole and crushes the white paper bag into a ball. "I don't want to talk about it here. You've got school, and I need to get to the work site."

I take a deep breath. "Okay, so tell me when and where you want to talk."

"Friday night? You, me, the Cumberland Science Museum?"

I'm scared to put myself back out there again, but this is Ezra. The guy I've known forever. The friend I can talk to.

The one I can trust?

119

Queen Bee

"I don't understand how we're getting away with this."

I'm walking with Ezra through the deserted Cumberland Science Museum on Friday evening, drinking a chocolate milk shake. I feel like I'm breaking every rule of museum etiquette.

"The curator owes Dad a favor."

"I thought things are weird with your father."

Ezra winks. "The curator doesn't know that."

We sit on a bench by the human body exhibit. Mechanical displays demonstrate how the intestine digests food and the heart pumps blood. It's a little grotesque and probably not the best thing to watch while eating, but there aren't many places to sit. I squint, trying to read the placards next to the displays. Ezra reaches into a white paper bag that's spotted with grease and pulls out a shrimp Caesar salad (for me) and a cheeseburger and fries (for him).

When I snap the lid off my salad, Ezra shares a few of his fries, setting them on top of my lettuce. It makes me grin. I eat one of the fries immediately but decide to save the other two for last. He bites into his cheeseburger, then licks mustard off his finger. Oh, to be that mustard. Maybe if I "accidentally" get some salad dressing on the side of my mouth, he'd lick it off.

I nearly groan at the thought. I shouldn't be thinking such things. I should be protecting my heart, but Ezra's intoxicating, spicy smell has me under a spell. He's wearing dark jeans and a gray *Iron Man* T-shirt he's had for years that looks soft and comfortable from being washed so many times.

"What'd you do after school today?" he asks between bites. "Soccer practice?"

"No, this coach doesn't make us practice on Fridays."

Ezra's eyebrows scrunch together. "How's he expect you to win?"

"I asked the same thing." I pop a crouton in my mouth and chew. "After school, I worked on my college essays. I'm having a tough time with the prompts. I keep trashing what I've written and starting over."

Ezra starts to bite into his burger but then he stops and pauses. "Yeah, they're hard."

"I'm so worried," I say quietly. "What if I don't get into Yale? I got kicked out of St. Andrew's. What if they question my character? What if—"

"Tease." He sets a gentle hand on my shoulder. "You're one of the smartest people I know."

I smile sadly. "I just don't know what I'll do if I don't get into Yale."

"Why do you want to go there?"

"It's what I've been working toward forever."

"So?"

"So?" I snap. "It's important to me."

"But why?"

"It's a great school where I'll learn a lot so I can help at my family's firm. Plus, my dad expects it."

Ezra removes his hand from my shoulder and rips into his burger. We chew in silence.

"Why're you having trouble with your essays?" he asks through a mouthful.

"I'm supposed to write about a time I took a big risk and what I learned from it. Other than getting kicked out of St. Andrew's, I haven't really done anything bad."

Ezra is thoughtful. "Risk doesn't always have to be a negative, you know. Sometimes, it's good to take risks—calculated risks—and hope you get a payoff. Life is a lot like poker."

I see what he's getting at. "You took a risk leaving school. Was it worth it?"

"Ultimately, I think so. I mean, I'm happier overall, but my parents are really pissed at me. Dad took away my trust fund, and he's talking about writing me out of his will."

"What?" I screech, dropping my plastic fork on the floor. I lean over to pick it up. How could a father separate himself from his son like that?

"I don't care about the money. It just sucks how Dad is treating me."

I squeeze Ezra's knee. "I understand what it's like to disappoint your parents."

He stares at my hand and clears his throat. "It's the risk I took. I knew my dad would be pissed, but I couldn't stay at Cornell. I hated the classes."

"So you want to keep doing demolition and get promoted to construction?"

He focuses on the mechanical human heart urgently pumping blood—*whoosh, whoosh, whoosh*. "I would love to design houses. Like architecture."

"That sounds really cool," I say eagerly. "Have you told your dad that?"

With a shake of his head, Ezra eats the last bite of his burger. "To Dad, I either major in business and take over his company, or I'm not part of his life. He can be such a dick sometimes."

"Maybe you could go back to school and study architecture. Pick the school you want and pay for it yourself. Take out student loans."

His face flames red. "I'm not sure I want to go back to school, even to study architecture."

I steal a few more of his fries. "I don't see how you can give up college."

"Like I said, I took a risk. There are other options out there. I wish you'd consider them yourself."

"What do you mean?"

"You don't even know why you want to go Yale, other than it's where everyone in your family has gone to college. You don't even know what you want to study."

I set my fork down in my plastic bowl. I'm not hungry anymore. "I already have my parents judging me. I don't need you doing that too. I need a friend."

"I'm sorry. I shouldn't have said that—I just want you to be happy."

"That's what I want for you too."

Ezra takes my hand. Gazes into my eyes. The low museum lights emphasize his handsome face. He's a great work of art.

Then he says softly, "Let's walk around."

Our next stop is the beekeeping exhibit.

Hundreds of thousands of bees zoom around behind the glass, serving their queen by feeding young bees, collecting pollen and nectar, and making honey. The dripping honeycomb looks delicious. The little placard says the queen lays three thousand eggs per day! My stomach hurts just thinking about that.

"Bees scare me," I tell Ezra.

His lips curl into a smile. "Oh yeah? I love them."

"Of course you would, you weirdo. Next, you're gonna tell me you love rattlesnakes and black widow spiders." I tremble, recalling a time in my grandparents' backyard. "Once, at Nana and Grandpa's, I lifted this clay pot, and I found a black widow inside it."

Ezra shudders. "What happened?"

"The spider was so pretty and plastic looking, I nearly picked it up, 'cause I thought it was a toy! Mom and Dad were always on my case to share my toys, so I wanted to give it to Oliver."

Ezra laughs. "You tried to give Oliver a black widow? Why have I never heard about this?"

"Probably because when I handed him the pot, he screeched like a girl and peed his pants."

At that, Ezra barks out a laugh and gives me a hug. It starts as a friendly pat on the back, but then he wraps his arms around me, and I do the same to him. His warm hands slide across my shoulders and glide up and down my spine. I've been waiting years for this moment. Since the first time I met him when I was ten. The hug makes me feel like I'm lying in a field, enveloped by the sun. But bees are swarming nearby.

I gently pull out of his arms and avoid Ezra's gaze, trying to hide the fact that he steals my breath away.

"Why do you love bees?" I ask, so he'll talk while I get back in control of my faculties. And by faculties, I mean lady parts.

"I like that every bee has a job and knows what he's supposed to do."

"Wouldn't you rather have choices though?"

"Wouldn't you?" he asks bluntly.

I cross my arms. I should call him an ass, but he's not wrong.

"Bees don't know any better," he goes on. "It's all instinct for them. I wish all we had to do is follow our instincts."

"How would you follow them?"

"Well, I'd eat pizza every day for dinner. I'd design houses and help build them. I'd take apart whatever I want, and nobody would care. Weekends would consist of watching sports and maybe playing a few games of poker during the day. And then at night, I'd go out and listen to live music. And instead of wearing swim trunks, I'd always skinny-dip."

My face heats up at that visual, which I think was his intention, because he smirks.

"What about you?" he asks, leaning so close our foreheads nearly touch. I can feel his warm breath on my lips. "I mean, other than stealing all my fries."

I lean back against the guardrail surrounding the bee exhibit. It's Friday night. I'm not in the mood for hard questions. "Can I get back to you on that? I'm busy right now."

"Oh yeah?" he asks with a laugh. "Busy doing what?"

"Beating you at a museum race!" I take off in a sprint down the long, wide hallway. Ezra runs behind me, his boots nipping at mine. Our laughter rings out in the empty museum. It's then that I can't deny it anymore.

I like him chasing me.

When I get home from soccer practice on Monday afternoon, I sit down at the kitchen island to work on my homework and essays. I pull my notebooks out of my bag and set them on the counter on top of a newspaper. Today's *Tennessean*. I ignore it at first, but then notice Dad and Mom on the cover.

They're at Centennial Park in Nashville, waving to a large crowd. A campaign event. I scan the article. Blah blah, tax reform, blah blah, farm bill, blah blah. Nothing new there. I'm not mentioned at all. Tossing the newspaper aside, I let out a breath of relief.

My cell buzzes. Oliver.

Dad came to visit today.

Yeah? At Princeton?

He brought a camera crew.

What!

It was ridiculous. He wanted footage of us playing catch. We put on gloves and pretended to throw a ball around for 3 mins. Then he left.

Ha! Why?

New commercial. He took footage of Jenna this morning.

So Dad flew to Connecticut and then New Jersey to video

my brother and sister? Does this mean I need to be ready for a candid close-up? I rush to the powder room to check my skin. Thanks to stress, I have a few blemishes that might be visible on TV. Hopefully, a little concealer will do the trick. Wait—what if Dad doesn't want me in the ad? No, when he makes a campaign video, the whole family is in it.

I'd check with Mom, but she's at the Vanderbilt hospital today, meeting with young cancer patients. It's something she enjoys doing to honor her sister's memory.

Dad doesn't come home until later that night. I'm in bed, checking over my AP chemistry homework, when I hear him trudging up the stairs and going into the master suite, the door shutting with a loud click.

The next morning, I find him at the breakfast table.

"Good morning," we say to each other.

"Want your omelet?" Marina asks me.

"No, thanks. I'm meeting Ezra for doughnuts." If Mom were up already, she'd scowl about me not eating a healthy breakfast. What surprises me is that Dad scowls. He totally sneaks fancy cheeses and sweets when Mom isn't looking.

"Have you been hanging out a lot with Ezra?"

I shrug. "Yeah."

"I don't think he's the best influence for you right now. You should find someone else to spend time with."

"What are you talking about? Ezra's a great guy."

My father stares at me. "Everyone's saying he dropped out of college."

"He took a leave of absence," I say defensively.

"That sounds like dropping out to me."

"C'mon, Dad. Don't be like his parents. Ezra just didn't like his major."

"I don't want him filling your head with crazy ideas."

"That won't happen," I say, even though Ezra's already been pressuring me to think about what I truly want. "Look, Ezra's nice."

"You thought that boyfriend of yours was nice too. But you never once got in trouble before you met him. Then I started getting calls from the dean about you kissing under the stairs between classes. Sneaking out to meet him after dark. And then there were the pills."

I hesitate for a moment at the mention of the drugs. "Look, Dad, I don't understand why Ezra's acting the way he is, but it's not like he's out drag racing every night. He's a normal guy. He's just trying to figure things out."

"Until Ezra Carmichael gets his life in order, I suggest you spend time working on your applications. Do your homework."

"That's insulting. You know I always do my homework. I work really hard all the time!"

Dad puts his napkin on the table and stands up. "I know, I know." He pulls me into an awkward hug. If I weren't so angry, I might appreciate the grand display of fatherly affection.

"I love you," he says with a pat on the back.

"I love you too," I mumble. This is the first time I've talked to him in days. "Dad?"

"Yeah?"

"My interview with Yale Admissions is in two weeks. Um, are you still coming with me? If you can't, that's okay. Jenna said I can stay with her. She'll take me. Mom would come, but she has that big fund-raiser at Vanderbilt that day. It's been on her schedule for, like, a year," I ramble.

Dad looks down at me. "I'll take you up there. I'll visit with your sister while you're doing your interview."

Of course he'll spend his time with Jenna. I'm a lost cause.

I'm too pissed to even bring up the fact that Dad visited Jenna and Oliver to record them for a commercial. It's not like I'm about to offer my help now.

But it never occurs to me that he doesn't bring it up either.

A day later, I find out why.

Unintended Consequences

Besides *Game of Thrones*, I never miss that show *I Didn't Know I Was Pregnant*. Yes, it's trashy, but I just can't help myself.

I finished my homework an hour ago and spent some time noodling over my essays. I have the worst case of writer's block, so I decide to indulge in the most craptastic show of all time. I flop down on the den couch and flick on the TV. If only I had some popcorn... I don't think Mom keeps it in the house, because even though it's made of whole grains, she'd be tempted to slather it in butter, and we couldn't have that, because Mom doesn't eat anything edible.

The show switches to a commercial, so I check my phone. I have a new group text from Steph and Madison. They are gabbing about the show, because they love it too. Their snarky comments make me smile. No texts from Ezra. After the Cumberland Science Museum, we haven't talked much except for today's five-minute coffee break at Donut Palace.

I decide to text him: Do you watch I Didn't Know I Was Pregnant?

A minute later, he replies, What is that?

A reality show about women who are pregnant but don't know it.

Sounds terrible.

Oh stop. You'd love it!

It takes forever for Ezra to write back. You're as bad as Oll. He loves this show where ppl bid on storage units.

Storage Wars! It's great.

Oh, you.

I grin at my screen. I wish he were here on the couch, curled up with me.

I stopped talking to him after he missed my party to hook up with Mindy Roberts, but what if I had forgiven him? Would we have gotten together? But why would I want to be with a guy who hooks up with another girl?

On the other hand, why did I give up our friendship just because he made one mistake? I hate how my parents have been judging me after I made one mistake. But giving up my crush two years ago, giving up *him*—that was the only way to protect my heart.

Based on how Ezra's been acting since I came back to Franklin, it's like I'm the only girl in the world. I mean, except for Svetlana, the Russian spy dominatrix. I run my finger over my phone screen, touching Ezra's picture.

I'm distracted from Ezra's smile when Dad's voice spills from the TV speakers. It's one of his campaign commercials.

"My mother was a schoolteacher, and my father, a businessman.

They raised me in a middle-class neighborhood right here in Franklin, Tennessee. After high school, I joined the Air Force and served my country in Vietnam. Now I serve my country in a different way. As your senator for the past eighteen years, I've worked hard to bring jobs to Tennessee. In just the past two years, we've added one hundred government positions at the Arnold Engineering Development Complex, the most advanced flight simulation test facility in the entire world.

"I'm a lot like you. I have a family that I work to support. My son is prelaw and hopes to become a public prosecutor, to help keep Tennessee safe."

God, Dad will say anything for a vote. If Oll becomes a public prosecutor, I'll eat my hat. He's totally gonna get a job as general counsel at the family firm.

The commercial cuts to my brother throwing a baseball to my dad. Then the image of my dad sitting with Jenna on a park bench fills the screen.

"My daughter is carrying on the family tradition and is majoring in business, just like me and my father. My kids left Tennessee for college, but my goal is to keep creating good jobs here, so my kids and yours will come back to Tennessee after they graduate.

"Tennesseans, we stick together."

That's how the commercial ends. No mention of me. Nothing about me having a 4.2 GPA or being a kick-ass soccer player or that I'm hopefully headed to a good college…

I lean over and place my head between my legs. Tears fill my eyes. I've killed myself working hard for years. And now I am an embarrassment.

But wait. Why is this new commercial airing now? Why did Dad rush up to get footage of Jenna and Oliver?

I swipe on my phone and pull up the *Tennessean* home page. The headline reads, *Senator Lukens Admits Family Problems*.

The article reads, *Senator Edward Lukens released a statement today, acknowledging his underage daughter was recently found with pharmaceuticals that were not prescribed to her. Senator Lukens stressed that while this is a personal family matter, his stance on drugs has not changed, and he and his wife are taking the situation with their youngest daughter very seriously.*

My hand shakes as I stare at my phone.

I storm up the stairs. A tear rolls down my face. And then another. I bang my fist on the door to Dad's study.

"Come in." He sounds tired.

I walk over to Dad's media center, where's he's pecking away on the keyboard. Of course he's on the speakerphone with one of those bozos, Kevin or Randy.

"How could you?" I screech.

The clackity-clack of Dad's typing stops. "Randy, I'll call you back." *Click.*

"Taylor, I'm sorry," he says softly. He at least has the decency to look embarrassed. "You know I had to get out in front of this. If I didn't say something now, Wallace's people would've secretly encouraged the press to bring your issues to light a day or two before the election."

"My *issues*? How can Yale consider me with this splashed all over the papers? They make me sound like an addict."

"With your grades, you've still got a shot—"

"I have to get into college on my own merits, and you just took away any credibility I had left! No one is going to care about my grades or my résumé now. They'll just see what is printed in the headlines. You didn't even ask my permission before blasting my business all over the news!"

I stalk out of the room, slamming the door. I hurry to my bed, where I crawl under the sheets and cover my face.

If Yale didn't know about what happened at St. Andrew's, they will now. I shake my head. If only I'd thought through all the possible outcomes before I told the dorm mothers it was my backpack. But with the dorm mother shining a flashlight in my face, I froze. If I had thought it through, maybe I would've turned Ben in. I still could. But would anyone believe me, considering Adderall was found in my system? Oliver and Jenna would. Ezra too. They could help me set the record straight.

I'm fixing to call my brother when I think about the ramifications. Turning in Ben wouldn't take attention off me; it would just fuel the story. It would give the press more to blast me for and, in turn, would negatively affect Dad's campaign again. I can see the headlines now: *Senator's Daughter Snitches to Save Self.*

On top of the possibility I could further trash Dad's campaign, I'd almost rather be known as a druggie than a snitch. People will forget about pills, but a person's character isn't so easily forgotten.

When I was a freshman, the most popular guy in school was a senior lacrosse player named Davis. Everyone loved him, even though he was an asshole. One time during his senior year, he wasn't prepared to take his U.S. Constitution exam, so he called a bomb threat into the school. Everyone was terrified as we evacuated. Until I was safely at the University of the South up the road, I really thought I was about to die.

After the bomb dogs finished searching campus, freaked-out parents showed up and hauled their kids away until the situation was under control. Then a rumor spread that Davis was behind the bomb threat. Pretty soon, all the students knew what he did. Since no one got hurt, some people didn't think it was a big deal. Others, like me, thought it was a shitty thing to do. Just because nothing happened didn't mean it wasn't dangerous. What if someone had been trampled in the rush to escape? What if a real emergency happened and the cops were busy searching for a bomb that had never existed?

I gave Davis the stink eye whenever I saw him and muttered "jerk" under my breath, but I would never have the guts to tell a teacher. It didn't matter that lots of kids thought Davis was worse than a Lannister after what he did; no one would've ever trusted me again if I snitched. And you know anonymity wouldn't work—someone would eventually leak that I was the person who turned him in.

In Davis's case, a junior ended up stepping forward. He told the dean the truth about what happened. In return, someone put a dead fish in the ceiling above the boy's bed and scratched SNITCH into the side of his car.

What sucks is that the boy didn't do anything wrong. Ultimately, he did what was right.

But nobody saw it that way.

All they saw was a tattletale.

The next morning's headlines:

Antidrug Senator Admits Daughter Is Drug User

Wallace Passes Lukens in Polls

I can't breathe.

Out of Context

Apparently, when your name is splashed all over the news, your classmates revert to middle schoolers.

Before first period, when I walk down the hall, other students say, "Ooh" and "Busted!" like seventh graders.

Some guy I've never spoken to corners me in the hall. His eyes dart around. "Do you have any Ritalin? I can pay."

I throw my tote bag over my shoulder to block him from getting any closer and dash away, trying to make it to calculus unscathed. Up until today, most people ignored me. Now, teachers shoot me glances—some of pity, some of suspicion. Have none of these people ever made a mistake before?

Nicole and Chloe see me, and Nicole starts whispering. Then she blurts out, "Do you use steroids too, Taylor? I'm gonna have to tell Coach."

"You do that," I snap back. "I'll recommend that we all get tested. Hope your aim into a cup is better than your shots on goal!"

Her face goes white.

Chloe bites down on her lip as if to keep from laughing.

I charge away and don't start breathing normally again until I'm sitting in class, thinking solely about equations. Things must be fucked up if I actually want to do math.

Third period, I have Crucial Life Lessons, which is the sorriest excuse for a class ever. We're learning how to balance our bank accounts, when a paper wad hits me in the head. It falls onto my desk, so I unwrinkle it.

Ritalin? Can you hook me up?

I glance around to see who threw it. It's the same guy from earlier this morning. I write NO!! in big letters, wad up the paper, and throw it back at him, but Coach Lynn—our teacher and girls' softball coach—intercepts it with the finesse of a catcher.

She smooths out the paper. My heart is racing, and—oh God!—she's going to call my dad, and he's going to think I'm *still* involved in drugs.

But Coach Lynn looks up with a smile. "Good job, Taylor. Excellent life choice!"

"Teacher's pet," some girl whispers loud enough for everyone to hear, and the class snickers. Jeez, I was wrong. They didn't revert to middle schoolers but to first graders.

Coach Lynn pockets the note and speaks to the boy who wrote it: "Caleb, may I see you after class?"

I look over my shoulder at Caleb. His *need* for Ritalin is scary. I never considered that prescription drugs could make a person behave this way. Between classes, I lean against my locker, swipe on my phone, and look up Ritalin addictions. I scroll through a webpage about it. Shit. This particular prescription drug acts like cocaine. Some people snort it to get high. I hope Coach Lynn tries to help Caleb.

Next I text Oliver. Dad is such an asshole.

I'm sorry, T.

I wait for him to say something else, something encouraging. But Oliver doesn't text again. What else is there to say? This is not how I expected my senior year to be. All anyone sees is my one mistake.

Later in the day, as I change into shorts and a T-shirt, then slip on my shin guards, socks, and cleats, my hands shake like I've had ten cups of coffee. My eye twitches as I braid my hair into a plait. I stare at myself in the mirror. How did this happen? How did things get so out of hand so fast?

When I walk out onto the field, I'm the first person there, as always. Danny arrives a few minutes later to set up cones. Today, he's wearing a T-shirt that says *I'm Kind of a Big Deal*.

I grab a ball and start juggling, then run up and down the field, dribbling. I lean back, strike the ball with my laces, and plant a shot in the upper right of the goal, putting all my rage into it. Nailing that shot feels great.

I grin as I retrieve the ball from the net. The other players start arriving and doing their random warm-ups. Alyson heads to the goal, jumping to slap the overhead beam. It's her tradition.

"Can I take some shots on you?" I ask, and she claps, appearing happy for the practice.

For the next several minutes, I run hard, dribble hard, and kick the ball at our goalie. She stops four out of my seven shots. We smile at each other.

Then Coach steps out onto the field, and for once, he's not having a love affair with his phone.

He calls, "Taylor!" and gestures for me to run his way.

I pick up my ball and jog with it. "What's up, Coach?"

"Listen," he starts. He sighs, looking everywhere but at me as he chews his gum. "I can't let you practice today."

"Um, what?" I've been looking forward to practice all day!

"Your father made a statement about what happened at your old school."

No shit, Sherlock. "Yeah, so? What's that got to do with soccer?"

"I've had parents calling. They want to make sure you're not sharing drugs with their kids."

"Excuse me? You're joking, right?"

"Three upset parents called. I can't let you practice. Not until this is sorted out."

"What does the principal say?" I demand, because there's no way I'm quitting without a school professional telling me that I have to. And Coach Walker is not a professional anything, particularly the way he's handling this.

"I haven't spoken with Dr. Salter yet, because he was unavailable this afternoon, but I have an appointment to talk with the school board at their Monday meeting. That's when we'll decide if you can stay on the team."

Coach Walker went over the principal's head? Really? "But we have a game against Hendersonville on Saturday!"

"I'm sorry, but you should sit the game out. Come to think about it, you should probably come to Monday's meeting too, so you can explain to the board that you're clean now."

Clean now.

Great, just great.

"We need you on the team, Taylor," Coach says. *What he needs is the extra paycheck he gets for coaching.*

I storm off the field, trying not to listen to Nicole's laughter. Alyson and Chloe stare over at me.

"Coach, what's going on?" I hear Alyson ask, her voice full of desperation. I'm upset too. We were starting to form a really good defense together.

I retrieve my bag from my locker and head for the Swamp. Students don't have assigned parking spaces at Hundred Oaks, but all the seniors park around this sunken expanse of concrete that's filled with water and mud. It's gross. As I trudge through the Everglades to my car, I see a crowd of people waiting.

"That's her!"

"There she is!"

People charge at me with microphones, cameras, and notepads.

They start taking pictures of me. *Flash, flash, flash, flash.* I lift my hand to shield my eyes.

"Taylor! Do you have any comment about your father's statement?"

"Do you take pills?"

"Do you sell them?"

"How is your father handling your addiction?"

"Do you think your father could still run for governor after this?"

I try to break through the reporters and run back toward the school, but it's a mob. They're too close. Doesn't this school have security or something?

"Get away from me!" I shout, trying to pass two men.

"Talk to us then!" one of them retorts.

"Look, what I did is not a big deal compared to what's happening in Yemen or the homeless problem in our country. And what about veterans' affairs? There's an issue you can focus on. Now go away."

The reporters suddenly let me pass, but the cameras keep clicking as I enter the school.

As soon as I'm inside, I go straight to the school office to report what happened. The principal isn't in, but his assistant assures me that she'll inform him, and the police department will put up signs warning the press not to come on school property.

That helps me breathe a little easier, but anger still rumbles below my skin. How could Dad talk to the press like that? Whenever anyone googles me in the future, this is what they'll find. What college would consider me now?

I go home to a nearly empty house. Mom is at a Nashville nursing home volunteering. Dad has meetings in his Chattanooga office, which is more than two hours from here, so he won't be home anytime soon.

Marina emerges from the pantry and lays her clipboard on the granite countertop. "Want me to start making dinner, baby?"

"I'm not hungry."

"Very good. Just let me know when you're ready." Then she picks up her clipboard and returns to the pantry, where's she no doubt doing some sort of complex inventorying process.

I sniffle. I'm terrified that if I let myself really cry, I'll catch a cold, and I won't get rid of it for weeks. That happened to me last January. I was so stressed out over school, I couldn't stop crying, which in turn kept making me sick.

My eye twitches. I take a long, deep breath. I need to calm down. Get my mind off everything that happened today.

I need a friend.

My phone buzzes at that very moment. Ezra sent me a picture of a cute German shepherd puppy and a text: you ok??

How sweet…

The next thing I know, I find myself jogging up the stairs

to my bathroom. I yank off my soccer clothes and take a quick shower, then pull on jeans and a clean, white button-up blouse.

I hop in the Beast and take off for Brentwood—to the Carmichael residence. Brentwood is a Nashville suburb about twenty minutes from where I live. The drive there is lined with trees and mansions that get progressively bigger and bigger.

When I arrive at Ezra's house, or should I say castle, I park in the semicircular driveway next to the fountain and stare up at the white mansion, which was rebuilt in 1866 after being almost completely destroyed in the Civil War. Ezra's dad loves telling the story to anyone who will listen. Even though Mr. Carmichael is very important to my father's work, Dad always dreads going to their parties, because he knows Mr. Carmichael will corner him and tell him about the house for the gazillionth time.

I climb the porch steps, passing between two behemoth white columns, and ring the doorbell. A maid dressed in a blue uniform answers the door, and after I tell her my name, she ushers me into a yellow parlor. This room, with its cherry hardwood floors and lush white sofas, makes me feel warm and relaxed.

A minute later, Mrs. Carmichael sails into the parlor, looking fabulous as always in a pink dress-suit the color of a ballet slipper, beige pumps, and perfect makeup. I've always admired her work. She travels all over the country doing serious fund-raising for St. Jude's pediatric cancer research.

Like a perfect lady, I stand to greet her.

"Taylor!" she says, graciously shaking my hand. "What a wonderful surprise. How are your mother and father?"

"Great," I lie.

"We've been following his campaign. A few bumps here and there, but everything seems to be going smoothly for the most part."

Lies, lies, and more lies.

She's still awkwardly shaking my hand. I hold my breath, waiting for her to chastise me for my behavior. But she doesn't, probably because Mrs. Carmichael is waaaay too formal to say anything to my face. Instead, she and her friends will gossip about me later, like when they whisper about Jack Goodwin dating *the help.*

Mrs. Carmichael finally releases my hand. "To what do I owe the pleasure of your visit?"

"I stopped by to see Ezra. Is he home?"

Her perfectly shaped eyebrows pinch together. "He doesn't live here anymore. You didn't know?"

How could I possibly know that with a brother who keeps secrets like a defense attorney and Ezra being an Internet-phobe?

"Where can I find him?"

"He has an apartment over on Ragswood Road." She sniffs.

Is she sniffing because Ezra's living in an apartment, or because the apartment is on Ragswood Road? Probably both. "I need to see him."

Her eyes light up. "Let me write down the address for you, Taylor. Lord knows, maybe you can talk some sense and get him to move home."

Mrs. Carmichael must be desperate for Ezra to come home if she's willing to let me—a person on the front page for abusing prescription drugs—go see her son.

Twenty minutes later, I arrive at his building. A "Checks Cashed Here!" establishment is on the opposite corner. The train tracks are on the other side of that. A heavy freight train chugs by, rattling the apartment building's windows.

This must be the place, because Ezra's shiny black Range Rover is parked out front between a rusted red Nissan Sentra and a Ford pickup with faded white paint. It looks like a diamond nestled between two lumps of coal. The SUV was a high school graduation gift from Ezra's father.

My boots clang against the metal stairs as I climb an outdoor staircase four flights to 4B. I knock on the door. A few seconds later, a curtain moves in the window to my right. Suddenly, the door is whipped open. Ezra's face is blazing with confusion and embarrassment, especially when he spots the overflowing bag of trash outside his neighbor's place.

With a deep breath, he pulls the door open to let me in. He's wearing dark, frayed jeans and a gray Henley. He's barefoot. He looks so good. I swallow hard.

I walk into the living room. It's about the size of our foyer, but it's nicely furnished with a leather couch, beautiful wooden end tables, and a glass coffee table. Unlike his clothes, I doubt his mother picked out this furniture. It's masculine and very much Ezra. Especially the large TV tuned to ESPN. I smile when I see a bunch of random bolts, screws, circuit boards, and gears strewn across the coffee table. What's he taking apart and putting back together?

He looks around the living room as if embarrassed.

"I like your place," I say. "But you need some throw pillows."

"What are you doing here?" he asks.

"I needed to see you."

He clears his throat and gestures at the couch. We sit. I scan the walls—he's hung a few pictures of friends. I spot one taken in Mexico, when he, Oliver, and Jenna were on that mission trip in high school. I smile when I see one of me, him, and Chickadee as a baby chick.

"Your couch is really comfortable. Did you buy the furniture yourself?"

"Yeah." He shrugs a little. "I had some money left over from graduation, and construction pays okay… So what's going on? Why'd you stop by?"

At his look of deep concern, I lean over and bury my face in my hands. "You saw the news today."

He sets a hand on my shoulder. "Yeah. That sucks."

Somehow, he knows the right thing to say. He doesn't tell me it will all blow over soon or that my dad's just saying this shit because he wants to be reelected. It is what it is.

"People at school were such dicks today. I hate it there. And now my soccer coach is questioning whether I should still be on the team, because parents think I'm gonna give their kids drugs. *God!*"

His hand continues to massage my shoulder.

"I fucked up. My future is over."

"It's not." He gently rubs my back; it feels so good. "You can do anything you want. Unlike me…"

That's new.

His comment makes me think I don't know the whole story about him leaving school.

"Why'd you take a leave of absence from Cornell?" I ask. "For real this time."

"I can't talk about it."

Taking his hand, I weave our fingers together. "You can talk about anything with me, Ez. You know that."

"Not about this."

"Why not?"

"My father…he would get pissed."

"So what? You're an adult. You don't even live with him anymore." I check out the little apartment. It's not bad. The privacy and independence seem great. A bag of potato chips sits on the coffee table. I love the idea of having potato chips in the house.

"C'mon, tell me what's up," I plead.

"It's not easy for me to talk about."

"Hey," I say quietly. "You can trust me."

He cups the back of his neck, his green eyes filling with tears. I've rarely seen him like this. He's always cheerful and in control. This is the opposite of the Ezra Carmichael I know. The only other time I've seen him so upset was the Monday after my birthday party. But I sure as hell didn't care about him that day.

I squeeze his hand, and it must give him the strength he needs to speak.

"I'm pretty sure that I'm dyslexic."

How could I not know this? Ezra didn't take special classes or get any extra tutoring that I know of. Does my brother know?

I grip his hand harder, trying to show I support him no matter what. "Have you talked to anyone about it?"

"My father told me not to tell anybody."

"Wait, so Cornell doesn't know?"

He shakes his head.

"Is that why you were having problems with your classes?"

"Yeah." He drops my hand and folds his arms across his stomach, looking ashamed. "I couldn't remember what I read half the time, even after reading the material over and over. At St. Andrew's, the teachers just let me skate by. They knew who my father was—hell, the *library* is named after him. So they passed me."

It makes sense. If Dad had made a fuss, I bet St. Andrew's wouldn't have expelled me.

Ezra goes on, "That didn't work when I got to Cornell. I couldn't keep up with the homework, no matter how hard I tried. I'd study all night long, and I'd still fail tests. The highest grade I made my first semester was a C."

I rest my hand on his knee, worried if I let him go, he'll never talk to me again like this.

"You've never been tested?" I whisper.

"No. Dad says that there's no way I could have dyslexia, because I'm a Carmichael. According to him, it's *genetically impossible*. He says my problem is that I'm lazy, but I know that's not it."

"Of course you're not lazy. But why didn't you just get the tests yourself?"

"I was embarrassed…and scared, I guess. And even with doctor-patient confidentiality, you know how people gossip."

"Why do you think you're dyslexic?"

"My writing is fine, but I misread things…I forget a lot…and I've fucked up some really important things in my life because of that."

"Such as?"

He looks into my eyes. "I missed your sixteenth birthday party."

Out of This World

"What do you mean?"

He stands up from the couch, folding his hands behind his head. He pads to the front window and looks out, then walks to the kitchen, seemingly for no reason. I let him pace; he needs to work through this at his own speed.

"I misread the date on your invitation," he says. "I know your birthday is November 15, but I got confused about when your party was. I read the invite a few times, but I wrote down the 25th on my calendar instead of the 12th. I made a stupid mistake."

He mixed up the numbers? He wanted to come to my party? "Wait, but didn't you go to Chattanooga that night? With Mindy Roberts?"

"I did."

"I heard you hooked up with her, and that's why you didn't show."

He shakes his head. "We were just friends. I never hooked up with her. She was helping me pick out a birthday gift for you... I wanted it to be just right."

He wanted my gift to be just right.

I place a hand over my chest, trying to calm my racing heart. For nearly two years, I've thought the worst of him.

I slowly get to my feet. "Why didn't you tell me?"

"I couldn't admit I'd messed up the dates. Dad told me never to tell anyone about my...*problem*...and it was a lame excuse. The day before, Oliver had even mentioned he was heading home for the weekend, and I still didn't put two and two together. I was so mad at myself. How could you forgive me?"

I slide my fingers onto his hip and look up at him. "I would have forgiven you then. I forgive you now."

He smiles sadly. "Stay right here." He turns to jog down the little hallway to what I presume is his bedroom. When he returns, he hands me a box wrapped in silver paper. "Happy late birthday. This is what I meant to give you that night."

"Thank you." I open the card first. It's a picture of a golden retriever.

Happy Birthday, Tease.

Love, Ezra

I rip off the paper and slide the box open. Inside, I find a pair of soft, pink, silk pajamas—a tank top and shorts with a delicate strawberry print. *How intimate.* I understand now why he took Mindy to buy my gift. He wanted a girl's help in picking out a present that would show he was interested in me.

Tucked under the pajamas, I find a bunch of notepads, pens, and pencils decorated with cartoon soccer balls and dogs, and a homemade "gift certificate" written on an index card. One coffee on me! it reads.

He knows me so well.

"Thank you," I say, running my fingers over the pajamas.

"You like it?"

"I love it…" I pause for a long moment. "Ez, you could've told me you mixed up the date on the invitation. I would've forgiven you."

"I wish I had. I was just too embarrassed. And ashamed. I had been planning to ask you out the night of your birthday."

"I would've said yes."

An angry tone fills his voice. "If you had said yes, maybe you wouldn't have dated Ben."

I loved Ben while we were dating, but I'd be a lot better off if we had never gone out. I wouldn't be living with a terrible secret that's my shadow.

Ezra just told me his big secret. I should tell him mine. But what if I tell him I covered for Ben and then he spills the news to Oliver? Oliver might tell Dad. I can't even imagine how upset my family and friends will be that I lied. Especially given how it's affected Dad's campaign. Unraveling this mistake might cause more trouble than just staying silent.

Bad news is only interesting for so long. The press will get over it soon.

I shake my head to clear my thoughts—I came to Ezra's place to get my mind off the media, not to rehash what happened. I look down into my box of birthday gifts. "I can't wait to use my soccer ball pens." When I gaze up at him to say thank you again, his eyes are low-lidded and filled with longing.

Without a word, I set the birthday box down on his coffee table and gently press my lips to his.

When I was younger, I imagined that kissing him would be like an electric shock. But the spark I once dreamed of turns out to be *lightning*.

I pull away, and we stare at each other for several heartbeats. Then he crushes his mouth to mine.

Our lips are warm, full, and hungry. His hands trail up and down my arms, caressing my skin. My hands are everywhere. I pull him hard against me, leading him to the couch. We land in a tangle of arms and legs. I kick off my boots, and he lifts me onto his lap so that I'm straddling him. He continues to kiss me as he wraps his arms around my waist.

"Tee," he says breathily. "We need to talk."

"So talk."

But he doesn't. He's too busy using his mouth for other, more important things. I sweep my tongue between his lips, loving this. Kissing Ben was always good, but kissing Ezra feels *vital*.

The first time I set foot in the Louvre in Paris, saw its grand passageways filled with art and history, I thought, *This is it. Now I'm alive.* But that was just a precursor for this moment, because it feels as if my heart is beating for the first time.

We kiss, each of us unleashing years of pent-up attraction, until he suddenly pulls back. His gaze grows heated as his fingers gently caress my breast through my shirt. Having a guy's hand there has never done much for me, but with him, it's different. I unbutton my shirt so he can have full access. His lips part in breathless excitement when I reveal my bra, baring myself to him. His warm hands send sparks scattering through me. I push my hips into his. Pull his T-shirt off over his head. Cup his cheeks. I can't get close enough. I need him to touch me *everywhere*.

He slowly unzips my jeans. If I'd known this would be happening, I would've worn something sexier than my white underwear with the little blue dogs on them.

He laughs, gently tracing the waistband, making me shiver. "I love these." He leans his head back and stares up at me. "Have you considered becoming a vet?"

"I've never thought about that."

"Maybe you should. I bet you'd enjoy it."

"Like how you enjoy working with your hands?"

"Yes."

"Well, what are you waiting for? Use those hands on me."

With a relaxed smile, he kisses me again and flips me onto my back, then edges my jeans down and onto the floor. He discovers the bluebird tattoo on my ankle, kissing it once before his lips begin working their way back up my legs and between them.

His hand joins his mouth, and together, they fly me out of this world.

In bed with Ben, I spent a lot of time worrying about whether my stomach was flat, if my boobs looked awesome, if I was making him feel good and doing the right things with my hands.

It is not like that with Ezra. There's no time for thinking. I'm too busy kissing his neck. Too busy exploring his chest and abs. I make noises that should be embarrassing, but they're not, because I'm not self-conscious like with Ben. All I care about is giving him the same pleasure he gave me. He threads a hand through my hair, and his eyes flare as they meet mine.

When we're finished, we lie crushed together on his couch, staring at the ceiling, silent except for our heavy breathing. I'm in my bra and panties, and he's in his boxer briefs. I've never gone from zero to sixty with a guy in one day. I figured I might feel guilty or maybe a little naughty, but I just feel good. Happy.

Grinning, I reach out to pull him in for another kiss and maybe round two, but he suddenly sits up and leans over, putting his elbows on his knees.

"You okay?" I ask.

Ezra drags a hand through his dark hair. "Oll is going to kill me. He told me that if I ever fuck with you, he'd fuck me up."

I smile at my brother's protective nature. "It's none of his business what we do. That was great, by the way." Ezra's still looking away from me, so I get up onto my knees, press my chest against his back, and wrap my arms around him. I kiss his ear and neck. "Want to go to your bed?"

"This was a mistake."

I stop breathing. "What?"

"Look, I was just trying to be there for you as a friend. I thought I could keep my feelings under control."

I give him a little smile. "I'm glad you didn't."

"I don't want to lead you on. I'm not right for you."

We can't end now. We can't. "Why don't you let me decide who's right for me?"

He twines and untwines his fingers nervously. "Your life isn't right for me."

The air conditioner rattles on, blasting cold air over my body. I shiver. "What are you talking about?"

"I'm not going back to college. I won't ever take over my father's company. I'm never going to fit in at our families' parties again. People will talk about you like they do Jack Goodwin, wondering why you're slumming it with me."

"*Slumming it?*"

"Yeah."

"That's ridiculous. And rude toward Savannah. Screw them. Who cares?"

"I care. You're gonna go to college and do whatever you want with your life, and all I'm ever gonna be is a construction rat." He finds his jeans on the floor, steps into the legs, and zips them up.

I start rasping for breath. I just went down on him—I would've slept with him if he'd asked. And now he says *this*?

I grab my jeans and yank them on. My foot gets caught in the fabric, and I have to sit down to jerk it free. "This sucks. You care more about what other people think than about giving us a chance."

"I'm sorry," he replies quietly. "I didn't mean for this to happen. I just want something different for both of us."

"You don't get to decide what I want," I snap. "I'm sorry I'm not worth suffering through a little gossip at parties. Not that I give a shit about those things."

He looks out his window. Through the front windows of my house, all you can see are green grass and lush trees. From Ezra's windows, you get asphalt.

"If you didn't want this," I say, "why have you been hanging around? Meeting me for coffee?"

"I told you… I was lonely."

"Then why don't you go make new friends at your construction site?" My voice is mean. Rage-y. He deserves it.

I tug on my shirt and try to button it as quickly as I can, but my fingers are shaky and feel clumsy, like bloated sausages. When he sees I'm having problems, he helps me. His fingers make quick work of the buttons.

Angry as I am, I can't help but tell the truth. "Ez, I don't care what people think. I've wanted you for so long."

"But you were with Ben."

"Because I was heartbroken after I thought you hooked up with Mindy."

"Still, you were into him."

"Yes, I was, but I've *always* wanted you, Ezra." My words make his lips part. I set my hands on his bare waist. His skin is soft like satin. I find his eyes. "Honestly, I can't say I want a relationship right now either. It's not smart after what happ—" I shut my mouth quickly.

Ezra's eyebrow shoots up. "After what happened?"

How could I be so stupid as to almost let the truth slip? I regroup. "Breaking up with Ben was hard, and I told myself I wasn't going to get involved with anyone else…but I care about you."

"I care about you too." He leans his forehead against mine. "You've really always wanted me?"

I can tell he's scared, that he doubts himself thanks to his parents. That's why he tried to push me away. "Yes, I want you more than anything. Now don't make me beg."

A smile edges on his face. "Why don't we see where this goes?"

"Finally." I reward him with a long, slow kiss. Then, "Can I see your room already?"

"Sassy."

He leads me there by a hand. His bed is neatly made with a comfortable, navy-blue quilt, which we promptly mess up in a kissing storm of the century, and later, when we're cuddling between his sheets, I whisper to him, "Thanks for telling me what happened that night."

He links his pinkie with mine. "I trust you. No more secrets between us, okay?"

I freeze. "Okay," I say quietly. Another lie.

They keep piling up.

But it's too late to tell the truth about Ben and the pills.

Friday morning, as I'm getting dressed for school, I'm still in a smiling daze thanks to Ezra.

All I can think about is when I get to kiss him again. Maybe this morning, at Donut Palace? What if we start and can't stop and I skip school and he misses work and we end up back at his place, messing up his bed again—

Someone bangs loudly on my bedroom door, distracting me from my daydream.

"Taylor!" Mom shouts. "Your father and I need to see you downstairs right now!"

What in the world? My hairbrush clatters when I drop it on my vanity in a rush. I hurry down the stairs and to the breakfast nook where my parents are sitting in front of untouched plates of eggs.

"What the hell is this?" Dad asks in a low tone, shoving a newspaper at me.

The front page features a picture of me at school, standing in front of the Swamp. It was taken yesterday. The headline reads: *Lukens' Daughter Says Drug Use 'Not a big deal!'*

"But that's not what I said."

"You know you should never speak to the press," Mom says. "Never! How many times have your father and I told you that?"

"They wouldn't let me get into my car. I was angry."

"You *never* show emotion to these people, Taylor," Dad says. "You know better than this. You don't speak to the press without media coaching from my publicist."

I crush the newspaper between my hands. "This isn't what I said at all! I said that what I did isn't a big deal compared with what's happening in Yemen and with veterans' affairs. They took it out of context."

"That's what the media does," Dad says, his voice suddenly gentle. "It's happened to me before." Dad's cell phone rings, and he answers. "Randy?" He listens for a moment before hanging up. "Polls went down by two points."

Mom scowls at me. "We'll be lucky to salvage this election thanks to you. Two points!"

She storms out of the kitchen. Part of me wonders if she's taking this harder than Dad. It wouldn't surprise me. His political career is her whole life too. I don't blame her for being upset though. My actions are messing up our family's reputation.

Dad packs his laptop into his briefcase and leaves the house without another word.

I cover my eyes with the heels of my hands. Mom always said Ben wasn't good for me; if she found out the truth, she'd rub it in my face for eternity, and I don't think I can handle any more shame.

I've already made a mess of Dad's campaign. The situation is way past me not wanting to be a snitch. If I tell the truth now, it would only hurt my family more—the press would skin us alive: *Antidrug Senator's Daughter Covers for Drug Dealer Boyfriend.*

I'm so jittery, caffeine is probably the last thing I need, but I get in line at Donut Palace anyway. I keep my head down in case somebody recognizes me from the paper this morning and check my phone as I wait to reach the counter.

My sister sent me a text: get your shit together. My brother told me: you need to lay low for a while.

Damn.

I inhale deeply. The smell of coffee always soothes me.

"Hey, Tease." Ezra elbows me.

"Hey," I reply softly.

"I saw the news. Those people are bastards."

I try to smile, but my lip quivers instead. When he sees, he sweeps me into his arms and hugs me in front of the entire coffee shop.

"Thank you for not yelling at me," I say.

"Huh?"

"That's all anyone has done so far today."

With a concerned look, he touches my cheek. "I'll get your drink. Go grab us a seat, okay?"

I sit down in our usual booth, the one overlooking the cornfields.

Once he has our coffees, he slides onto my bench, bumping his hip against mine. Our thighs touch.

I lift an eyebrow at him. "We're going to be those people? The ones who sit on the same side of the booth?"

"Well, *yeah*."

I lean to my left so I can reach into the back pocket of my jeans and pass him the handmade coupon from his birthday gift: One coffee on me!

He laughs when he sees it, seeming so much happier and lighter now that we talked about our past. He pushes my coffee in front of me, then opens Miss Brady's daily envelope.

"My guidance counselor takes her job waaaay too seriously."

Ezra pulls out the slips of paper and gives me a few.

I read the first one. "What is your favorite memory?"

"What we did last night," he says with no hesitation.

My cheeks heat up. And don't even ask about the lady parts.

He holds up another of Miss Brady's papers. "What does your perfect day look like?"

"What we did last night," I say with a giggle. He wraps an arm around me and kisses my neck. I could get used to this. I place a hand on his chest, feeling his strong muscles.

"School sucked so bad yesterday," I say. "I don't want to go today. I just want to sit here with you."

"I wish I could blow off work and hang out too, Tease, but you can't hide."

"Can't I?"

"I know things are hard right now, but everybody will forget about all this crap soon. The press always loses interest quickly. They'll find some other drama to glom on to."

"I know, but I keep messing things up for my dad."

Ezra massages my thigh. "For real though. What does your perfect day look like?"

"I'd sleep in. Lie around in bed for a while. Meet up with you. We'd get some coffee and French toast in Nashville, then walk along the waterfront. Maybe go in some shops or a bookstore. Then you'd buy me a present," I say cheekily.

He smirks. "What kind of present?"

"Something not alive. Mom would kill you if you bought me another pet."

"Would this work?" He passes over the One coffee on me! coupon.

I pluck it from his fingers and slip it back into my pocket. "No, but nice try."

"Okay, so I'll buy you something nonliving. Then what would we do?"

"We'd go back to your place and watch some really bad TV."

He wraps an arm around my shoulders, pulling me close. "We'll do all that on Sunday, okay?" he murmurs. "If today gets sucky, just keep your perfect day in mind…just keep *me* in mind."

Superglue

School passes by in a blur.

More kids ask me for pills. More kids make fun of me. More teachers give me suspicious looks.

But Alyson the goalie stops by my locker before lunch to see if I'm okay. "I'm sorry about Coach. My parents are upset you weren't allowed to practice yesterday. They're going to call Dr. Salter about it. I don't want to play without you."

I give her a small smile. "Thank you. I like playing with you too."

She points over her shoulder with her thumb. "You coming to lunch?"

"I think I'll hit the library. I'm not in the mood to deal with Nicole."

Alyson grins at that. "I don't blame you."

In class that afternoon, I can't focus, because I keep thinking about how much I've hurt my family. Jenna and Oliver aren't perfect. I mean, Jenna cheated on Jack Goodwin, and one time, Oliver drank so much he puked out the window all over

Mom's rosebushes. But neither one has ever done anything *this bad*. Why can't I get what happened off my mind? Why do bad memories stick like superglue?

In the past, I've seen news stories where people have gotten themselves into crazy predicaments because they didn't tell the truth up front, and as a viewer, I always wondered why they let their story, their situation, get out of control. I get it now. Sometimes, problems grow like a crack in the ceiling that starts out small but expands if you're not paying careful attention. Then the roof caves in.

They say the cover-up is worse than the crime. Don't I know it.

I smile, however, when Ezra sends me a text about halfway through this interminably hellish American history class: You ok?

Yeah. Thanks.

Miss you.

He's so sweet, I can't help but text: xo

He sends back a picture of a golden retriever puppy. I needed that. Last night, he confessed the reason he doesn't use social media is because reading online makes his brain hurt. He spends more time questioning what he reads than actually reading, so he doesn't bother anymore. I'm glad he's willing to text with me.

I also get a group text from Steph and Madison.

Mads: Tee, how are you?

Steph: We love you!

Me: love you too, girls. Things suck.

Steph: :-/ what can we do?

Me: Talk to me about anything besides my dad's campaign

Mads: Tell us something that makes you happy!

Me: Went to Ezra's last night. Found out why he missed my party.

Steph: !!!!!! why!?

Me: It's not my story to tell, but it was a good reason and I forgave him. And I think we're together now…

Mads: OMG!!!!

Steph: Is he lick-able?

Me: Totally lick-able

Steph: Eeeeeeeeeeeeee! What happened?

Mads: Did you hook up?

My girlfriends and I have never kept the details from each other, so I give them a rundown of what it was like being in Ezra's arms and in his bed. My friends are probably giggling at my texts. Especially when I admit: He knows exactly what he's doing.

Steph: Hehehe. Does he find you lick-able?

Me: Classified info ;-) ok. Fine. YES!

Mads: I'm happy for you, Tee.

Me: I miss you guys…

Steph: Miss you more!

Mads: Yep! Time for class. chat soon.

The rest of the day slugs by. I drive home from school, looking forward to a quiet night. I don't want to work on applications or study for Monday's calculus exam. All I want is to relax.

When I'm safely in my driveway, I send Ezra a text: Can we do something fun tonight?

Bowling?

Bowling?!

What's wrong with bowling? Snob.

I snort. Fine, let's bowl.

We'll get dinner first. I'll come pick you up after I shower.

I go inside my mausoleum of a house, glad that Mom and Dad aren't here. Marina tells me my parents went to a campaign event in Nashville and won't be home until late. She gives me my snack of cheese and crackers.

Rather than wallow in my own pity, I need to do something constructive. I hop onto a stool, open my iPad, and pull up the Internet. I search for *dyslexia*, then click on a link to dyslexia.org.

Who has dyslexia? the site says. *Anyone can have it, even very smart people.* Like Ezra.

The website says people with dyslexia read with the right side of their brain instead of their left, but it's the left side of the brain that can keep sequences straight. This is why dyslexics don't read things correctly sometimes. It's hard to diagnose after grade school, because most kids stop accidentally transposing letters and numbers when writing by the time they are seven or eight. Reading, however, can remain a problem.

There's no cure.

With a deep breath, I read on, finally finding some good

news. Specialized education and training programs can help. Emotional support is also important though, and while I can give him that, I doubt his parents ever will. How will he believe he can get better if the people around him aren't encouraging him? Hiding it won't help.

I bring up the Cornell website, search for the keywords *learning disability*, and click the result that says *Student Disability Services*. I scan the page. *Cornell strives to create and sustain a welcoming, accessible, and supportive environment.*

The webpage has a lot of complicated information about diagnostic interviews and assessments, but I can tell that the school is willing—and wants—to help its students. Maybe I can show this to Ezra. Explain that he's not alone and that he doesn't have to give up his education just because he thinks he can't succeed.

"Miss Taylor?"

I turn around on my stool to face Marina.

"You have a guest."

I push the home button on the iPad, clearing the screen. "Who?"

"Ben Cooper."

I gasp and cover my mouth. *What is he doing here?* Slowly, I climb down from my stool and make my way into the living room. There's Ben in his St. Andrew's white button-down shirt, blue plaid tie, and khakis, staring at one of our abstract paintings that Mom bought in Paris. The few times Ben visited our house when we were dating, he always had this dazzled reaction, like when Dorothy steps into the land of Oz for the first time.

"Ben."

He turns and rushes toward me—to hug me like he used to. But I give him the Heisman. He stares at my outstretched palms, shocked.

"Why are you here?" I ask.

His Adam's apple shifts as he swallows, and that's when I see the tears in his eyes. "I needed to see you. You haven't been answering my texts."

"I blocked your number."

He takes a step back. "I'm so sorry, Tee. I never thought this would happen. I was so grateful when you helped me, but I didn't think it would turn out this way."

"Neither did I."

"I saw the news today."

I cross my arms. "So did everybody else."

"I'm going to fix it."

"What? How?" I reply, panicked. The situation is already sticky enough!

"I'm going to come forward to the school. Tell them the drugs were mine."

"You can't! Then what I did would all be for nothing."

"They'd let you come back to school," he cries.

"St. Andrew's might take me back, but it doesn't matter now. My father's campaign has gone to shit because of me. My reputation is ruined. My family is already angry and disappointed. Can you imagine how pissed off they'll be if they find out I was covering for you? The press would be even worse if they find out I covered for a drug dealer."

He grasps his dark curls. "I can't live with this, Tee. I hate what the news is saying about you. It's not true."

"Then you should've said something when I got kicked out of school."

"I fucked up. But I'm going to say something *now*."

"You know what really sucks? You should've come forward before, because you care about me, because you love me. The only thing driving you now is your guilt."

That shuts him up. An embarrassed flush fills his face. "I need to tell the truth."

"And what about what I need? Isn't this all screwed up enough? Don't you dare mess things up with my family."

The living room suddenly darkens; outside the window, a cloud passes over the sun. "I need to know something," Ben says. "When your dad didn't get you out of it, why didn't you admit they were my pills?"

"Because I'm not a snitch."

When he picked me up at Card House for last year's homecoming dance, holding a pink corsage, his blue eyes were wide and excited. Now tears threaten to leak out of them. How did our relationship come to this?

"You should leave now," I say quietly.

The antique grandfather clock strikes loudly five times.

Marina reenters the room. "Miss Taylor, Ezra just arrived."

Jesus. Nobody has worse luck than I do.

Ezra appears in the doorway with a lazy smile. It turns into a hard scowl when he sees I'm not alone.

"Taylor," he says, coming to my side, placing a protective hand on my shoulder, because every guy's M.O. is to act all caveman in front of others. He lightly pecks my cheek and gives Ben a cool glare. "What is he doing here?"

I'm a little annoyed that Ezra would kiss me in front of my ex. That's a dick move. On the other hand, I sort of enjoy seeing Ben's face flare up in rage.

"Carmichael," Ben says with a tilt of his chin. They weren't in school together at the same time, since Ben didn't start St. Andrew's until junior year and Ezra was a freshman in college at that point, but Ezra met Ben at Easter lunch last spring when my family celebrated with the Carmichaels. That whole day was a clown show.

Mom wasn't happy I brought Ben home, because she thought he wasn't good enough for me. Mr. and Mrs. Carmichael ignored Ben, since they didn't know who his parents were. Jenna flirted with him, and Oliver was happy that I was happy. Dad didn't seem to care one way or the other, because he was upset Mom forgot to order mint jelly for the lamb.

Ezra didn't crack a smile that entire day. He just kept stabbing his carrots and shoving them into his mouth, all the while giving Ben stink eye. After lunch, I told Ben not to worry about Ezra, referring to him as a "Cro-Magnon" (mature, yes, I know), and then Ben and I spent the rest of the afternoon making out in the basement.

Here, now, Ezra laces his fingers with mine. It's not lost on Ben. He flinches at the sight of me holding hands with another guy.

Ben scrubs a hand through his curls. "Can we please talk in private?"

I never officially said good-bye before I had to leave St. Andrew's, but everything has changed between us. Seeing him hurts too much. My voice cracks when I say, "You need to go."

"Taylor, please," Ben begs. "It wasn't easy to get a ride here. I had to sneak off campus. I don't know when I'll be able to see you again, and we need to finish our conversation."

"There's nothing left to talk about," I say.

"I'll walk Ben out," Ezra says. "Then we can go get dinner."

Ben looks from me to Ezra. "Are you with him now?"

Ezra and I didn't have the relationship talk last night. He said, *"Let's see where this goes."* To me, that means we're exclusive, but I won't be the first to admit it. Not today, at least. I don't want to feel any more vulnerable than I already do. Also, I don't want to hurt Ben. I'm not a bitch like that.

But I don't want to hurt Ezra either. So I just stay quiet, gnawing on my lower lip, trying to decide what to say. I guess my silence is the answer.

Ben shoves his hands in his pockets. "I deserve this."

Ezra scrunches his eyebrows together, giving me a questioning look.

"I'm sorry, Ben," I say and turn my back as Ezra walks him out. It's weird seeing someone I used to be so close with but who now seems so far away. Tears drip out of my eyes, making me sniffle.

When Ezra returns, he gives me a long hug. "You're shaking. You scared I'm gonna beat you at bowling?"

"Yup, that's totally it." I laugh quietly, then wipe my nose with the back of my hand. So attractive.

He pushes the hair away from my forehead, focusing on the little white scar near my hairline. "I remember this. You cut it on a rock when we were playing football."

I smile when he presses his lips to the scar.

"Can I ask you something?" he asks.

"Yeah."

"Oliver told me that you and Ben broke up because you didn't want a long-distance boyfriend. But that's not true, is it?"

"No," I whisper.

"What happened?"

I shake my head.

"I won't push you…just tell me one thing: did he hurt you?"

"Physically, no. It's that he…he wasn't who I thought he was."

"Did Ben give you the pills?"

I pause before responding, to play this carefully. "I needed them, Ez. To stay awake to study."

"I understand that. I know what it's like to feel that kind of pressure."

He pulls me into his arms and hugs me long and hard, cocooning me in a safe place.

At the bowling alley, I rent a pair of red, white, and blue shoes and put them on. Ezra does the same. He's the only guy I know who can make ugly bowling shoes look hot.

I sit down behind the computer to type in our names. *Tee* and *Ez* appear on the TV screen above our lane.

"Should we flip a coin to see who goes first?" I ask.

"Ladies first."

From the racks of balls behind the lanes, I choose a neon-orange one that doesn't weigh too much. My arm muscles are good enough to throw a soccer ball in during games, but that's about all they're good for.

Lugging my orange ball, I approach the lane, aim, and roll it toward the pins. Seven fall down on my first try.

"Yay!" I yell, hopping up and down. Ezra gives me an easy smile. When I bend over to pick up my ball from the return, I catch him checking out my butt. I grin, pushing my auburn hair over my shoulder to get it out of the way.

I knock down two more pins on my second try, leaving one. *Bollocks.*

"My turn," Ezra says and proceeds to knock nine down on his first try. Damn.

I cup my hands around my mouth to shout at him. "Show-off."

When he retrieves his ball from the return, I let him catch me staring at his butt. That makes him laugh, but then his gaze grows more heated, and I know he's thinking about what we did last night.

I can't believe how lucky I am. Sophomore year, Steph had a crush on this guy Gordon. She talked about him constantly and went out of her way to run into him in the hallway. This went on for months until he finally caught wind that she wanted him. The next weekend at a mixer in Harvey House, Steph and Gordon finally made out.

Later that night when we were getting ready for bed, I asked her how it was.

She stuck out her tongue and proclaimed in her fancy British accent, "It was like kissing white bread. Boring and limp!"

Madison and I giggled with her, but I remember freaking out inside. If I ever got to kiss Ezra, would it be like white bread?

Now I know. He's like mint chocolate truffles: succulent and rich. And I want another helping already.

Right as I'm about to go steal a kiss, I hear, "Taylor, hey!"

I twirl around to find Chloe approaching our lane.

Ezra sets his chin on my shoulder, hugging me from behind. His large masculine hands grip my waist. "I changed my mind," he says in a low rumble. "Let's forget bowling and go find a bed."

Chloe walks up right in time to hear Ezra's colorful suggestion. Her eyes flash with amusement.

"Hi, Chloe," I choke out. "Um, this is my, um, my Ezra."

Over my shoulder, he stretches out a hand to Chloe. "I'm Tee's boyfriend."

Chloe laughs. "Does she know that?"

He holds me tighter. "I hope so. Otherwise, I just struck out."

I pat his hand that's on my hip. "Chlo, this is my boyfriend, Ezra. Ez, I know Chloe from Hundred Oaks. Who're you here with?" I ask her.

She points at three people bowling a couple lanes down from us—Alyson and two guys from the basketball team. I wave at them, and they wave back.

"How are you?" Chloe asks, studying my eyes.

"It's been a long couple of days. I'm glad it's Friday night."

"I'm sorry about what happened with the team yesterday. It really sucks. We need you."

I nod. There's nothing else to say, so I just stand here in an awkward silence. Ezra kneads my shoulder.

"Do y'all want to join us?" Alyson calls out.

Ezra bends down and whispers in my ear. "It's up to you."

"Yeah," I tell her, excited about the prospect of hanging out with them. "That'd be great."

Ezra and I retrieve our balls from the ball return and move down two lanes, where we meet Alyson, Thomas, and John. Thomas adds our names to their computer.

Ezra has always been competitive, so he gets a little too into the game with Thomas. "I bet twenty bucks I'll beat your score," Ezra tells Thomas.

"You're on."

According to Chloe, Alyson and John are on the verge of getting together, so they spend most of the game flirting and chasing each other around. That leaves me to chat with Chloe, which is a little nerve-racking, because she hasn't been totally welcoming so far, but I've also missed being around girls. I haven't seen Madison and Steph in forever.

"I was surprised to see you here," I tell Chloe. "And without Nicole."

"Honestly? Lately, Alyson and I feel like Nicole is acting really immature." She shrugs. "And a bunch of our friends graduated last year."

"But you still have friends on the soccer team, right?"

"Yeah, but I'm not really enjoying this season. What's the point in playing if Nicole doesn't pass me the ball?"

I nod in understanding. "I try to pass it to you whenever I can."

She grins at that. "I know. It pisses Nicole off when you do that. I love it though."

We laugh together.

I change the subject. "So are you here with Thomas?"

Chloe bites her lower lip and musses her short hair. "We've hooked up a few times, but it's not serious. I kind of like it that way."

"Yeah?"

"I like that he isn't looking for *forever*. I want to travel after graduation, and I don't want to be tied down by a boyfriend."

That's different. Most girls I know want relationships.

"My brother and Ezra traveled after they graduated," I say. "They bought Eurail passes and spent three months getting lost in Europe. I was so jealous—they went to a bunch of museums I can't wait to see one day."

"That sounds amazing."

"Where do you want to go?"

"I'd love to backpack around Nicaragua and Guatemala. I want to take a year off before going to college. My parents aren't wild about that idea, but I feel like I need to do it. What about you? What are you doing after you graduate?"

"Going to college…I hope." I trace a line on my palm to avoid looking at her.

Her voice drops to a whisper. "We don't have to talk about this if you don't want, but are the rumors true?"

I lower my head. "It's not as bad as people are saying."

"I didn't figure it was. I mean, I don't know you very well, but you seem so…normal."

I give her an amused smile. "Thanks, I think."

Alyson and John are staring deep into each other's eyes and whispering God knows what, and Ezra and Thomas want to play one-on-one, because the rest of us are not *serious bowlers*, so Chloe and I decide to get some nachos from the concession stand.

While waiting on the fry cook to serve them up, we sit on bar stools and swirl in circles like we're little girls. Chloe cracks up when I nearly fall off my stool. I catch myself on the counter, giggling.

The fry cook rolls his eyes at me, flipping his spatula up in the air and catching it as if he's in the Chef Olympics.

Chloe twirls around again, then suddenly grunts and grabs her knee. She stretches her leg out in front of her and bends it carefully.

"You all right?" I ask.

"Yeah. Sometimes when I accidentally move my knee in an awkward way, I get scared."

"Can I ask what happened?"

"Between sophomore and junior year, I went to soccer camp at Western Kentucky."

"Oh! I've been there. It's a great program."

Chloe nods. "I was playing in a scrimmage, running really fast, when I heard a pop. Then I fell on the ground." She shakes her head, lost in the memory. "I'd never felt pain like that before. The emergency room said I needed to see a specialist. An orthopedist. Dr. C., I mean Dr. Carpenter—he said I had to have surgery."

"Was it scary?"

"Before I got the anesthesia, I freaked out that I wouldn't wake up, but when I did wake up, I wanted to go back to sleep because my leg hurt so much. I had to take this pill, Percocet, for a month to help with the pain. It made me drowsy all the time and messed up my stomach. But the worst part was when I had to give it up. I wanted it all the time. I'd wake up in the morning thinking about it."

After using Adderall, I often felt twitchy and nervous. Sometimes I couldn't fall asleep, even when I wanted to. I'm lucky I never started to crave them. Was staying awake to study really worth the risk of becoming addicted? It makes me think of Caleb, the boy at school who's desperate for Ritalin.

I rest a hand on Chloe's forearm. "What happened next?"

She gives me a weak smile and takes a deep breath, then continues her story.

"Last year, I was in therapy the entire season, so I didn't get to play at all. I could barely walk. I just sat on the bench and watched. I couldn't wait to play again this year, but without Lilian as captain—she was in charge last year—Nicole's just taken over, and she obviously has no clue how to lead."

"That sucks," I say quietly.

"The worst part is I was actually pretty good before I got hurt. Now I'm too scared to take any risks on the field. Don't get me wrong, I love it when you pass me the ball, but I also sort of panic. What if I step in a hole or plant my foot the wrong way and I hear that awful *pop* again? I can't handle the thought of needing more surgery."

"I think you're brave for playing," I reply, remembering what Ezra said about risks not necessarily being a negative. Chloe playing soccer again is a positive.

The cook passes us our nachos, and we take them back to our lane, where Ezra and Thomas are still trying to one-up each other. Thomas is leading 220 to Ezra's 212. Close match.

Chloe dips a chip into the melted cheese and pops it in her mouth. "This has been fun."

I take a deep breath, gathering my courage to open up to her. "Do you want to hang out again sometime?"

"Sure," she says with a smile.

"Great," I reply, feeling a rush of happiness.

Thomas barely beats Ezra. Grumbling, my boyfriend takes twenty bucks out of his wallet and passes it to Thomas. In the next game, I bowl an all-time low of 85, but I don't care. I'm having too nice of a time lounging on my boyfriend's lap and hanging out with Chloe and Alyson. Then I glance down at my phone and see it's nearly eleven. At first I panic because I have to wake up early, but then I remember that I don't. Coach asked me to skip the game tomorrow. Which makes me sad and a little ashamed.

Until I realize…I can sleep in!

When Ezra drives me home, it's nearly midnight, and my parents still aren't back from Nashville.

"Want to come in for a while?" I ask.

"Is that a real question?" he jokes, sweeping me into his arms for a kiss. "Of course I want to come inside."

He nervously jingles his keys as we go in through the back door; he leaves them on the counter. The lights are turned down throughout most of the house. Marina's probably either already in bed or holed up with a novel in her room.

I lead him up the stairs. I can tell it's an effort for him to control his breathing. For me too. Sneaking him in makes me nervous. So does anticipating what will happen once we're in my room.

Then we're in each other's arms. Unlike last night, tonight we're not rushed. We're not as impatient. We take our time, gently kissing and hugging and getting to know each other again. I don't make any moves to take his clothes off, but we do lie down on my bed.

"You are terrible at bowling," he says, kissing my lips.

"Next time, we're doing something I'm good at."

"Oh yeah?" I can feel him smiling against my teeth. "Like what?"

"Trivia night at Freddie's Oyster Bar."

"Oh good God," he mutters.

He crawls on top of me, moving his hips against mine. I grip his bottom, pulling him closer. He groans at the sensation. I can't believe he's mine. All mine. I grin, but it fades when I remember.

"Can I ask a question? Who is Svetlana? To you, I mean?"

Ezra sets his elbows to either side of my head, propping himself up, and looks down at me. "A friend."

"Were you ever more than friends?"

He shrugs a little. "We fooled around some, but we never dated."

"Why not?"

"She wanted to, but I stopped hooking up with her when she said she wanted more."

"But you didn't?"

A long pause. "I guess by then I had given up on you and me… I wasn't unwilling to date somebody. I just hadn't met anyone I liked as much as you, Tease."

Smiling broadly, I trace the freckles on his tan nose. "I was worried you might like Svetlana more than me. She's a Russian gymnast, right? I bet she does it in fancy Kama Sutra positions. How can I compete with *that*?"

Ezra laughs hard. "She's from Russia, yes, but you're more of a gymnast than she is."

"A spy then?"

"No."

"Dominatrix?"

With a laugh, he pins me down by the wrists. "If you're so jealous, why don't you show me your gymnastics skills?"

I take the challenge.

Dodging his tickles, I fight to get on top. I press my hips to his and rock, loving the intimate feel of him. Closing my eyes, I get so into our grinding, I'll die without another kiss. I lean down to take his mouth at the same moment as he pops up to wrap his arms around me. I lose my balance, and with an unsexy "Eeeeee!" I fall from his lap, topple off my bed, and land spread-eagle.

Ezra peeks over the edge of the bed. "Seriously great gymnastics, Tease."

Name-Dropping

Saturday morning, I'm eating cereal in the kitchen and reading a book about the Vatican Museums when Dad appears. Dark circles rim his eyes.

I glance at my phone. It's nearly 10:00 a.m., and he's just coming downstairs? He must've had a late night. He wasn't home when I kicked Ezra out around 1:00 a.m.

Dad startles when he notices me. "Tee. What are you doing here?"

I swallow my bite of raisin bran and set down my spoon. "What do you mean?"

"Don't you have a game? It's Saturday."

I bite my bottom lip. I can't stop my eyes from watering. "Coach told me to sit this one out."

"What? Why?"

"Your press release…when my teammates' parents found out about me, they called the coach to complain."

"Shit," Dad murmurs, running a hand over his head. For a moment, he looks apologetic, but that quickly turns to rage. He makes a fist and slams it down on the island. I've never seen him mad enough to punch anything. Then he barricades himself up in his office all day, only opening his door to accept lunch and dinner on a tray from Marina.

On Monday morning, Dad accompanies me to school, because he wants to speak to the principal about my "soccer situation." I direct Dad to the office, where he yanks open the door and strides in, suit jacket thrown over his arm.

"May I speak with Dr. Salter, please?" he asks with a patient smile.

"Your name?"

"Senator Edward Lukens," his voice booms.

Damn. Dad's name-dropping himself. He must be angry.

The admin assistant sits up straight. She reaches to use her intercom, but she misses the *on* button on the first attempt. Dad must be making her nervous. She hits the button on her second try.

"Dr. Salter. Senator Lukens is here to see you."

Several seconds go by before the principal responds. "Please send him in." I distinctly hear him clearing his throat before he shuts off the intercom.

The assistant ushers us into Dr. Salter's office. The principal is straightening his bow tie when Dad charges forward to shake his hand. Dr. Salter smiles warmly and gestures for us to have a seat.

"What can I do for you, Senator?"

"My daughter wasn't allowed to play in Saturday's game against Hendersonville, and I'd like to know why. Before she enrolled here, you assured me that any activities she chose to pursue would be open to her, that the reasons for her leaving St. Andrew's wouldn't be held against her. You told me she could be happy here."

I gasp. Gaze over at my father. He talked to Dr. Salter before my first day?

"Senator, I'm sorry you had to come down here," Dr. Salter says, folding his hands in front of him. "I'll be speaking with the school board today about my decision to let Taylor keep playing. Coach Walker made a unilateral decision without clearing it with me first. The situation is under control now."

"So my daughter will get to stay on the team?"

"Yes, Senator. So long as she wants to play. I don't withhold opportunities from our students if they haven't done anything wrong at Hundred Oaks."

"Thank you," Dad says in an annoyed tone, checking his watch. "I need to get to work."

After shaking Dr. Salter's hand, Dad vamooses as quickly as he arrived, leaving me alone with the principal.

"Are you okay, Taylor?" he asks.

I shrug. I keep causing more and more problems for my parents. Dad's usually at work by now or at least on his way to his office in Nashville, but he had to come deal with me again.

"Listen," Dr. Salter starts, "if anyone, and that includes Coach Walker, gives you any problems, you come straight to me, okay?"

"Are you saying that because of who my dad is?"

"I'm saying that because you deserve every chance to succeed."

The way he says that makes me feel like an at-risk student or something, but it's nice to have someone looking out for me. Also, it was pretty badass how Dad came down here and took care of business.

That afternoon when I get to practice, I find Dr. Salter sitting on the bleachers. He waves at me. I let out a deep breath and wave back, glad he's here. Coach Walker, however, is another story.

For once, the coach isn't obsessed with his phone. He actually directs practice. He makes us do drills! Amazing what the presence of a school principal will do for productivity, eh?

The next evening, we have a home game against St. Andrew's.

My old team.

Dressed in my red-and-black Raiders uniform, I'm pumped to play, but my old friends are about to see me playing with a team that isn't a team at all. That deflates me a little.

I pull my hair back into a ponytail, nod once at my reflection in the locker-room mirror, then head out onto the field, where four mothers and a father are surrounding Coach Walker, giving him the third degree.

"I don't understand," one says. "You told us Taylor Lukens wouldn't be playing. I don't feel comfortable with Nicole being around a drug user."

She must be Nicole's mom, because *damn, like mother like daughter*. This is more humiliating than the time I begged my teacher to pull over the bus during a field trip when I had to use the bathroom really bad. I remind myself that I can help this team play better. It's not like I'm a burden. My eye twitches.

"The school board and Dr. Salter said she could stay on the team," Coach Walker replies in a rush.

"I demand an explanation!" Nicole's mom insists.

Jeez, if my mom pulled a stunt like this, I'd be embarrassed out of my mind, but Nicole seems to find it hilarious. She hovers next to her mom, listening in on the conversation.

During the drama, Chloe joins me. "Want to pair up for drills?"

"Yes, please."

We start kicking the ball back and forth, and I smile, excited I'm finally getting to warm up with a serious player.

When Nicole glances away from her mom chewing out Coach, she notices Chloe warming up with me. A hurt look crosses her face. "Chlo! What the hell? You're my partner."

"Not today," Chloe replies. "You were messing around when I needed to warm up."

Nicole's eyes grow dark. "Beth!" she calls to the girl digging through her mobile hospital of a backpack. "Warm up with me."

Chloe ignores her and goes back to passing with me.

As more parents arrive to watch the game, a few trickle over to speak with Coach. Luckily, Dr. Salter is there to help put out the fires. Which apparently are flaming, because many of the parents are yelling and gesturing at me.

How did it come to this?

Madison, Steph, and my former teammates are watching the commotion from their bench across the field, seeing me at my lowest.

Madison gives me a small wave, and I wave back. Steph blows me a kiss. I return it. Earlier today, they group-texted me about catching up after the game. No matter what has happened, they still care. They love me. And that means pretty much everything.

As I'm kicking the ball back to Chloe, my parents appear on the side of the field. So does my boyfriend.

Mom gives Ezra a big hug and pats his back. Then he scratches the back of his neck before stretching out a hand to shake Dad's. What are they talking about? Knowing Ezra, I wouldn't be surprised if he's asking Dad permission to date me. When it comes to behaving like a gentleman, the guy's as old-fashioned as a typewriter.

Alyson comes to stand with Chloe and me.

"Your man's here, huh?" Alyson says, watching as Ezra escorts my mom over to the stands.

"I didn't know he was coming."

"I coulda told you he would," Chloe says. "He was eye-fucking you like crazy the other night at the bowling alley."

I laugh at Chloe's brashness. "I'm more shocked that my father is here."

The girls raise their eyebrows and follow me over to the bench to meet my dad. He has this purposeful way of walking: I can tell he's on a charge into battle, but he moves like a swan. An angry swan ready to jab Coach with his beak.

"Soccer is supposed to be a wholesome school activity!" Nicole's mother rages on. "How can we uphold its sacredness with Taylor on the team?"

"Sacredness?" Chloe snorts.

Coach holds up both hands. "Calm down."

"If we could all lower our voices," Dr. Salter starts.

I reach the bench right as Dad does.

Dr. Salter sucks in a breath. "Senator."

At that, all the parents startle and turn to Dad, who is standing tall in a black suit with his jacket draped over his arm. It's not every day a United States senator is in their midst.

The principal continues, "I apologize for the commotion, Senator. We're getting it worked out."

"What is that supposed to mean?" Nicole's mom says.

Dad pastes on his *I'm-annoyed-but-I-have-to-be-nice* smile that other people eat up. But I can tell he's pissed. He loosens his tie and begins smiling directly at each parent in turn.

"It's been tough for my little girl, having to start at a new school. Soccer has always been Taylor's favorite activity, and her mother and I were so pleased she found a spot on the soccer team here.

"Now, I know we've had some trouble in the last week, but Taylor needs this team. She *needs* your kids in her life." He looks around at everyone again. "I'd be grateful if you'd give my daughter another chance."

He's brilliant. He made it seem as if we can't live without *them*. Which is total bullshit and embarrassing if you ask me, but hey, it works. The parents all gaze at Dad in adoration.

"Well, um," Nicole's mother starts. She pauses, looking to the other parents.

"I think we can help you out, Senator," a father says, putting his hand out to shake Dad's. Dad takes it, of course, always on the prowl for votes.

"We can give Taylor a chance," another mom says. This makes Nicole's mom storm off like she's just been fired from a job.

"Thank you all," Dad says, bowing his head slightly. "I'm looking forward to seeing the team play today."

With sweat rolling down his forehead, Coach looks like he might pass out. After dealing with all these parents, will he ask for a pay raise?

I go to my father, and he gives me a side hug. "Think your mom would notice if I sneak a hot dog from the concession stand?"

I nearly trip over my feet. "You're actually staying for the game?"

"Of course. I want to see you play. I rarely get to do that."

I walk him toward the bleachers where the other Hundred Oaks parents sit.

"So Ezra Carmichael is here?" Dad asks.

"Yeah…"

"Remember what I said."

"Dad, Ezra's a great guy. I know he's had some trouble, but he *needs* us in his life," I say, fluttering my eyelashes, mimicking his political mumbo jumbo. "I'd be ever so grateful if you'd give Ezra a chance."

A big grin crosses Dad's face. "You kill me."

"Dad?"

"Hmm?"

I wrap an arm around his waist. "Thank you."

For the first time in forever, he kisses my forehead. "No problem."

We lose to my old school 3–1.

Which isn't all that bad. When Chloe scored on a header, I ran screaming down the field and joined in the group hug.

After the game, while Mom and Dad chat with the other soccer parents, Ezra and I catch up with Steph and Madison. Ezra hugs me from behind, but he lets me go when he sees Dad glaring at him in that Dad way of his.

"I knew you guys would eventually get together!" Steph says in her British accent.

"Now maybe Mads will stop calling me The Asshole," he replies with a playful grin.

"You knew about that?" Madison mumbles.

He winks at her. "I heard all sorts of stuff during poker night at St. Andrew's."

"Hey, Ez," Steph says, poking him in the bicep. "Do you have any construction worker friends you can set me up with?"

"No, but Taylor can introduce you to a landscaping lion," he replies, and I groan.

Back at home, Dad hauls ass up to his office so he can get to work. Mom sets her purse down on the kitchen island and sighs.

"You okay?" I ask.

She seems distracted when she replies, "I heard parents talking in the stands. They mentioned some of your teammates weren't happy you joined the team. I'm sorry if they've been mean to you."

My face burns with embarrassment. "They're not all so bad."

"Why didn't you mention it to me and your father?"

I set my tote bag on a stool and unzip it, unpacking my empty lunch containers and iPad. "I don't know. I've caused you and Dad enough trouble, so I didn't want to bother you with this. And I guess I'm just used to figuring out stuff myself. If I had a problem at St. Andrew's, I dealt with it on my own."

Mom picks up my lunch containers and carries them to the

sink. "I know your father has always put a lot of pressure on you kids to be independent, but you can talk to me, okay?"

I nod, wishing that soccer were my biggest problem, when really it's this lie holding me hostage. If I tell the truth, my family will be pissed at me. It could do further damage to Dad's campaign. My friends and family may not look at me the same way anymore. They'd see me as a liar. But what I wouldn't give to go back to being the smart, studious girl, the one colleges would kill to have at their schools.

Mom goes on, "I know what it's like to feel lonely." I can tell she's thinking of Aunt Virginia. "It's not good to keep those feelings bottled up inside."

My mother's gaze meets mine, and in that moment, I can feel I'm loved. I should tell her the truth. I open my mouth to say the words, but then Mom rubs the tears from her eyes and takes a deep breath. I don't want to give her even more to worry about right now.

I decide to make a pact with myself. The election is a month away. Once that is over, I can come clean to my family.

The Interview

Dad kept his word: he actually takes a Friday off work to accompany me on my Yale visit.

While I meet with the admissions officer, Dad and Jenna have plans to get coffee. They need to get their fix when Mom isn't around too.

Dad parks the rental car outside my sister's apartment, which is nothing like Ezra's on Ragswood Road. The condo is a quaint first-floor unit in a classic redbrick building on State Street. I feel like I'm at Bilbo Baggins's place in Hobbiton.

If Yale accepts me, I'll live in the dorms freshman year, but I might be able to move off-campus for sophomore year like my sister did. I love the idea of having my own little place with a dog, a Keurig, and a Hobbit front door.

Dad and I walk up the cobbled path framed by lush green bushes to the curved, wooden front door. I knock, and Jenna appears. When I see her, I always feel like I'm gazing into a mirror. We have the same ivory skin tone, same auburn hair.

"You're early!" she says, giving us a panicked smile. She hops up on tiptoes to kiss Dad's cheek and hug him, and he grins down at her.

Then she turns to me. "What the hell is wrong with you? How could you get kicked out of school?"

"Nice to see you too," I mutter. Like I said, she always gives you her opinion straight.

She turns to our father and gives him a smile. "Dad, I'm glad you're here. I want to talk to you about a paper I'm writing for philosophy. I'm having trouble grasping some concepts."

Brownnoser.

Inside Jenna's chic condo with the white sofa, matching loveseat, and light-yellow walls with cream crown molding, we discover she's not alone. A guy is sitting in her armchair, putting on his tennis shoe.

Dad's nostrils flare as he takes in the scene. "Did your boyfriend spend the night?"

"Oh, he's not my boyfriend."

The guy gulps.

"Excuse me?" Dad's hands go to his hips.

My sister waves dismissively. "C'mon, Dad. I'm an adult."

"And a horny one at that," I murmur.

"At least I didn't get kicked out of school," Jenna retorts.

The guy rushes to put on his other shoe, then jumps to his feet and pulls on a *Yale Lacrosse* hoodie. Jenna shows him out, saying good-bye to him—whoever he is—at the door and clicking it shut. Given that she didn't introduce him to us, I imagine this was a one-night stand. I don't blame her though. That lacrosse player is *cute*.

"I don't pay for this condo so you can entertain boys here," Dad says, and I can barely contain my laughter.

Jenna ignores his red-faced glare. "Ready to go?" she asks, picking up her purse.

She makes a big deal of showing us around campus, even though Dad went to school here and I attended family day last year with my parents. Dad speaks to Randy on his cell phone about campaign tactics while Jenna plays tour guide.

"There's the bell tower." Jenna points at it. "I always forget its name."

I roll my eyes. "Great tour, Jen."

She ignores me. "And there's the Commons."

"Jack Goodwin asked me to tell you he said hi, by the way."

This distracts her from the tour. "Is he still dating that girl Savannah?" She looks at me sideways, and I nod. "I really screwed up with him, huh?"

"Yeah, kinda," I reply.

"Is he happy though?"

"I only met her for a few minutes, but they seem happy. Savannah was nice."

Jenna gives me a tiny, sad smile. Jack was the first boy she ever loved. I feel kinship with her at the moment, because even though she's incredibly smart and confident, she's made mistakes. Just like me.

"So Oll told me you broke up with Ben," she says softly. "Are you okay?"

"I'm getting there, thanks."

"Why'd you do it?"

If I don't give her some other juicy tidbit, she'll interrogate me until I'm begging *her* to listen to all my deepest, darkest secrets. "Have you ever thought about hooking up with a construction worker?"

Her eyes light up. "You did not."

"Did."

"Oh my God, I want all the details! Go you." She elbows me.

Luckily, Dad finishes his conversation and pockets his phone. He rubs his eyes. He suddenly looks tired.

"You okay?" I ask him.

"I'm sure the polls will go back up. If not, your mother will kill me." He laughs nervously and won't meet my gaze. Guilt presses on my heart.

I suddenly don't feel like doing this college interview. I don't feel like doing much of anything.

Jenna leads me to the admissions building, where I have an appointment with the director of admissions, Gregory Brandon. I googled him last night and found out he attended Georgetown University in DC, where he was on the crew team. I didn't find much else. I wish I knew more about him, so I can schmooze if I have to.

"Good luck," Dad says, squeezing my shoulder. "Just stick to the script, and you'll do great. You plan to major in business, and you know Yale has the best program to help you achieve your goals. Be honest about why you were expelled."

"Thanks, Dad," I choke out.

"I'll be back to pick you up in half an hour."

I watch as he walks off with my sister, sliding an arm around her shoulder, listening as she talks. She's not perfect by any means, but she's never dragged our family into the headlines. Meanwhile, I did something so stupid Dad's poll numbers are dropping faster than rain in a monsoon.

I try to shake it off. Concentrate. The biggest moment of my life is about to happen—the moment I've been working toward for years.

My college interview.

I pull open the door to the admissions building. The blue Yale logo is painted on every wall, and sunlight pours in through the windows. The atmosphere instantly improves my mood. I confidently walk up to the receptionist, a woman wearing a Yale Bulldogs sweatshirt.

"I'm Taylor Lukens. Here to see Mr. Brandon."

"I'll tell him you're here," the lady says with a smile. "Please have a seat."

I sit down and smooth out my gray pencil skirt. I paired it with a white satin blouse and heels. It's a sophisticated outfit, one I picked out myself. Even Mom approved it, which means the sky is falling.

This interview is a chance to make sure I have my ducks in a row before I submit my application in a few weeks. I can ask the admissions officer questions about my draft essays and review which extracurriculars I should highlight above others. It's also my chance to make a great impression.

Unbuttoning my tote bag, I quickly check my portfolio for the thousandth time to make sure I packed copies of my résumé. I run through answers in my head. *"I plan to major in business with a minor in politics. I love community service—I've been on three different Habitat for Humanity projects."*

When I make sure my phone's ringer is turned off, I find a text from Ezra: Good luck. xo.

Best. Boyfriend. Ever.

I watch five minutes tick by on the clock. I flip through a copy of last year's yearbook, the *Yale Banner*, sitting on the coffee table. The pictures of students laughing in the stands at homecoming make me smile.

Finally a tall African-American man emerges from an office. He wears round glasses that remind me of Harry Potter's, a Yale lapel pin on his suit jacket, and a black, white, and blue Yale-themed tie.

"Taylor?"

"Yes, sir," I say, standing to shake his hand. He introduces himself and invites me into his office. He gestures at a seat in front of his desk and sits down in front of an open file folder labeled with my name. Probably my test scores, transcripts, and résumé I sent ahead of time. My entire life is in there.

"I'm glad you could stop by," Mr. Brandon says. "I understand several of your family members attended Yale."

"Yes, and my sister's here now. She and my father are grabbing coffee while I meet with you."

Mr. Brandon clicks his pen. "Have you been to Blue State Coffee yet?"

"No."

"You should go try their mocha latte. They sprinkle chocolate chips on top of the whipped crème."

"Can we go there now?" I ask, making him chuckle.

Mr. Brandon looks down at my file. "So you'll be applying early admission in a couple weeks?"

"Yes, sir. If accepted, I plan to major in business with a minor in politics."

"Well, you've got great test scores. A perfect GPA." He scans the papers in front of him. "Superb community service and extracurricular activities. I imagine our admissions committee will be very impressed by your application."

"Thank you. I've worked really hard."

He looks up at me, clicking his pen on and off. He hesitates. "I did an Internet search on you before you arrived."

"I did one on you too, sir."

This surprises him. "Find anything good?"

"I know that you did crew in college…but I don't know anything about crew, so I probably shouldn't have brought that up."

He smiles. "I like that you're straightforward. Honesty is very important to us." I fidget in my seat as he keeps speaking. "Normally, I prefer to respect our applicants' privacy, but sometimes we can't help but hear something in the news."

I feel like he's sizing me up. "Yes, sir."

"So I understand you've been in some trouble recently. The articles I read said you were taking Adderall that wasn't prescribed to you, and you were forced to leave your school."

"I made a mistake," I say, clasping my hands in a bid to make them stop shaking. "I shouldn't have taken the pills, but I take responsibility for what I did. And I won't let my bad decision define me. I will keep working hard."

He makes a note in my file. "Thank you for being honest. That tells me a lot about you." Mr. Brandon sets his pen down and leans back in his chair to look at me. "We consider each applicant on a case-by-case basis, Taylor. As a matter of practice, we don't admit any applicants who have a record of hard drug use. We can't afford that kind of liability here on campus."

"I understand that, sir." My voice is now shaking along with my hands.

"Adderall is a bit of a different case," Mr. Brandon says. "It's not an illegal drug like cocaine or heroin, but it's still serious. Use of prescription drugs by someone other than the intended recipient is happening more and more, and it's not something we want to see here on campus. We'll have to carefully consider your circumstances before agreeing to accept you as a student here."

"I admit I've taken it a few times in the past, but I haven't in over a month, and I don't plan to again. I've been seeing a counselor."

He makes a note in the file. "That's good to know. Yale is a tough school, but we try to have fun here as well. We don't want our students feeling like they are under so much pressure to succeed that they have to take pills."

I bite my pinkie nail. "No, sir. I don't want that either."

I nearly do a cheer when he changes the subject. "So how do you like your new high school?"

"It's okay, but I miss St. Andrew's. Especially my soccer team."

He picks up a paper from my file and studies it. "But you're playing for your new school now?"

"Yeah, but we aren't very good. Haven't won a game yet."

"Are you having fun at least?"

After thinking for a moment, I shake my head. "It's hit or miss."

"But you're still playing?"

"I'm not a quitter." *Not this close to when college applications are due.* "I really do love the game…just not this team. Some girls don't pass the ball. They don't work together. It's not very fun."

"Then why are you still playing for the school?"

Good question. I love soccer, but at this point, it's just something to put on my résumé. That sounds shallow, and any other answer would ring false, so I choose not to respond.

Mr. Brandon picks up his pen again. "After you graduate high school, life is going to get a lot tougher."

"That's hard to imagine," I say quietly.

"It's important to do things you enjoy. You don't want to end up on a path that you hate."

"I don't want that either."

"So what do you plan to do with your business major?"

I nod, prepared for the question. "I want to work for my family's investment firm."

He looks a little bored by my answer. I don't blame him. It bores me too.

"What about your minor in politics?"

I should say that I will run for office one day, but he must hear this same drivel all day long. He probably looks forward to hearing the random—like a guy who wants to major in art because he's on a graffiti crew, or a girl who wants to join the Yale sailing team but might have to take a semester or two off because it's her dream to sail around the world.

"I'm not totally sure what I want to do with the politics

minor," I say. He appreciated when I told the truth earlier, so I decide to just lay it all out there. "I'm not wild about business either, to tell you the truth. I hate math."

"So do I," he replies with a smile.

"Whatever I do, Yale is the best school to help me achieve my goals."

"I can't disagree with you there. All of our students take general education courses during their first two years here. It helps kids learn more about who they are and what they like."

"That's good to know. I don't really know what I like."

"That's okay. I just turned forty, and I still don't know what I want to do with my life." He stares out the window at a parking lot.

I follow his eyes. A black car reverses out of its space and drives out onto the road. I worry my life is just like that car, reversing and heading out to some unknown destination. I don't like the idea of not knowing where I'm going.

We sit in an awkward silence.

"I totally bombed this interview, huh?" I say.

He shakes his head. "It's been a good eye-opener for me, to be honest."

"How so?"

"Based on your background and what I've seen in the news, I figured you'd make excuses for your behavior, but you were completely open with me. I appreciate that. When you send in your application, make sure to include a detailed letter explaining why you were expelled and what you've learned from it."

"I can do that."

"Good. There have been times when we've accepted a student only to find out later he'd forged his transcript or she lied about her extracurricular activities. We had to rescind their acceptance letters. So it's best to get everything out in the open from the start."

Mr. Brandon puts his pen back in the cup on his desk and closes my folder.

I shut my eyes. I still haven't been completely honest with him. The election is in three weeks. I am planning to tell Mom and Dad the whole truth right after that.

I thought the worst thing would be not getting into Yale, but what if I got in and then they rescinded my acceptance?

I have no idea what to do next.

I won't lie.

Call me a snob, but being my father's daughter has its perks.

On the flight home from Connecticut, I stretch out my feet in first class. Dad upgraded us using his frequent flier miles. The flight attendant serves me sparkling water, steak and mashed potatoes, and chocolate-covered strawberries for dessert.

Dad reads briefing paper after briefing paper on his iPad. He's on the Senate Appropriations Committee on Foreign Relations, so his staff is always forwarding him information about overseas development. I glance over his shoulder. He's reading a paper titled *PEPFAR FUNDING CUTS.* That's the President's Emergency Plan for AIDS Relief.

"What's going on with AIDS funding?" I ask.

Dad lets out a long sigh. "I'm trying to keep it going at current levels, but some of the guys want to cut it. They don't want to spend so much money on Africa when we could use the funding domestically."

PEPFAR has always been a favorite project of Dad's. At first, I didn't completely understand why Dad would fight for it so hard when we have homeless, hungry people here in the United States, but then he explained that over the past thirty years, AIDS ran rampant in Africa, leaving twenty-five percent of kids without parents. Kids without homes are more likely to join groups that promote violence. Without PEPFAR, the entire African continent could've destabilized.

But still, what about hungry people here in America? It's a hard balance. It would be great to help everyone, but funding has its limits.

"Do you think funding will be cut?" I ask.

"I'll get the guys to change their minds, but not without giving up something else I want."

"That doesn't seem right, Dad."

"That's politics for you. But don't worry, we'll figure out a way to keep it funded. It's the right thing to do." Dad flips the lid on his iPad, covering the screen. He nods at my laptop. "What are you working on?"

"Just finishing up my English essay that's due Monday. It's on Chaucer."

"Ahh, the Cadbury Tales."

I laugh softly. "No, *The Canterbury Tales*."

"I know. But I always thought about Cadbury eggs when we were reading it in class."

"Sounds delicious."

Dad elbows me. "If only your mom would buy them for us."

It's such a comfortable moment between us, I rest my head on his shoulder. I can't remember the last time I did this. I must've been a little girl?

He pats the back of my hand, then keeps his fingers there. Again, something that hasn't happened in a long time. It feels awkward, but I like it too.

"So how'd your interview go?" he asks quietly. He must've been waiting for me to bring it up, because he hadn't asked until now, even though we left Yale a few hours ago.

"Mr. Brandon was really nice," I say. "Our conversation was very real."

Dad nods. "I've heard that about the admissions office. They're no bullshitters."

"Exactly."

"What did he think of your résumé?"

"He said it looks great. He didn't mention any ways I need to improve it, but he said the committee will have to carefully consider my application, you know, because of what happened at St. Andrew's… I may not get in." My voice cracks. A tear slips down my cheek.

Dad squeezes my hand. "I'm proud of you no matter what."

I wipe my nose. It's nice to hear that.

"So what's going on with Ezra Carmichael?" he asks.

Hearing my boyfriend's name always puts a smile on my face. I shrug at Dad, hoping he won't make a big deal of it. "We're dating, I guess."

"Does your brother know?" Dad asks.

"Not yet. I'm trying to figure out how to tell him. Ezra wants to do it in person."

"Don't wait too long. He deserves to hear it from you and Ezra and not somebody else."

I take a long sip of my drink. "I like him a lot, Dad. I have for a long time. I know he's got some stuff to work out, but he's a great guy—"

"Of course he is," Dad interrupts. "You forget I've known him since he was a little boy. Other than taking apart my lawnmower and always winning all your brother's money at poker, I admire his character. What teenage boy asks permission from a girl's father before starting a relationship?"

That makes my heart race. "Seriously?"

"Yes, he asked once a couple of years ago and again last week."

I laugh. "What did you say?"

"I said okay. But I told him he'd better follow through and ask you out, because I won't say yes for a third time."

With a smile, I snuggle my head against Dad's shoulder, and he leans his head back against the seat. His black hair has a lot more gray in it than it used to. Frown lines accentuate his mouth. I can't help but think those lines are my fault. My mistake is blotting out everything my dad has worked for for eighteen years.

"Dad?"

"Yeah?"

"I'm really sorry. For everything."

"I know," he replies quietly. "I hate how the press is portraying you."

The guilt might drown me.

"I'm worried about you," he adds.

"You have nothing to worry about. I'm good. But I feel terrible about what's going on with your campaign," I say. "I wish I could help somehow."

"I want you to focus on you, okay?"

"Okay," I say with a small smile.

After that college interview and all my conversations with Ezra, I like the idea of figuring out what I want. What I need.

I just hope I figure it out before it's too late.

Relaxing

"I don't think Ezra and I need your prompts anymore," I tell Miss Brady.

"Oh?"

"Yeah, we're dating now."

Miss Brady smiles. "I'm glad you have someone to talk to. How about friends?"

"I'm getting closer with Alyson and Chloe from the soccer team. They're different from my old friends, but I like them."

"Different how?"

"They're more laid-back. Like, Chloe never talks about her plans for the future except for how she wants to travel. With my old friends, and with Ezra—my boyfriend—it seems like we only talk about the future."

"There's nothing wrong with that, if that's what you want to concentrate on. But don't spend so much time thinking about the future that you forget to live *now*. High school needs to be a balance of serious and fun, just like life."

It's Friday night, and Ezra is coming over to hang out. When he arrives, Marina answers the door and calls up the stairs, "Taylor! Ezra's here."

I love how when my parents are here, Marina walks from room to room and makes quiet announcements, but when they're gone, she shouts like a normal person. It makes this house feel more like a home.

I finish my makeup and check my hair in the mirror, then jog down the stairs. Ezra's not in the foyer. I poke my head into the living room. He's not in there either. Then I hear his voice coming from the kitchen.

"Mustard, please. Thanks."

I find him standing at the island, relaxed in a navy-blue pullover and loose, worn jeans. Marina hands him a sandwich cut into triangles.

When he sees me, he sets the plate down and gives me a broad smile. I rush into his arms for a long hug.

"Mmm," he says into my hair. "I missed you. It's been too long."

"I just saw you this morning for coffee."

"I was going into withdrawals. I need a kiss."

I grin and get up on tiptoes to give him what he wants.

Marina clucks her tongue. "None of that hanky-panky in my kitchen."

I break away from my boyfriend but keep my arms stretched around his neck. "Did you just say hanky-panky?"

Marina's response is to shoo us out of the room.

We twine our fingers and go down the steps into the basement, taking his sandwich with us. Ezra slips off his work boots, and I turn on the TV.

It's campaign season, so of course, the first commercial to pop up is one for Harrison Wallace. *"Like you, the most important thing in my life is my family."* The commercial cuts to pictures of Wallace's perfect blond wife and three perfect blond kids. They're in a kitchen, cooking together. *"This election, my vote is for better healthcare. I want to build more hospitals and bring better healthcare funding to Tennessee. Vote for me, Harrison Wallace, for senator, because your family matters."*

I shut my eyes. It's a brilliant commercial. It would be in poor taste for Wallace's campaign to come right out and attack me for being a drug user, but he can get away with playing up his own family. That commercial was the most wholesome thing I've ever seen. I wouldn't be surprised if homemade apple pies and lemonade started flying out of the TV.

There's no room for error in Dad's campaign. I understand enough about politics to know that if we were in any other part of the country, say New York or California, my mistakes wouldn't become as major a campaign point. Because let's be honest, elections in the South are all about family values. They're about tradition.

Ezra bumps his knee against mine. "You all right?"

I paste on a fake smile. "Definitely."

"Liar. You don't have to pretend with me."

"Fine. It's been a long week, I'm tired, and I'm hungry." I side-eye his sandwich.

With a laugh, he passes me a triangle, and we chew, content in the silence.

Since Mom and Dad aren't coming home tonight, there's no rush to fool around before they get back. I love just relaxing with Ezra on the couch, on the rug, in the armchair. We keep moving around the room as he play-wrestles with me and tickles me, but I always end up in his lap again, kissing his lips, curling my fingers into his hair.

My smile is real now.

He slightly lifts my top and runs his warm fingers over my lower back. Heat flares in his green eyes. I want to take this further, but Marina could walk through the basement on her way to the laundry. I hope she wouldn't be doing a load of clothes on a Friday night, but you never know.

"Let's go to my room," I say between kisses.

"You are insatiable."

I playfully push his chest. "You say that like it's a bad thing."

"No, it's a very, very good thing. I love that about you."

"You love that I'm horny?" I tease.

He bursts out laughing. "I love that you always go for what you want. I wish I could do that."

I roll my eyes. "I hate it when you sell yourself short. You can do whatever you want, Ez."

"You don't get it. I can't."

I take a deep breath and lay it out there. "I was doing research online, and most colleges offer help for people who have learning disabilities."

He winces when I say that, although I don't entirely get why. It's not like it's something he can help; it's a genetic thing. I guess it's sort of like mental illness. It's not rare by any means, and it's not anything to be ashamed of, but people are still scared of the stigma that comes along with it.

But I don't know what else to call dyslexia other than a learning disability. I certainly can't call it a problem or an *issue*. Because it's not.

"I think if you explain your situation to Cornell, they would help. You could go back to school."

"Are you trying to get rid of me, Tease? I thought you were horny."

I pinch his arm. "I'm being serious!"

"You're serious all the time."

"I am not," I reply, even though the guidance counselor said something very similar.

I'll show them who's serious.

I launch an attack, tackling him to the carpet. He retaliates with tickles. I squeal and escape by crawling away. Laughing, he chases after me on his hands and knees. He snatches my ankle, pulling me up close to him, pinning me to the floor and pushing his hips to mine with a sexy grin. I can feel his hardness through my leggings; it makes me gasp. Gasp—and think naughty thoughts. We're still getting to know each other again and haven't slept together, but that doesn't mean I don't think about it.

He softly kisses my lips, cupping my cheek with his hand. When he opens his eyes and smiles lazily, I flip him onto his back and straddle his hips.

"I have one more thing to say," I announce.

"Jesus, Mary, and Joseph," he mutters.

"I'll stop being serious after I say this."

"Fine, go ahead."

"Please call Cornell and ask how they can help."

"Taylor, seriously. We've been through this. I hate classes. I hate taking notes. I hate writing papers. I hate reading. I'm happy now."

"But you want to be an architect."

"What I want and what's going to happen are very different things. You think my dad would pay for me to go to school to become an architect?"

"You could always get student loans."

With his hands wrapped around my waist, we sit in silence, looking at each other.

He's right. I am being way too serious for a Friday night.

So I start another wrestling-tickling fight, and for a second time, I end up in his lap with his arms straitjacketed around me. He kisses my nose.

That's when I hear a throat being cleared.

I fall off Ezra's lap backward, then scramble to a sitting position. I swivel around to find Oliver.

"Oll!" I squeal, jumping to my feet and hurtling myself into his arms. It's so good to see my brother. I hug him hard, then step back to take him in. Same disheveled auburn hair. Dark jeans, a corduroy jacket with elbow patches, a white button-down, and brown loafers. Totally an outfit my mother bought him. His eyes glare from behind his glasses.

He pats my back stiffly. "What's going on here?"

"Creepy," I say. "Your voice sounds just like Dad's."

No one laughs at my joke.

I start, "Ezra and I—"

"Oll, I need to speak with you in private," Ezra interjects.

"Oh, come on," I complain. "Just tell him now."

"Tell me what? That my best friend is fooling around with my baby sister?"

"We need to talk," Ezra repeats.

Oliver nods at Ezra. "Upstairs."

My brother storms out of the room. Ezra takes a few long, steadying breaths, stands, and adjusts the front of his jeans. He blushes when he notices me staring. Then he trudges up the steps after Oliver.

I blow out a puff of air and cross my arms. Then uncross them. I look up at the ceiling. Chew on my thumb.

I'd hate to mess up their friendship. Oliver and Ezra have known each other for almost fifteen years. I had been planning to tell Oliver about me and Ezra, but I wasn't honestly sure how to tell him yet. Our relationship is still new. Shaky. Fragile. I mean, I know we're really into each other, but what if I can convince him to go back to school for second semester? What if he decides we can't date because of that distance, or if he continues to spout nonsense about feeling inferior?

Then I remember what he said a few minutes ago: "*I like that you take what you want.*"

I can do that.

I charge up the stairs to the kitchen, where I find Oliver pouring tequila into shot glasses and Ezra shuffling a deck of cards.

"I don't care what you say," I snap at my brother. "I want Ezra, and nobody's going to stop me from dating him. Not you. Not Dad. Not Svetlana, the Russian gymnast."

"Rawr," Oliver says.

My little speech lights up Ezra's eyes.

"Bottoms up, man," Oliver says, pushing one of the shots in front of Ezra. They sprinkle salt onto their wrists, toast their glasses, throw back their liquor, grimace, then lick their wrists. Next, Ezra deals Oliver a card. *Are they playing blackjack?*

"Seriously?" I say. "Were you just going to leave me down there all night while you get trashed and gamble?"

They both have the decency to look sheepish. Ezra sweeps the cards back into a neat pile.

Oliver holds an arm out to me. I slide up against him and accept his hug. "I wish you'd given me a heads-up that you're with Ez now. Why didn't you tell me?"

"I was trying to figure out how. I didn't want to mess up your friendship, but I'm not giving up Ezra either."

"It sucks to know you didn't feel comfortable telling me."

I nod. "I'm sorry. I love you."

My brother gives me a small smile. "Love you too."

"So you're okay with us dating?"

Oliver looks from me to Ezra. "I trust him with my life. Why wouldn't I trust him with my sister's?"

Aww. Ezra nods once at my brother, and Oliver nods back. Then they glance away, because they are guys, and guys seemingly can't be seen showing affection toward one another.

"What are you doing home?" I ask my brother.

"Fall break."

"I thought you were going to Alana's house in Miami," I say, and Ezra nods. He must've been under the same impression.

"Eh, Alana and I broke things off yesterday. I got cold feet about spending five days alone with her and her parents, and that got us talking about how we'd both rather be single for now. So I decided to come home. I needed to see how you're doing…but I guess I know, since I caught you and Ez practically bumping uglies."

"Ugh!" I shout.

Ezra makes a face. "Dude, never say 'bumping uglies' again."

"If you don't want me to say it, you shouldn't have been trying to do that with my sister." Oliver pours himself another tequila shot. He tosses it back, then grimaces.

"Hey, where's mine?" I ask.

"I don't think so," Oliver says.

I snake an arm around Ezra's waist. "Where's mine?"

With a smile, he surrenders his shot glass to me, and I reward him with a kiss on the cheek.

"Gross. Just because I've given Ez permission to date you doesn't mean I want to see any PDA."

I shoot my brother a withering look. "Permission?"

Oliver ignores me and turns to Ezra. "Do you want to head up to Nashville? There's a new nightclub I want to check out. It's called Tunnel Vision."

My brother absolutely loves clubbing. I'm surprised he didn't head to Miami on his own so he could hit up the night scene. Honestly, I'm shocked he hasn't tried to get a role in one of those *Step Up* movies.

Ezra has always been more of the listening-to-live-music type, but the boy can dance. Like, seriously dance. I've never actually fast-danced with him, but I remember watching him at St.

Andrew's dances, and of course, I've seen my brother's videos from their trips to Mexico and Europe. I nearly groan at the thought of Ezra behind me, swaying his hips against mine. God, I'm a complete perv. But at least I own it.

"I'm up for dancing if you are," I say to Ezra. "I can use Jenna's old license to try to get in, but it might be risky."

He takes my hand, caressing my fingers. "Not tonight. I'd rather just hang out here."

With a roll of his eyes, Oliver pours Ezra another shot. I steal it and drink before either can protest. It tastes horrible. I can barely swallow it. I cough hard and let out a burst of laughter once I've recovered. Then I burp accidentally.

"She's all yours, bud," Oliver says to Ezra.

"Hey!" I slap my brother's hand.

My phone buzzes with a new text from Chloe.

What r u doing?

Hanging out w Ezra and my brother. Want to come over?

Can Alyson come too?

By the time they arrive, Ezra and Oliver are tipsy, and we're having our own dance party in the formal living room. When Marina shows Chloe and Alyson in, Oliver has unplugged a decorative lamp and is singing into it, pretending it's a microphone.

I say, "If Mom saw this, she'd have a coronary."

"*I'm* going to have a coronary," Marina says, and Oliver

placates her by setting down the lamp and making her dance with him.

"Um, is this typical at your house?" Alyson shouts over the music, watching my brother dance with our housekeeper.

"The Oliver Dance Party happens every night," Ezra says.

Once my brother has stopped doing the tango with Marina, I turn the music down and introduce everyone. Oliver checks out Chloe and vice versa.

We turn the music back up, and I dance with Ezra, which makes Oliver cover his eyes and whine. You'd never know my brother is about to turn twenty, given how childish he's acting. The good news is that he and my new soccer friends seem to hit it off, and they distract him from our dancing. Ezra draws me up against his chest and grips my waist, moving his hips in time with mine. I get lost in his green eyes. We dance for so long, I lose track of how many songs have played.

"Do you have work in the morning?" I whisper in his ear.

"Day off. You?"

"Soccer game at noon."

"Nice, you can sleep in a little."

Mom and Dad are in Washington and won't be back until tomorrow afternoon, so I take a deep breath and do something I've never done before. Something my parents would never allow.

"Want to stay over?"

He raises his eyebrows and glances at my brother, who's now passed out on the floor. He smacks his lips, then snores. Classy.

"Yeah," Ezra says with a thick voice. "But we probably shouldn't fool around, since Oll is here."

As if Oliver would notice. He belts out another snore. Chloe and Alyson are curled up asleep together on a love seat. I wake them up to show them to one of our guest rooms.

Then I take advantage of Oliver's drunken obliviousness and lead Ezra to my room, praying Marina doesn't notice. He follows me into my bathroom, where I find a new toothbrush under the sink. He accepts it with a smile, and then we brush our teeth together. Ezra goes to steal a pair of basketball shorts and a T-shirt from Oliver's room while I change into the pink strawberry pajamas he bought me for my sixteenth birthday.

When he walks back into the room and sees what I'm wearing, his eyes take me in, and he swallows hard. "You're beautiful, Taylor."

"You are too."

His hands skim over my back to settle on my waist. "I like your strawberries," he says with a wicked grin.

"Behave."

As I'm crawling under the covers with him, cuddling and kissing, loving the feel of his body against mine, it occurs to me that I never could've planned such a wonderful evening if I'd tried to orchestrate it.

Find the Coupon

About an hour before the soccer game is to start, I'm at the field warming up. I want to get in a run and stretch my legs really well so I'm limber for the game.

Chloe appears ten minutes late, wearing dark sunglasses. "Never. Again."

I laugh.

"Your brother's crazy."

"He definitely knows how to party."

We look over into the stands, where Oliver and Ezra are sitting together. Oliver waves at us, happy as can be. He has a Tylenol/Gatorade/McDonald's breakfast sandwich hangover cure that works for him every single time. He looks like he's never had a drink in his entire life. Ezra, like Chloe, is also wearing sunglasses and looks grumpy as hell.

"Um, are you interested in Oliver?" I ask her. "I don't really care, just wondering, since you and I are friends—"

"No. I think he's great, but I'm still not interested in anything serious with anyone."

I touch her elbow. "Do you want to warm up with me?"

She groans. "I don't want to do anything right now, but sure." We begin kicking the ball around in a half-assed manner. Then I manage to squeeze in my run before joining the rest of the team to stretch.

Nicole gets up in front of everyone and gives her typical pregame speech. "Let's play hard, everybody."

I can't help myself—maybe there's leftover tequila in my bloodstream—but I have to speak up. "Let's have fun today too, y'all!"

A bunch of heads turn my way.

"Nobody asked you," Nicole says.

"Oh, so you don't want to have fun? I don't believe that, especially considering how much you hog the ball."

Coach Walker just stands there. He's probably wishing Dr. Salter were here to help him.

"Don't you think it would be more fun if we pass the ball to each other?" I ask. "Give everyone a chance to play?"

"I agree," Alyson says.

"Me too," Sydney adds.

"Because otherwise, what's the point?" I say. "I'm not having fun, Nicole. I'm tempted to walk away."

"Me too," Chloe says.

"Then why don't you?" Nicole snaps.

"Because then you'd have no subs," I tell her. "C'mon, y'all. Let's pass the ball. Communicate. Have fun."

"Yeah!" Chloe says, and Sydney joins in.

A smile appears on Brittany's face. "I'm in."

Slowly, all the other girls begin to clap and smile, and I haven't felt this good about soccer since I left St. Andrew's.

Nicole puts her hand out, and we pile ours on top. "One, two, three, team!"

During the game, we pass the ball and overall have a good time. I don't even mind playing defense instead of forward, because Sydney rocks it.

At halftime, we're down 1–0 against Tullahoma, but we've been playing great. Well, everyone except for Chloe, who gets sick behind the bleachers. She should've tried Oliver's hangover cure.

During the second half, Sydney is on fire. With an assist from a momentarily revitalized Chloe, she rockets a shot into the upper left of Tullahoma's goal.

"Goal!" I scream, running up the field. The other girls hustle toward Sydney, surrounding her with hugs. She blushes and grins, laughing. I jump up and down. Chloe smiles but places a hand over her stomach.

"You need grease ASAP," I tell her.

"That's the first thing I'm going to do right after the game. Obtain grease."

The ref blows her whistle. Tullahoma kicks off, and Nicole runs up to meet the ball. She passes it off to Chloe. She dribbles a few feet before it's stolen from her. A Tullahoma player boots it down the field my way. I stop it with my chest, and it falls to the ground in front of me with a bounce. I dribble a few feet, faking out a forward, then pass it up the left side of the field to Sydney. She's like lightning as she attacks the ball and heads for the goal. She sidesteps a defender, rears back, and boots the ball. The Tullahoma goalie lunges for it but misses.

"Ahh!" I yell, running for Sydney. By the time I reach her, she's beet red but jumping up and down. We encircle her again, patting her back. I bet the scouts will be keeping an eye on her from now on.

"Wooooo!" Coach Walker hollers from the sidelines. Even he's clapping.

The rest of the game goes great. We pass the ball and call each other's names. Alyson stops a ton of shots on goal. I'm grinning my butt off, even when Tullahoma scores a second time. But hey, a tie is great!

When it's all over, I throw an arm around Chloe. "You know what this tie means, right? You have to get trashed before every game from here on out. For good luck."

Chloe gives me an evil look to end all evil looks.

After the game, Oliver wants to go out, just the two of us, so I give Ezra a kiss good-bye, and he makes plans for tonight to go to that dance club Oll is desperate to try. For now, I'm excited to spend time with my brother alone. I haven't seen him since he went back to school at the end of summer, and talking on the phone is just not the same.

My brother's car is not much better than my Buick, but he loves it. Dad bought him a 1999 Mustang convertible. Oliver puts the top down before we peel out of the school parking lot. As always, he drives waaay too fast, and we argue over the radio station. I turn it to rock, and he keeps flipping back to rap.

"Would you stop it?" I snap, pushing his fingers away from the radio.

He smacks my hand.

I let my hair out of its braid to feel it blowing in the wind.

A cop car is up the street, so Oliver slams on the brakes, slowing way the hell down.

"How was Jenna when you saw her last week?" Oliver shouts over the music.

"Pretty good. She was her usual crass self."

"Hey, that's my twin you're talking about."

"I'm surprised she didn't devour you in the womb."

"Hey!" Oliver puffs out his chest. "We didn't share an amniotic sac, so there's no way she could've devoured me."

"Well, this conversation just got weird."

Oliver snorts.

"Jenna had a guy over—he'd spent the night—and Dad was pissed." I lower my voice and do an imitation. "*I don't pay for this condo so you can entertain boys here. Grrr.*"

My brother laughs hysterically. "Dad really said that?"

"Yep."

Oliver parks outside Pizza Hut. Other than clubbing, his other favorite thing is eating poorly. With an arm around my shoulders, he leads me inside. The pizza is great, of course, but his real reason for coming here is the mini arcade, which has ancient games, like the original Donkey Kong. He orders us a large cheese pizza, then ushers me into the arcade to play while we wait. Two little boys are playing air hockey, but otherwise, we have the place to ourselves. Oliver commandeers Contra, and I decide on Super Mario.

We talk as our fingers work the buttons. "How's your Yale application coming? Need me to read your draft?"

"It's going fine."

"You don't sound all that excited."

I make Mario jump over a hole in the ground. "It's just the admissions director got me thinking about what I want to do with my life, and I don't really know."

Oliver's fingers frantically tap away on the controls. "That's pretty typical, Tee."

"I don't even know if I want to go to Yale. All I know is I've been working my ass off for years."

"And it's going to pay off."

During this entire conversation, Oliver doesn't look up from Contra. I love him, but he's just like Dad. Ambitious. Focused. Eyes always on the prize.

But should you play a game if you don't know what the prize is? Life is not like *The Price Is Right*, where they show you three doors and tell you to pick one. The prize might be a new car, but sometimes it's a month's supply of paper towels. What if I pick the wrong door by going to Yale, majoring in business, getting a job at the family firm, and end up living a miserable life because I did what was *expected* of me?

I'm proud of my family, and I want to help continue the business Grandpa started, but shouldn't I listen to my heart too? I was born with an insane amount of privilege, and I know I'm lucky, but with that privilege comes responsibility to do important things in my life.

I jab a button, and Mario bumps a brick box with his head. It bursts, and a coin pops out.

"I'm worried about you," Oliver says. "You're questioning Yale? That's where you've always wanted to go. And then you had all those pills… Is something else driving this? Are you depressed?"

I accidentally run into a Koopa who shrinks me back to Little Mario. "No, I'm not depressed."

"This is all just so weird."

"Oll, I already talk to a counselor four days a week. Can't we just eat and hang out?"

We go back to tapping on our games until the pizza and a pitcher of Coke come. We take a break to eat, and I'm hopeful the pizza will keep him from talking, but he chatters on with his mouth full.

"I still can't believe Ezra took a leave of absence from Cornell,"

Oliver says, ripping off a bite of crust. "I'm worried he's going to drop out."

"I hope he goes back too."

"So wait. You want Ezra to go back to school, but you're weirded out about applying to Yale? That doesn't make sense."

"Ezra knows what he wants to do—"

"Yeah, he wants to work in construction. He doesn't have to go to Cornell for that."

"He wants more…"

Oliver scrunches his forehead. "What else does he want?"

"It's not my place to say."

He takes another bite and chews. "Would y'all stay together if he went back to Cornell?"

I don't hesitate. "Definitely."

"But you broke up with Ben because you didn't want to do long distance. And I know you loved him."

I rush to cover up my lie about Ben. "Ezra's different."

I hate that about lies, how you constantly have to stay on your toes. Telling the truth is so much better. It allows you freedom.

Oliver sets down his second slice. "Ezra's my best friend. I know he's serious about you, and I don't want you hurting him, okay?"

"I won't. I care about him so much."

Great. Not only do people think I take drugs, they doubt my character. The lie I told to cover my breakup with Ben doesn't really reflect how I feel. If I loved a person, I would make it work, no matter the distance. If Ben hadn't betrayed me and one of us had moved away, I would've worked hard to keep our relationship intact.

Now my brother thinks I'll dump his friend. Probably thinks I'm still taking pills. Soon, his opinion of me will be in the toilet. I need to get us back to normal.

"How about some two-player Mario?" I challenge him.

He wads up his napkin. "Oh, it's on like Donkey Kong."

Ezra and I have settled into a routine. We meet up every morning before he goes to work and I go to school, and whenever we can, we meet up after soccer practice in the evenings. He started wanting to play again himself, so he joined an intramural rec league in town. His team is made up of mostly Spanish-speaking guys who barely speak any English but rock at soccer. Ezra's been holding his own in goal. I love going to cheer him on, especially when they play shirts versus skins and Ezra is on skins.

Even with soccer, and even though he has me, I can tell he's restless. He may love working on the construction crew, but I know it's not enough for him. He's too smart, too ambitious. He has dreams he's too scared to reach out and take.

Before school one day, I meet up with him for our usual coffee. But I got there a few minutes earlier than usual and caught him doodling and writing in a sketchpad with a pencil. He hates writing and reading, so it shocks me to find him like this.

I pass him the **One coffee on me!** coupon to "pay" for my cup. He slips the coupon into his front jeans pocket, raising his eyebrows at me. At some point, I'll steal that coupon out of his pocket so he'll buy me another coffee tomorrow. He loves it when I put my hands all over him looking for it. *Find the coupon* has become a game for us.

"What were you working on?"

He shuts the sketchbook. "It's nothing."

I snatch his white paper bag. "If you don't tell me, I'm gonna eat all your doughnuts."

He grabs at the bag, trying to steal it back from me, but I hold it behind our booth.

"You're evil, Tease. Hey, I'm gonna start calling you that. Evil Tease."

"Stop trying to distract me. What were you writing?"

"I wasn't writing anything."

"You sending a love note to another girl?"

He lifts an eyebrow mischievously. "I think after last Friday night, we've established I don't want anybody else."

My face blazes at the memory. Even though we said we weren't going to fool around because my brother was in the house, we ended up kissing for what felt like hours, and his shorts and my pajamas ended up on the rug. Suddenly, I need to fan myself.

"Stop trying to distract me," I say again, more sternly this time.

He pushes the sketchpad over to me. I open it. He's been drawing a house.

"Is this a Colonial?"

"Yes."

"It's beautiful."

He smiles. "They're my favorite design."

"Did you draw this?"

He shrugs a little, then nods.

"It's great! Do you have others in here?"

"Yeah." His voice is strained and thick. "When I was little, I loved drawing floor plans. I loved using a ruler and deciding where to put doors and windows. I liked designing impossible houses with six stories, ten bedrooms, a game room, and an indoor swimming pool."

"Can it also have a big doghouse?"

He smiles. "As long as I get my doughnuts back."

I pass him the bag. "Thanks for showing me your drawing. Have you checked out schools with good architecture programs? The University of Tennessee at Knoxville has one."

He gives me a long, annoyed look, and for a moment, I feel guilty for being a nagging girlfriend, but it seems to me that a serious relationship comes with an obligation to be truthful, and sometimes that means nagging.

"Let's talk about something else, okay?" he asks.

"I won't bring it up again. Just promise me you'll consider it."

He nods curtly, and stares at his Colonial drawing, then picks up his pencil to work on it a little more.

"You seem distracted."

"I am," I tell the guidance counselor. After I told her how things are getting better at soccer and it's a lot more fun now, we spent most of this period going over my essays and application for Yale. But my life still feels weird. I twine and untwine my fingers.

"What's wrong?" Miss Brady asks.

"I've been thinking…"

"Go on," she encourages.

"I hate math. Why would I major in business?"

"Isn't that what people in your family do?"

"Yes, but it's not what I want."

A smile blooms on Miss Brady's face. "So what do you want then?"

"I'm not totally sure."

"You should play to your strengths."

There's an inspirational poster behind her desk that says *Strength*, but it's just a picture of Mount Everest. I've never understood what those posters are about. "What do you mean, play to my strengths?"

"What are you good at? What do you enjoy?"

I think for a long moment. "Museums."

"Museums?"

"I love any kind of museum, but my favorite is the National Gallery in Vienna. I could see myself being a curator, but I love art, science, and history equally—I'm not sure how I'd choose. I just like learning." Miss Brady smiles, so I keep going. "I also love animals…my boyfriend says I should become a vet. I kind of like that idea, but I don't know that I could handle putting pets to sleep. I just know I'm good at history and that I love museums."

"Great. Well, I'm glad that you are open to other options."

"It's kind of scary though, you know? One time, I told my dad it might be cool to be a museum curator, and he said there's no money in that."

Miss Brady looks around at her office, focusing on the patch of wall where the white paint is peeling away. "I could've used my psychology degree to work in a fancy practice and make lots of money, but I wanted to work with kids. It's your life. If you want to live, you need to do what you love."

I think back to what Ezra said about taking risks. Taking a risk can be scary, but it can also be worthwhile.

Museums are one prize I think I could keep my eyes on. But can I give up my desire to fulfill my family's expectations?

Stupid, but Ballsy

The election is less than a week away.

The last time Dad was up for reelection, I was eleven years old. Back then, my biggest problem was being freaked out about having to shave my legs and wear a bra on election night. Dad's campaign managers were constantly trotting me around in front of voters. I brought the *cute factor*.

Now, I'm under orders not to speak to anyone or do anything out of the ordinary for the next seven days, but I wish I could help Dad in some way. He's barely sleeping. Neither is Mom.

My brother and sister are coming home this weekend to join him for speeches around the state and will stay until after the election on Tuesday. I can't wait until it's over, because then I'm going to tell Mom and Dad the truth about what happened at St. Andrew's. The best thing I can do right now is lay low.

On the Wednesday night before the election, Ezra picks me up for his intramural soccer game. They're down a man, so I end up playing right forward for them. It is so nice to take shots on goal again. I love just playing to play. When I score a goal, the team lifts me up on their shoulders and parades me around the field, laughing. Ezra grumbles at that, but I'm having a ball.

After the game, he and I grab dinner at Jiffy Burger. I always like going there, because it's full of trucker guys cursing up a storm. It's highly entertaining when they say things like, "I had to pull the truck over 'cause my engine got hotter than a billy goat's ass in a pepper patch."

When we're finished eating, Ezra asks if I want to go back to his place.

"I wish I could, but my Yale application is due Friday. I should proofread it a few more times."

Ezra opens the passenger door of his Range Rover, then helps me inside. He jogs around to his side of the SUV and climbs into the driver's seat.

"Are you sure about applying there?"

I nod. "It's what I've been working toward forever, Ez."

"But if you get in early decision, you *have* to go there." He starts the ignition. "Shouldn't you take some time to try to figure out what you want?"

"People in my family go to Ivy League schools. My parents expect me to do something important with my life."

He shakes his head. "You can still do something important even if you don't go to Yale. Look at Jack Goodwin. His parents were pissed when he started dating somebody who works for him, but his life isn't over."

"There's nothing wrong with me going to Yale, you know."

"But what's *right* about it? Tell me one good reason you want to go to there, and I will stop bothering you about this."

"I don't understand why you get to press me about my future, but I can't even suggest you go back to school without you snapping at me to drop it."

Ezra drums his hands on the steering wheel, agitated. "I just want what's best for you."

"That's all I want for you too."

I'm so close to telling him I love him.

We ride in silence all the way back to my house, and when we arrive, there's a familiar-looking silver Jaguar in the driveway. Is that Michael Williamson's car? We went to school together at St. Andrew's. I climb out of the Range Rover and move to get a closer look. Sure enough, when I peer in the front window, he's sitting in the driver's seat, playing with his phone.

I knock on the window. He rolls it down. "Tee!"

I throw Ezra a nervous glance and shrug. "Michael, hi. What are you doing here?"

"Ben agreed to let me copy his chemistry homework if I gave him a ride. I guess he wants to win you back or something." He gives Ezra a sly smile. "But something tells me I got the better end of my deal with Ben."

"How long have you been here?" I rush to ask.

"Five minutes or so."

My phone beeps in my hand. A text from Mom. Come home NOW.

Then my phone buzzes. *Dad Calling. Dad Calling.*

I gaze up at my house.

Leaving Michael and Ezra behind, I feel as if I'm floating—and not in a good way.

"Tee!" Ezra calls out behind me.

When I reach the front steps, I break into a jog. I crash through the front door.

Marina heads me off in the foyer. "Your parents want to see you in the senator's office."

I rush up the stairs and into Dad's study. The lights are low. Burning wood crackles in the fireplace, snapping under the intense heat.

Ben is standing there, shifting from foot to foot. Mom's face is redder than a fire extinguisher. Dad has his glasses off and is rubbing his eyes.

"*Taylor Lukens. What have you done?*" Mom says in a low voice. Then it turns into a screech. "Are you out of your goddamned mind?"

Ezra suddenly appears beside me and places his hand on my shoulder. When Ben sees him touching me, the look on his face morphs from pain to torture.

"What's going on?" Ezra asks, taking in the scene. "Why are you shouting, Mrs. Lukens?"

"Ask Taylor!" Mom yells. "How could you? You've ruined your father's career! And for nothing!"

Ezra pulls me toward him.

Dad still hasn't said a word.

"What did you do?" I ask Ben.

"I had to tell the truth, Tee." His words come out in a rush. "I'm sorry. I just had to make things right. Before your father's election."

"It's a bit late for that, isn't it?" Mom snaps. "Polls are down by three points, and the election's in six days! What good does your little confession do us *now*?"

Ben winces. "I thought maybe if the press knew the truth—"

Ezra's hand tenses on my shoulder. I can feel his body stiffen.

"The last thing we need is for the press to rehash this," Mom interrupts. "We need good news, not bad."

"Dad?" I say with a shaky voice.

He pulls his hand away from his eyes but still won't acknowledge me.

"Will someone please tell me what's going on?" Ezra asks.

I turn, place a hand on his chest, and look up at him. "The pills weren't mine."

Shock fills his face. It slowly turns to understanding. Then anger.

He lets me go, stalks toward Ben, lifts his hand, and makes a fist.

Ben puts his hands up to protect himself, but he's too slow. Ezra punches him square in the jaw. Ben stumbles to the side, nearly taking out an antique vase on his way to the hardwood floor. Dad rushes over, pulling Ezra off Ben. Ezra tries to break free from Dad's arms, but Dad keeps a firm grip.

"Son, stop it," Dad says to Ezra. "Go sit down." He jerks his pointer finger at a sofa on the other side of the office. Ben clutches the side of his face, rasping for breath.

"Tee, tell me you're lying," Ezra gasps. "Tell me you didn't cover for this little sh—"

"Ezra," Dad commands. "Go sit down, *now*." He turns to me with betrayed eyes. "Taylor, I'd like an explanation."

"How could you?" Mom cries again, and Dad sighs.

"Donna, please let Taylor speak."

I square my shoulders and stand up straight. "Ben and I were out in the woods. He brought his backpack. When he left to go to the bathroom, that's when the dorm mothers found me and thought the pills were mine. I knew that Ben would get kicked out of school, but I thought I'd be fine, Dad…because of who you are."

Dad hangs his head, disappointed.

"I know now I was wrong. I shouldn't have tried to use you and your position to get out of trouble."

"But you wouldn't have been in trouble!" Dad says. "They weren't your pills!"

"I know," I say quietly. "Things got out of hand. I never expected all of this to happen."

"Well, what did you expect?" Mom asks. "I can't believe you'd do something so dumb."

"Stop talking to Taylor like that," Ezra says, but he looks furious with me. His angry eyes bore into mine. "We said no more secrets."

"I'm sorry—" I start, but he's already storming out of the room. "Ezra!" I call. He leaves me alone with the firing squad.

"Mom, Dad, if I had known this would get so crazy, I never would've covered for Ben. And I didn't tell you afterward because I found out Ben was selling the pills, and I thought it would make things worse if people knew I was covering for a drug dealer. I was planning to tell you the truth as soon as the election was over. I knew it wouldn't do any good right now—"

Dad holds up a hand to quiet me.

"Ben," Dad says quietly, "thank you for coming to tell us the truth. But I don't want to see you at my home again. And if you try to contact my daughter, I'll be asking the police to investigate you."

"Yes, sir."

"Please leave."

Ben gazes over at me with tears in his eyes. He nods once, mouthing *good-bye*, then disappears out the door.

Mom stalks over to Dad's wet bar and pours herself a scotch. With a shaky hand, she brings the glass to her mouth. She sips, closing her eyes.

We're all quiet, but Mom interrupts the silence. "This will cost us the election, Edward. You shouldn't have let St. Andrew's expel her."

Dad sits down on the sofa and puts a hand over his face.

"Dad?"

"Go on," he says softly, gesturing at the door.

"Don't you want to talk this through?" I ask.

He shakes his head. "Not now."

With tears streaming down my face, I climb the stairs to my bedroom. I doubt my parents will ever look at me the way they used to. Will they ever trust me again?

And what about Ezra? I betrayed him. We promised there wouldn't be secrets between us, and I kept this from him—from everyone.

I open the door to my room and gasp. He's sitting on my bed, staring down at his hands. He lifts his head to stare at me.

"Are you kidding me?" Ezra starts. "You'd throw away your future for that asshole? Why? Why didn't you tell the truth?"

"Ezra—"

"You could do anything you want with your life, and you gave up St. Andrew's for some loser who didn't even have the balls to stand up for his own mistake!"

"Things got out of control. I didn't mean for this to happen—"

"I thought you were better than this."

"I am—I didn't want to be a tattletale!"

"You should've confronted Ben and told him to fix the situation before it got out of hand! I am so mad at you right now."

"Ezra—"

"We said no more secrets. That includes the big, dark ones."

"Now you know everything. We've both made mistakes. Please, let's just get past this, Ezra. Please."

He drags a hand through his hair and stands. "I need time."

He strides by me without another word and leaves.

I'm scared to go downstairs.

Scared to face Mom and Dad.

Scared to read the texts from Oliver and Jenna.

Scared to turn on the news to check the polls.

Scared to go to school.

This feels like that time in elementary school when our parents took us to Six Flags Over Georgia, and Oliver went missing. I ran around searching for him. What if he got kidnapped? What if he fell down a manhole? What if he fell off the Mine Train ride and got trapped in a tunnel?

It turned out he was gorging on ice cream sundaes at Big Mo's, but my heart didn't stop racing until we arrived safely home in Franklin that night.

This morning, I wait until I see Dad's car pulling out of the drive, and then I rush downstairs and out to my car before Mom or Marina can stop me.

I sent Ezra a couple of texts, including one that said Donut Palace? No response.

I decide to skip coffee today.

By lunchtime, I'm yawning my ass off thanks to no sleep and no caffeine. I join Chloe and Alyson at a round table and unpack the lunch Marina made for me. Alyson starts chattering about Maya Henry, a musician who graduated from Hundred Oaks last year. Apparently, Maya uploaded a new song she wrote to YouTube last night, and it's just amazing. I nod in response.

"What's wrong, Tee?" Chloe asks. She started calling me that after hanging around my brother and Ezra.

I shrug. "My parents and Ezra are pissed at me."

"How come?" she asks, popping a baby carrot in her mouth.

"I did something super stupid and didn't fix it when I had the chance…" Since we've become close over the past couple months, I take a deep breath and explain what happened to my new friends. Their eyes grow wide at the story, and they both place a hand on my arms, supporting me.

"That sucks," Chloe says, and Alyson agrees. I'm grateful neither of them judges me for what happened.

"Can we do anything to help?" Alyson asks.

"Distract me," I reply with a tiny smile.

Alyson tells me how she's planning to dress up like a sexy train conductor tonight for Halloween. Chloe's going as a butterfly.

Halloween. I forgot it's Halloween. I glance around the cafeteria. A bunch of girls are wearing cute mouse ears. One guy has on devil horns. Another is dressed up like Barack

Obama. I really must be out of it if I missed all that in my morning classes.

Ezra and I didn't make plans to go to any parties or anything, but we were going to trick-or-treat in my neighborhood this evening. I figured it would be my last time to do so, since I'm going to college next year and all. I won't be a kid anymore.

While Chloe chatters away, I check texts under the table to see if Ezra sent anything. *Nada.* With a deep breath, I gather the courage to read the texts from Jenna and Oliver.

Jenna: Are you under the influence of hot construction worker sex or something? I can't believe you protected Ben. Ballsy. Stupid, but ballsy.

Oliver's one-word text: Seriously?

I start trembling. He must be furious. I excuse myself from the table to go out into the courtyard to call him. At first, I worry he won't pick up. The phone rings and rings, but finally he answers.

I begin to say hi, but he starts right in on me. "You lied to me. I asked if the drugs were yours, and you said yes."

"I know."

"It's like you cared more about Ben than being honest with me. With your family."

"That's not true! The situation just…got out of hand. I never meant for any of this to happen."

"You made us think you had a drug problem, Taylor. Do you know how much I've worried? Sometimes I don't sleep. I call

Mom and Dad every day to see how you are. To get the results of your goddamned pee tests. I considered coming home this semester to be with you because I was scared you were worse than you and Mom and Dad let on."

Oh my God. "I didn't want to be a snitch."

"I'd rather be a snitch than a liar."

Touché.

"Oll, please, I'm sorry."

Click.

My big brother hung up on me. I bury my phone deep in my bag and wipe away a tear.

And Ezra… He still hasn't answered my texts or calls, and I've reached out to him so many times, I'm beginning to feel like a psycho. I decide to go over to his house after school. He's told me he appreciates that I go after what I want, and to me, this situation is no exception.

When the final bell rings, I go to the bathroom to freshen up. My eyes are still puffy, still red, and still rimmed by dark circles. I splash my face with water and straighten my ponytail.

I drive to Ezra's apartment. When I get there, I can't hold it in anymore—it's been such a long day that I start choking back sobs. His apartment lights appear blurry through my tears. Like watching a rainstorm through foggy windows.

I climb the four flights of stairs and knock on the door. His curtains shift a little, and I see him peeking out. For a heartbreaking moment, I think he's not going to answer the door, but then it slowly swings open.

He's barefoot, and his hair is wet, as if he just got out of the shower, and he's wearing a black T-shirt and jeans. His bloodshot eyes don't look much better than mine. He ushers me inside to stand in his living room. He stares at the floor with his arms crossed.

"Ezra," I start softly. "Can you ever forgive me?"

He looks up in surprise but says nothing. He chews on his lip, and I'm terrified this is it. He's going to break up with me, end our friendship.

Then he slowly pulls me against him, kissing the scar on my forehead. "Of course I can." He talks into my hair. "But I'm still really mad at you."

"I know." I gasp with relief, and my legs feel like they might give out. Ezra holds me up, helping me to stand.

"What you did for Ben…you will never, *ever* do anything like that for me, understand? If I've learned anything in the past two years, it's that a man takes care of his own mistakes. He owns up. Got it?"

"Got it."

We hug each other, and I sink my fingers in his wet hair, inhaling his scent of lemon soap. He places a warm hand on my lower back beneath my shirt, tracing circles with his thumb.

"You didn't think I'd forgive you?" he whispers.

"You left so abruptly, and you said you needed time. I didn't know what that meant."

"I'm sorry." His big hands sweep over my back. "I needed to process this. I still do."

My eyes start watering all over again. "You scared me."

"I just hope you know that whatever happens between us or outside of our relationship, we can work it out. Okay?"

"I love you," I blurt, not caring whether it's too soon to say it and whether he'll say it back. It doesn't matter. "I love you so much."

I'm speaking into his chest, so I can't see his reaction, but his arms around me grow tense. I hold my breath.

His hands weave through my hair. "I love you too, Tease."

I relax against his chest and gaze up at him. "Thank you for forgiving me."

"Always." A mischievous smirk takes over his face. "Now are we gonna make up or what?"

I playfully shove his chest. "Get your mind out of the gutter."

"Everyone knows the best part of fighting is making up afterward. I want to make up with you every day from here on out."

His fingertips slide up and down my spine, spreading shivers over my skin. His lips are wanting as they devour mine in a kiss. He cradles my neck in his hand and presses his body to mine, leaving no space between us. He edges me toward his bedroom. He lifts me into his arms, pinning me to the wall, kissing me. I didn't know he was this strong. I grasp his biceps.

"I changed my mind. Never stop doing manual labor."

He smiles against my lips.

Lowering my feet to the floor, he guides me to the bed. I climb onto his navy-blue quilt. Eyes blazing, he yanks his T-shirt over his head and joins me. He straddles my waist, burying his face in my neck. His warm skin feels smooth against mine. He lifts my sweater off.

I'm not sure when he loses his jeans or when I lose mine, but all our clothes wind up on the floor. Up until now, we've never been completely naked together, and I'm a little scared—like that first time you jump off a high dive into the water. But I know the fall will be so much fun.

He takes in every bit of me. And then he presses his hot mouth against my core. I tangle my fingers in his hair until I can't wait any longer. I need him. *All of him.*

Subconsciously, I guess I had been waiting to take our relationship to this level until there were no secrets between us, because now I have no hesitations whatsoever.

"Do you have protection?" I whisper, and he nods, reaching into the drawer of his nightstand to get a condom.

"You're sure?" he asks.

"Please."

He hesitates, looking away for a moment, then his green eyes rejoin mine. "I'm not your first, right?"

"No," I whisper.

"I should've been."

"Make it up to me now."

"Bossy." He grins and wraps my legs around his waist, and we finish what we started years ago.

When we finished showing how much we love each other, Ezra passed out.

Passed out.

I grin to myself.

Knowing I wore him out does great things for my ego, but I want to cuddle. I wake him up with a long, soft kiss and lean on an elbow, staring down at him as a smile appears on his face.

"That was nice," he says.

"That was verrry nice."

He groans with a laugh. "If Oliver ever finds out, he's going to fuck me up."

"You're damn right he will. Unless you agree to do tequila shots and go dancing with him. Then everything'll be just fine," I tease.

We grin at each other, intertwining our fingers.

"I've wanted to do that with you for a long time," he whispers, weaving his other hand through my hair.

"How long?"

He grins. "Since the summer before senior year. I was at your house swimming in the pool with Oliver, and you were sitting on the side reading a magazine."

"*Seventeen*. I was getting advice on how to talk to guys so I would have something to say to you." I nudge him with my elbow. "I remember you checking me out."

"Yeah, Oliver noticed too. He said, 'Stop staring at my sister, dipshit.'"

"So you liked what you saw?"

His eyes flick over my body. "I liked your little bikini. The red one with polka dots."

I punch him in the arm. "You did a cannonball and soaked me. Asshole!"

"I was trying to get your attention."

"You were?"

"Constantly."

I smile, cuddle closer to him, and yawn, finding that he wore me out too.

We nap together for a bit, and when I wake up, it's completely dark outside. I look over at the red glowing numbers on the alarm clock. It's seven. Mom and Dad are probably wondering where I am.

I am not ready to face them, but my early decision application for Yale is due tomorrow.

I have to go home to press Send.

It's five minutes to midnight.

I'm staring at the blinding white of my laptop screen.

Applications are due tomorrow. Friday, November 1.

My pristine application, which I've double- and triple-checked a hundred times, is ready to be submitted.

My dad expects me to apply.

So does Mom.

And Oliver.

I let out a sob. None of them are talking to me after what happened with Ben.

What do I expect of myself?

I have no clue.

I've never felt so lost, but the more I think about it, I wonder if I've ever actually *found* myself to begin with.

Maybe I've always been lost.

Coming Clean

Three days before the election, I bundle into a warm down jacket, boots, and jeans, and drive out to Cedar Hill Farms.

After remembering how Ezra said Jack Goodwin went against his family's expectations and everything turned out okay, I sent him a text, asking to meet.

When I pull into the circular driveway in front of the mansion, Jack is standing on the front porch with his hands stuffed in the front pockets of his jeans. He's wearing a red plaid shirt, dirty work boots, and a cowboy hat. He must've had a busy day with the horses.

As I'm shutting off my car, Jack, ever the gentleman, jogs down the steps and opens my door for me.

"Tee, hey. Come on in."

He leads me inside to a creamy white parlor with windows overlooking one of the paddocks, where a mare and her foal stand grazing. A tea service is set up next to the fireplace. My parents have money, but the Goodwins have serious cash. Cedar Hill isn't just a mansion; it's an estate. Accordingly, they have servants out the wazoo.

Jack takes off his cowboy hat, then fusses with a china coffeepot decorated with a rose design. "You want a coffee or anything?"

"Uh, *yeah*."

"I figured you might. When Jenna and I were dating, she always complained that your mother hated coffee."

"One of the very few topics Jenna and I agree on."

Jack and I fix ourselves coffees and grab a couple of brownies, then sit down in armchairs next to the window.

"So what'd you want to talk about?" he asks, chewing.

"Savannah."

He sets his cup and saucer on the coffee table. With a cautious expression, he asks, "What about her?"

"Was it hard when you started dating her? Like, were your parents mad?"

He nods. "Oh yeah. They didn't want me fooling around with a member of our staff. It took me a while to convince them I was serious about Savannah." He pauses and picks up his coffee cup again. "It also took me a while to realize *I* was serious about her."

"But it's been worth it?"

He smiles. "Yeah, of course. I mean, we've been dating almost two years, and we still can't keep our hands to ourselves."

"TMI."

He laughs, but the mood turns solemn again. "Why are you asking about this? Is it something to do with Ezra? I heard you're dating."

"We're dating, yeah, but that's not why I'm asking." I sip my coffee. "I just…how did you go up against your parents like that? How did you get the courage?"

"It wasn't easy. I had to lay it all out there. I had to tell them it didn't matter what they thought, that I was going to date Savannah."

"Were you scared to talk to your parents?"

"I was so scared, I didn't speak up for weeks, and I nearly lost Savannah in the process. I hesitated about going public with our relationship, and she wouldn't put up with that." He smiles, looking out the window, as if lost in a memory. Then he shakes his head. "Tell me what's up, Tee. Why are you asking about this?"

"I've been thinking about my future. Everyone in my family went to Ivy League schools, and Oliver and Jenna are going to work at the firm. I'm not sure what I want to do with my life, but I'm pretty sure I don't want to do that." I take a deep breath. "The application for Yale's early decision was due yesterday, and I didn't turn mine in… I don't know how my parents will react when I tell them."

"They're good people. I think you could be upfront with them."

"Even after all the trouble I've caused with my father's campaign?"

He sips from his coffee cup, thinking. "Last winter, my mom had lunch with the governor's wife. All Mrs. Harrington wanted to talk about was how I was dating one of our jockeys and how *odd* that was." I expect to hear anger in Jack's voice, but it's calm. "By the time summer rolled around, Mrs. Harrington couldn't wait to meet Savannah and introduce her to her daughters. She thought Savannah would be a good role model for feminism or something." Jack smiles at that.

"So Mrs. Harrington got over it?"

"Some people just don't like change, and it takes time for them to accept it. They've gotten used to me dating Savannah. After a while, no one cared anymore. At least not the people who really matter, like my mom and dad. They came to understand how much I love Savannah."

I think of Ezra. Will people get used to him doing construction instead of joining the family business? Will they grow to accept it? I certainly have, because it makes him happy. Even though I wish he'd reconsider, I respect his wishes.

"Your advice is to just come clean? Let my family know I'm a big ole mess and have no direction?"

Jack smiles. "Yeah, and the sooner the better. Then you can start figuring out what you want to do instead of worrying about what your parents will say and pretending everything is fine. Just come clean."

Jack walks me out to my car and opens the door for me.

He gives me a quick hug. "Let me know how it goes, okay?"

"Will do." I slide into the driver's seat, and he shuts the door.

I wave good-bye to him as he heads toward the pasture to help round up the horses; the sun is beginning to set into a haze of gold and purple. After talking with Jack, I'm still scared to veer from the path I've been on for years, but the desire to take control of my life outweighs that fear.

First things first: I send Dad a text. I really need to see you. Can we please talk?

Then I turn the key, start my engine, and drive home. Once I'm in my driveway, I check my phone and see I have a bunch of missed calls from Dad. He didn't leave a voice mail, but he did send a text.

Can you please come home? I'm here.

I take a deep, quivering breath and clutch my phone in my hands, relieved that Dad wants to talk to me. For him to go two days without speaking to me just about broke my heart.

With three days until the election, I'm surprised Dad's at home this evening. When I arrive in his study, the door is open, and he's sitting in his armchair by the fire, nursing a scotch.

"Dad?"

He waves for me to enter and gestures at the couch for me to sit down. After a moment, Dad joins me, bringing his drink with him.

"This must've been a rough couple months, huh?" he asks.

"The worst." A few tears leak out. "I worried you weren't going to talk to me again."

He pulls me into a hug. "I'm sorry. Your mom and I needed time to think about what you did. All of this is so unlike you, Tee."

"I know…"

"Why did you cover for Ben?"

"His parents don't have a lot of money, and going to St. Andrew's was his big chance."

"If he hadn't been your boyfriend, would you have covered for him?" Dad asks.

I carefully consider the question. "I think I would've tried to help any of my friends. But I didn't think it would get so out of control… I know now that I should have told the truth from the start. I'm so sorry about your campaign, Dad. So sorry. I wanted to come forward and tell you what happened, but I thought it would just make the situation worse."

"Your instincts are right. It's too late to do anything about the election now. Any statement we put out will look like a last-ditch effort to win back voters."

I nod, continuing to cry, and Dad pats my back.

"I know I shouldn't start our conversation this way," I say, "but I have to, because I need to get this off my chest. I'm really upset with you, Dad."

He goes still.

"I've been killing myself at school for years. And it's like the minute I made one mistake, you were so ashamed, you didn't want to be seen with me anymore. You never once asked me to join you at a campaign event, and that made me feel like I wasn't part of the family—like you weren't proud of me. I'm really sorry for what I did, but it was even worse knowing that you and Mom were so pissed you didn't want me by your sides anymore."

His eyes never leave mine as I pour out my soul.

"I make great grades all the time, and my SAT score was almost perfect, even though math is hard for me. I was exhausted all the time because I took on so many activities, and you didn't even mention my hard work in your campaign commercial! In it, you were so proud of Jenna and Oliver, but it was as if I didn't exist. That hurt so bad, Dad." My voice is high pitched and shaky. He reaches over and squeezes my shoulder.

I pull a deep breath. "I didn't send in my Yale application."

Dad's eyes widen. "You didn't?"

"I wasn't sure why I should, other than that it was expected of me. I don't even know what I want to do with my life."

"You have to start somewhere. Why not Yale? It's a good liberal arts school. Besides, I thought you wanted to be an analyst at your grandfather's firm."

"I only said that because that's what I thought I was supposed to do. But, Dad, I don't have any interest in investing. I don't even like math."

He pauses at the bombshell I just dropped. "Well, what do you like?"

"Museums, soccer, animals, coffee. Ezra."

The corner of Dad's mouth lifts into a small smile. "Well, you absolutely cannot major in Ezra Carmichael. I forbid it."

I chuckle at his joke. "But what about the rest?"

"Tee, the reason I've always pushed you so hard is so you'll have options."

"I hate staying up so late to study. I feel like it's all I do. And I'm worried if I go to Yale, it would be more of the same. I'm not lazy…I'm just…tired."

For a moment, I wonder if I should copy Chloe and take a year off between high school and college, but that doesn't feel right for me. I need to do *something*.

"Shouldn't I have some idea of what I want to do before you spend all that money on college?" I ask.

"Honestly, Tee, you've got time to figure that out. Some days, I'm not sure what I want to do either, and I'm sixty years old. But I'm not sorry I've pushed you. You are so smart and so wonderful, and I want you to have all the options in the world."

My eyes water at his words.

I get what he's saying. But at the same time, I've been pushing myself so hard for so long that I resorted to pills to make it through. I never get eight hours of sleep. Is getting into the best school really worth it? I don't know. I really don't.

My eye twitches. I rush to cover it up with my hand.

"You should get some rest," Dad says, squeezing my shoulder. "Take a nap before dinner."

"Dad? If I didn't go to Yale, would you hate me?"

"Of course not. I'll always love you. But I'd want to know what you'd plan to do instead."

"I don't know, but I'm sure other colleges would take me with my grades and test scores." I puff out my chest in an imitation of Dad. "I'm so smart and so wonderful, and I will have all the options in the world."

He throws his head back to laugh. "Would you stop teasing me already?"

I give him a hug. "One of the good parts of being at Hundred Oaks is getting to be at home. I'm glad we're spending more time together, Dad."

My father gives me a sad smile. "Me too, Tee."

Election Day

In ninth grade, I worried that Madison and Steph were growing closer and that they didn't need me as a friend anymore. To feed my bruised ego, I started hanging around Gabriella, this girl from Spain who was glamorous and sophisticated. I wanted her to like me because I thought that would mean I was also glamorous and sophisticated. To get her attention, I told her things I shouldn't have, like that Madison had a crush on the basketball team's senior forward. Gabriella thought that a freshman having a crush on one of the most popular guys in school was funny and told just about everyone.

When he heard the gossip, the senior went up to Madison in the dining hall, patted her on the head, and said, "I'm flattered, but you're too young for me."

The embarrassment turned Madison's face purple.

She knew it was my fault, and for a while after the head-patting incident, I dreaded seeing her. I avoided her in the halls. I didn't want to see the disappointment on her face. I wanted to crawl into a hidey-hole and never come out. But

I apologized, and she forgave me, but that shame didn't just dissolve. It stuck around.

That's what I feel like on Election Day.

Six years ago, the last time Dad was up for reelection, I remember freaking out because mean girls at school kept saying, *"If your daddy doesn't win, he'll lose his job!"* That kept me up at night. I didn't understand that he could always go back to work for my grandfather's firm.

It wasn't the end of the world.

But today feels like the end of the world. Because regardless of whether or not he wins, his reputation will never be the same, thanks to me.

After school, Ezra and I head to Nashville to join my parents, Oliver, and Jenna for the election results.

Ezra looks over at me from the driver's seat. "You okay?"

"Not really."

He reaches for my hand and squeezes it.

We drive to the Opryland Hotel, where Dad's campaign rented out a ballroom. Tons of his supporters are here, waiting for the results that will come in over the next several hours. I take a peek inside to find an explosion of red, white, and blue balloons. Fun dance music is playing, and people seem to be having a great time.

Mom, my brother and sister, Dad, and his immediate staff have gathered in a smaller room next door. Unlike the ballroom, there is no party going on here. It feels like a funeral.

When Jenna and Oliver see we're here, they stand up. Oliver pats me on the back and shakes Ezra's hand, while Jenna gives Ezra a hug.

"Ezra, it's so good to see you," Jenna says in a sultry voice, her fingertips touching his chest.

"Well, aren't you handsy as ever," Ezra replies, extracting himself from her grip.

"Sometimes I worry you're a succubus," I tell her.

She winks. "Can you blame me? Your boyfriend's hot."

"That he is."

According to the TV, Dad is ahead. I bounce up and down on my toes at that.

Camera crews from CNN, MSNBC, AP, and a bunch of other news outlets are here to film Dad watching the results. A publicist from the campaign tells the camera guys, "No footage of Taylor, got it?"

Talk about things I thought I'd never hear. I mean, I get it. People will be voting over the next several hours, so it's best not to remind them that I exist. Still, I can feel my face getting redder and redder.

I sit down on a sofa near a television. Ezra gets me some crackers and water, but I'm too nervous to eat. All I can do is watch the results. Right now, with forty percent of precincts reporting, Dad is winning sixty-two percent to Wallace's thirty-five. Other candidates account for the remaining three percent.

I inhale and exhale. Inhale and exhale. I can't stop biting my thumbnail. After about an hour of watching results, it's ragged, and the polish is chipped off.

Ezra grabs my hand and kisses it, twining our fingers together. He leans over to whisper in my ear, "I'm here with you."

I nod and try to smile, but it hurts my face.

Over the next hour, Dad's lead falls from sixty-two to fifty-five percent. Wallace is gaining. Whenever I look over at Mom, she has a fake smile pasted on her face for the media.

Dad walks by me a few times and squeezes my shoulder, showing he still loves me. Part of me wishes I could go hide somewhere, but I got us into this mess.

I have to face it. I have to stand tall.

The room grows quiet when polls close at eight o'clock, and the next report shows Dad and Wallace are tied at forty-eight percent. Eighty percent of precincts have reported. I cross all my fingers. I start making promises in my mind. *If Dad wins, I'll never lie again. I'll be a good girl forever. I'll do whatever my parents say.*

An hour later, and with ninety-three percent of precincts reporting, the race is still too close to call. Mom and Dad are holding hands tightly, unable to tear their eyes from the TV. Jenna looks up at the ceiling, her lips moving as if she's talking to herself, doing math in her head, calculating our odds of success tonight. Oliver crosses his legs, shaking his ankle.

Then at nine thirty, the news says all precincts have reported:

Wallace pulled ahead by two percent.

With mouths gaping, Randy and Kevin look like they just found out the moon landings weren't real. Honestly, prior to me getting kicked out of school, that would've been more likely than Dad losing the election.

My brother stares down at his folded hands. Jenna's mouth hangs open.

Mom tries to keep a strong front, but tears roll down her cheeks. Being a senator's wife—working with Tennesseans and volunteering—has been her job for eighteen years.

Dad lost the election, and it is all my fault. I let out a sob.

Dad reaches a hand toward me, and I go sit with him on the couch. "It's okay, Tee. It's not the end of the world."

"But it's your job. I'm so sorry, Dad."

"I know." He wraps an arm around me and kisses my temple.

I wipe away the tear rolling down my cheek. "I love you."

"Love you too."

"Senator?" Randy says to Dad, still looking shell-shocked. "We need you to address the crowd."

Dad gives me a small smile and pats my knee. "Time for me to get back to work."

The morning after the election, Mom and Dad are up early to take Jenna to the airport so she doesn't miss her afternoon classes.

I go out to the front porch and wave as they are pulling out of the garage. My parents wave back, but my sister flips me off, then follows with a thumbs-up. I return the thumbs-up and roll my eyes.

Back inside, I climb the stairs to Oliver's room. He's heading for the airport later this afternoon, and I don't want to miss him before I leave for school. I take a deep breath, then knock.

"Come in."

I push open the door to find my brother lounging on his bed, reading a textbook.

"Hi," I say.

He sits up to face me. "Hi."

"What are you working on?"

"Studying for my classics test on Friday."

"Are you ready for it?"

"Yeah." He shuts the book but wedges his finger in it so he doesn't lose his page. "Did you need something?"

"I'm leaving for school. I wanted to say bye."

"I'll be down in a few weeks for Thanksgiving." Avoiding my eyes, Oliver shakes his textbook and proceeds to dismiss me. "I better get back to it. See you."

I look around his room, at the old-school record albums framed on the wall. At his stereo system. Anywhere but at him. Things have never been awkward between me and my brother before. I don't know how to handle it.

"Oll, I'm sorry I disappointed you. I screwed up. I didn't mean to hurt you or for you to think I didn't trust you with the truth. I love you."

He nods. "I love you too. We'll talk soon, okay?"

"Okay."

He goes back to studying, and I shut the door with a click. I lean my head against the wall, clenching my eyes shut. Will things ever go back to normal?

Will people ever think of me the way they used to? Will I need to prove myself trustworthy again? Once they doubt, can that ever be repaired?

The rest of my week mostly sucks, given how much Dad's campaign and my name are in the news, but I must say I feel better than before, when the lie was bottled up inside. It's nice not having to always be on my toes for fear that my lie might come out. And I'm glad my parents know I was never into serious drugs.

When I get home from school on Friday, Dad is already there. It shocks me to find him sitting in the sunroom, reading a newspaper.

"What are you doing here?" I ask.

"I left the office early. I want to take you and your mom out for dinner. Unless you already have plans with Ezra."

Wow, we haven't gone to eat together in forever. "We were going to see a movie, but I'll call him and cancel."

"Invite him along. I'll get a reservation for four."

After I text Ezra, I shower and change into a sleek black dress for dinner, but when I get downstairs, I find Dad in a pair of jeans and Mom in a casual flowered skirt and pink blouse.

"Dad, I didn't know you owned jeans."

He cracks a smile. "Neither did I."

"Tee, why don't you go put on something more comfortable?" Mom suggests.

This is all so weird. First of all, my family rarely eats together. Second, did Mom just tell me it was okay to dress down? I change into leggings, a white blouse, and leather boots, then meet my parents in the front parlor.

Ezra is here, dressed to the nines in a black suit and shiny red tie.

"Why did no one tell me this wasn't a formal dinner?" he grumbles.

Mom actually grins. "I'm sure you can find something to wear in Oliver's closet."

When we're all finally dressed appropriately, Dad drives us to the Roadhouse.

"This is where we're eating, Edward?" Mom asks, peering through the car window at the restaurant, which looks like a log cabin.

"I feel like a good steak and a baked potato." At the look of horror on Mom's face, Dad adds, "Don't worry, dear. I checked. They have salads."

Mom lets out a long breath of air.

"I didn't know the Roadhouse took reservations," I say.

"They don't. I found that out this afternoon," Dad admits, and Ezra and I laugh. "I learn something new every day," Dad says.

We go inside the restaurant, where people are cracking open peanuts and throwing the shells on the floor. The hostess seats us at a little round table by a window. The centerpiece is a lantern, its wick flickering in the dark room. Before we can even get drinks, people start converging on our table to shake Dad's hand. Everyone seems really sad about his loss, and some are pissed to have a Democrat in office. Dad is gracious and kind to everyone, even the nosy people who want to know what he plans to do next.

When everyone has gone back to their tables, the waitress takes our drink order. Mom seems a little horrified that they don't serve wine, so she settles for iced tea.

"Make that four iced teas," Dad says.

When the server is gone, Ezra clears his throat. "What *are* you going to do next, sir?"

Dad seems impressed Ezra has the balls to ask. "I have a lot of options, actually. I could teach or work at my father's firm. I might take some time off to travel. I saw an ad for a Caribbean cruise that looks relaxing." He glances over at Mom, whose eyes light up at that idea. "It's hard to believe I won't be in the Senate anymore… I'll miss Washington. I'll miss making a difference in people's lives." Dad's voice is so sad, I'm afraid I might cry.

"You don't need the title of senator to make a difference," I say quietly.

Dad leans back in his chair, thoughtful. "Maybe I'll consider the president's offer for a position over at Treasury. One of his people called earlier."

"But then you'll never be home," I say.

"You won't be either," he replies with a small smile. "It's off to college with you. Your mom and I will be bored at home without you around."

Since Dad was honest just now, I decide to do the same. "Mom, Dad, listen. I've decided I'm going to apply to some other schools...and not Yale."

Mom sits up straight, shocked. She looks over at my father. *He didn't tell her?* Dad doesn't say a word, so I take a deep breath and keep going.

"I'm not sure what I want to do with my life, but I like the idea of being a museum curator," I say, and before I know it, I'm totally word-barfing on my parents. "I love art history, and I think I want to major in it. That or history. Maybe minor in museum studies? Or major in museum studies and minor in business, like you want me to, Dad. That could be helpful if I'm running a museum one day. I'm still doing some research, but I think Boston University or GW or NYU could be a good fit. There's also Vanderbilt, which means I'd be closer to home. The University of Chicago has an intern program, and I could work at one of the museums there. There are so many good museums in Chicago, you know? Well, in New York, DC, and Boston too. Yale is a great school, but there wouldn't be as many internship opportunities in New Haven. That's why I don't want to apply there," I ramble.

Mom sets her tea glass down. "Life is short." Her eyebrows pinch together for a moment, and her eyes begin to water—she must be thinking of her sister. "You should do what you want to do."

Dad simply stares at me. Finally, he cracks a small smile. "It sounds like you have a well-thought-out plan. Let's talk about your college research tomorrow."

Ezra squeezes my leg under the table and grins at me.

"Ezra Carmichael," Dad says slowly. "Get your hands up where I can see 'em."

Ezra looks sheepish. "Yes, sir."

And I am all smiles for the rest of dinner.

When we get home, I invite Ezra inside.

"You can't stay too late because I have my last soccer game tomorrow. It's an early one. Eight a.m."

"That's fine. Shall we have dessert then?" He flashes me a killer smile.

"If by dessert you mean *dessert* dessert, sure."

"I was thinking of the *other* kind of dessert, but I could settle for an ice cream sandwich. Do you have those?"

We head into the kitchen. "I don't know what we have," I say, glancing in the freezer. "Green tea gelato?"

Ezra sticks out his tongue. "Never mind. Can we go downstairs? I need to talk to you about something."

My heart skips a beat out of nervousness. "Okay."

Once we're settled together in a cushy armchair with me sitting in his lap, Ezra speaks up. "I went to see my dad last night."

I suck in a deep breath. "How did that go?"

"I told him I want to go back to school. To study architecture."

I hug my boyfriend. "What did your father say?"

"He's so happy to hear that I want to go to school again, I think he'd be excited no matter what I wanted to study. I could've told him I want to be a gynecologist."

I punch Ezra's bicep.

"Ow."

"What made you change your mind?"

"Seeing what you did for Ben."

"Huh?"

"When you covered for him, you were living a lie. And even though you never meant for any of it to happen, it changed your whole life."

I draw tiny circles on my boyfriend's chest. "In some ways, that was good. Otherwise, I wouldn't be here with you now."

"I agree. But when you were lying, you were living a life that just wasn't right. Didn't you feel like something was off?"

"Yeah."

"I feel the same way. I mean, I'm happy working on houses, but there's always this nagging feeling. Something's off, and I don't think it will go away."

"Are you saying I'm a nagging feeling?" I joke.

He tickles my sides. "Yep. You are my little nagging feeling. But seriously, you made me realize that if I don't change something now, I could end up in a place I don't want to be, just because I didn't have the guts to tell the truth and ask for help. So I looked into resources for people like me and talked with my dad."

I touch Ezra's cheek. "Wow. What happened?"

"He was pissed, yeah, but I think he'd rather people find out I have a learning disability than us not speaking and me living on the other side of town. I'm getting tested for dyslexia and ADHD on Monday."

I suddenly feel like the day after Christmas, when all that anticipation finally pays off and you're happy, but also sad. "So you're going back to Cornell?"

"I think so…but I don't want to leave you either."

We hug each other tightly. "We will deal with it. You do whatever you need to do, and we'll work it out, okay?"

He nods. "I'm also looking into the architecture program at UT Knoxville. It looks like it may be a good fit for me. I might try to transfer. I'm waiting on a call back."

I kiss him. "You know what I'm thinking?"

His arms pull me close. "What?"

"Maybe your dad and mom wouldn't have a problem with your Ragswood Road apartment if you got some throw pillows."

"Jesus, Mary, and Joseph," he mutters, pecking my lips. "My little nagger."

Today is my eighteenth birthday.

Unlike my sixteenth, I don't have any big party plans for tonight. Ezra takes me to Jiffy Burger, so we can listen to all the trucker dudes talk smack. One bellows, "Well, that just dills my pickle!"

We eat burgers and fries and drink cherry cokes.

When we're finished, I feel like I will never be hungry again, but I look at the dessert menu anyway. "Want to split some pecan pie?"

He plucks the menu from my hand. "No dessert. I've got something for you back at your house."

I give him a pouty face. "I figured we could go to your place."

"Not tonight."

I raise my eyebrows. He won't have the apartment much longer, and I want to take advantage of the privacy while we still can. He's moving back home in December so he can spend the month working with an education specialist, who is going to help him get set up for college. He's transferring to UT Knoxville in January, and the school will pair him with tutors and the support he needs to succeed. He's excited to start and not scared, and that means everything to me.

His mom and dad are already telling people that the reason Ezra left Cornell is because he wanted to study architecture and his father was upset he wouldn't inherit the family business. I only hope that his parents will begin to accept that he has dyslexia and give him the emotional support he needs to succeed.

When Ezra drives me home, there are tons of cars parked along the street. *Wait—is that Chloe's Sentra? Hey, there's Steph's red Mercedes! What is she doing here?*

I hop out of Ezra's Range Rover and hustle up the front steps. Inside, rap music is pounding. The walls are shaking. Pulling my boyfriend along behind me, I jog through the house to the kitchen.

"Surprise!"

Tears flood my eyes when I see my family and friends standing around a cake with flickering candles. Chloe and Alyson are there from Hundred Oaks, and a few other girls from the soccer team, including Sydney and Brittany. Steph and Madison came down from St. Andrew's. Mom, Dad, and Marina. Even Oliver and Jenna are here. Wow. I guess I should've known, considering the loud club music.

I walk over to my brother and give him a big hug. "Any excuse for an Oliver Dance Party, huh?"

"You bet."

"I'm surprised to see you."

"Me too. I'm still pissed, but you're my little sister."

"Disappointing you has been one of the hardest parts of all this."

He pulls away from me and winks. "You'll have to make it up to me. There are several nightclubs I want to visit over Christmas break now that you're eighteen. Also, I'm thinking of a road trip over spring break. Think *Nightclubs across America.* Oh, and did I mention you're coming with me?"

I snort, leaving my brother to catch up with Chloe. "I have a new tequila you should try sometime," he tells her.

"Oh hell no. I'm not over the last time."

I spend most of the party gossiping with Steph and Madison. My sister won't stop hitting on Ezra, which I find hilarious. He keeps making excuses to hide from her.

At this point, I haven't seen my boyfriend in half an hour, and I'm starting to get worried he'll never reappear, when he suddenly materializes by my shoulder.

"Tease, your present is in the garage."

"The garage?" I place my hands on his chest. "Did you get me a Vespa?"

"Yes. I got you a Vespa." He rolls his eyes. "C'mon."

I go into the garage, where Ezra leads me to a cardboard box. There is a puppy inside.

"Eee!" I squeal. It's a yellow lab, and he can't be more than six or seven weeks old. I scoop him up. He fits in my hands, he's so tiny.

"He's so cute!"

Ezra smiles his gorgeous grin at me.

"Who's this?" I ask, accepting the puppy's kisses.

"He doesn't have a name yet, so I've been calling him Squeaks," Ezra replies.

I run my fingers through the dog's yellow fur and clutch him to my heart in a hug. "I love him, but do my parents know? Mom said I can't have a dog. The carpets!"

The dog is panting, his ears flopping all over the place. He barks a little puppy bark. Aww.

The garage door swings open, and Mom appears. "Taylor Lukens, you can't just leave your guests to sneak off with Ezra to kiss—" She stops chiding when she sees the puppy.

"Oh, Ezra," she says with a heavy sigh. "Not again."

"C'mon, Mrs. Lukens. Isn't Squeaks the best?"

Mom has always had a hard time saying no to Ezra. I mean, she caved when he gave me a rooster, for God's sake. She comes over and gives the dog a scratch behind his ears. "He'll chew my rugs." The puppy licks her hand, making a smile flit across her face. "He's awfully cute, Ezra."

"At least it's not a goat," I add. "I would love a baby goat."

Mom gives me a look.

"So Tee can keep him, right?" Ezra asks.

Mom sighs again. "As long as she takes care of him."

I lunge for my mother, folding her and Squeaks into a big bear hug. The dog makes a yipping noise. Mom takes the dog into her arms and goes back inside the house, either to show him off to our guests or to show *him* the rugs and tell him not to chew on them.

"Thank you for Squeaks," I tell my boyfriend. "I love him. But I bet Mom is going to steal him."

"No bet. Your mom looks tough, but she's going to love Squeaks like her fourth child."

"Where did you get him?"

"From Jack Goodwin's neighbors, the Whitfields. They breed them. You can go visit the mama dog if you want." He reaches into his back pocket and pulls out an envelope. "Here's the rest of your present."

I rip into the envelope to find a handmade birthday card; he drew a picture of a doghouse for me. I open the card, and little slips of paper fall out. More homemade coupons!

Doughnut holes on me!

I will watch exactly one chick-flick with you.

One free kiss!

"I love you," I tell him.

"I love you too."

"I want to cash this one in right now." I pass him the coupon for the kiss, and when his lips meet mine, this is officially the best birthday ever.

Spring Break

I kiss Mom and Dad good-bye and hug Leo's neck for the thousandth time this morning. I named my dog after Leonardo da Vinci because I've been on a total Renaissance kick. The puppy has grown from a tiny yellow furball that fit in my hands into a fifty-pound wrecking ball that loves romping all over the house. I haven't been away from him more than a day in the past five months, and now I'm leaving him for a week.

"Don't worry," Mom says, taking Leo's leash. "Leo will Skype with you every day while you're gone."

I smile, because that means I'll get to talk to my parents every day too.

"Be safe," Dad says. "We love you."

"I love you too."

"When you get back, we need to talk about what you're doing this fall," Dad adds.

I knew that was coming. He brings it up every single day. I need to decide which school I'm going to by May 1.

I imitate his voice. "When I get back, we need to talk about what *you're* doing this fall, Dad."

"Stop teasing me. I'm working on it."

After turning over his Senate seat to Harrison Wallace in January, Dad hasn't gone back to work. He and Mom took me to visit schools in New York, Boston, DC, and Chicago earlier this year, and then they went on a two-week cruise. They relaxed for the first time in forever. Dad even wore a Hawaiian shirt.

Still, I know he's sad about losing the election.

He hasn't decided if he wants to take a political appointment in DC or stay in Tennessee to work at Grandpa's firm. Either way, he loved setting his own agenda when he was in the Senate. He wouldn't get to do that at the Treasury, where the issues rarely change and it's all about money. He wouldn't get to interact with Tennesseans very much either.

Dad talks of running for governor, but I fear I damaged his legacy, and I'll never get over that. He says he forgives me and that it's not my responsibility, but still, I know what I did hurt his reelection. I live with that every day.

After giving Leo a final hug, I jog out to my brother's red convertible. I toss my bag in the open trunk.

"Shotgun," I tell Ezra.

He grumbles and climbs from the front seat into the back.

"Are you sure about that?" Oliver says. "You really want Jenna sitting in the back with him?"

"Good point." I crawl over the middle console into the backseat, accidentally kicking Oliver in the side of the face. His sunglasses fall off.

"I swear to God, Tee. I'll leave you home."

"Hell no, you won't," Ezra replies, draping a protective arm over my shoulders. Being away from him this semester has been difficult, but we're able to see each other most weekends. Our relationship is stronger than ever, and I know it will survive no matter where I wind up this fall.

Oliver honks the horn three times. "Jenna!"

My sister finally appears at the front door, lugging a suitcase, which she leaves on the stoop for someone else to deal with. She gives Mom and Dad kisses good-bye, then comes out to the car.

Dad helps with the suitcase, which takes up nearly all the room in Oliver's tiny trunk. Then it's finally time to go.

"Where to first?" Oliver asks, turning the key in the ignition.

"This is your road trip," I say. "Where's the nearest nightclub?"

"I'm thinking we head to Atlanta tonight, then on to Panama City tomorrow."

"And Miami!" Jenna says.

"Fine," Ezra says. "But I get to choose where we stop for snacks."

"And I want to hit the beach in Miami," I add.

Oliver carefully pulls the car out of the driveway as we all give one final wave. Once he's a good minute away from the house where my parents can't see him, he picks up speed.

"I bet Oll gets at least five speeding tickets on this trip," I say.

"No bet," Ezra and Jenna say simultaneously.

Oliver turns onto the four-lane, heading for the interstate. The road seems to stretch out forever. I look out at the rolling fields that blur by. The sun blazes down on us. Eminem blasts from the radio. I throw my head back, staring up at the wide blue sky.

Thanks to my grades and test scores (and the letter explaining why St. Andrew's expelled me), I got into the University of Chicago. I love the idea of being in a city with all those museums. I also applied to the University of Pennsylvania and got in. Being in the same place as the Liberty Bell and Constitution Hall and tons of other history is pretty enticing. Once I looked beyond Yale, I found so many options, and it's difficult to choose.

All I know for sure is that I want to dual major in history and museum studies.

Even after admitting why I got in trouble, the schools I applied to in Boston and New York didn't take me. And I can understand that. I know how lucky I am to have been given a second chance to make something of myself, but it's not just good karma. I have options because I worked hard at school. I gave classes and soccer my all. I still have no idea whether I should choose Chicago or Pennsylvania. I've still got a little time to decide. The future's wide open, filled with opportunity. But I've got a life to live in the meantime.

Today, I'm just along for the ride.

Acknowledgments

When I was growing up, kids at school made fun of me. As a result, I've spent most of my life working really, really hard in order to prove myself. Relaxing and fun always came second to hard work. Work, work, work! At twenty years old, I got my first real job working full-time for the U.S. Department of State. Simultaneously I was taking a full load of college courses at night. I spent what little free time I had with friends or trying to write poetry.

After I graduated college, I continued working at the State Department, only I began working overtime. I thought that in order to get ahead, I needed to "pay my dues" and to me that meant working twelve-hour days. I did that for years. In my free time, I kept writing. For some work projects, twelve-hour days became fifteen-hour days and long months living in hotels away from home. It was not a life. But I felt I had to push myself to the limit in order to get ahead professionally.

When I got married, I finally took a regular eight-to-five job. In my spare time, I went back to my writing and poetry. For years, I've continued to write for hours a night. One day a couple years ago, I realized I didn't have much of a life. I had few friends outside of work and the publishing world. No social life. My health wasn't the best because I didn't have time to go running. I was too busy working! Now I've made a point to schedule time to go to the gym. I make plans with friends and neighbors for drinks and dinner. I accept invitations, when in the past I would've declined. And most important, I make time to read the books I want to read, i.e. romance novels.

With *Defending Taylor*, I want to show readers that working hard is important—I wouldn't be where I am now if I hadn't worked hard, but living life is important too. I hope you live, live, live.

As always, I am so appreciative of my first readers who helped me shape this book: Julie Romeis Sanders, Sarah Cloots, Trish Doller, Andrea Soule, Christy Maier, Tiffany Smith, Michelle Kampmeier, Andrea Lepley, and Jen Fisher.

A very special thanks to Arturo Carrillo of George Washington University in Washington, DC, for telling me all about GW and letting me get an inside peek at the college admissions process! (And to Jim Core for introducing me to Arturo.) Arlington County Soccer in Arlington, Virginia, allowed me to visit practices and ask questions of their great players.

Thank you to Annette Pollert-Morgan, my amazing editor who challenges me and helps me enhance my stories. I'm grateful to everybody at Sourcebooks for their encouragement and for giving me this great writing career. Thanks to Sara Megibow and everyone at KT Literary and Nelson Literary Agency.

To my Washington, DC, writer friends: I love that you always believe in me: Jessica Spotswood, Robin Talley, Lindsay Smith, and Caroline Richmond. I want to give One More Page Books of Arlington, Virginia, a shout-out—thanks for all your support over the years!

I couldn't do anything without the support and love of my husband, Don.

Finally, I would be nowhere without my amazing readers! I love receiving your emails, Tweets, and messages on Facebook, Instagram, Wattpad, and Goodreads. You rock!

About the Author

Miranda Kenneally grew up in Manchester, Tennessee, a quaint little town where nothing cool ever happened until after she left. Now Manchester is the home of Bonnaroo. Growing up, Miranda wanted to become an author, a major league baseball player, a country music singer, or an interpreter for the United Nations. Instead, she became an author who also works for the U.S. Department of State in Washington, DC, and once acted as George W. Bush's armrest during a meeting. She enjoys reading and writing young adult literature and loves *Star Trek*, music, sports, Mexican food, Twitter, coffee, and her husband. Visit www.mirandakenneally.com.